The
STRANGER
IN MY
BED

BOOKS BY KAREN KING

Snowy Nights at the Lonely Hearts Hotel
The Year of Starting Over
Single All the Way

KAREN KING

THE STRANGER IN MY BED

bookouture

Published by Bookouture in 2020

An imprint of Storyfire Ltd.
Carmelite House
50 Victoria Embankment
London EC4Y 0DZ

www.bookouture.com

ISBN: 978-1-83888-961-6
eBook ISBN: 978-1-83888-960-9

To Sharon. Thank you for all the years of friendship and support.

PROLOGUE

I watch as he strides down the path, pressing the remote to unlock his car as he walks. He gets into the driver's seat, then he's off, speeding down the road. He shouldn't be speeding, not with the state of those brakes. But he thinks he's safe; he doesn't know that he's not.

I follow him, wanting to see it happen with my own eyes, wanting to see him dead. He deserves to die. He's a bully, a cheat, scum. He doesn't know that I know about him, know all the awful things he's done.

He's heading down the hill now and the lights are changing. I know he won't be able to stop in time. I can imagine his panic as he stamps down on the brake pedal and finds that it doesn't work, that he can't stop his descent down the hill, can't stop as a lorry emerges out of the side road. I pull over and watch as the lorry smashes into the side of his car. I hope the lorry driver is okay. I don't want anyone else to get hurt.

Only him.

I hope he dies.

CHAPTER ONE

Freya

Monday

'Wake up, Phil,' Freya whispered, holding her husband's hand as she sat beside the hospital bed. A place she'd barely left since that devasting moment on Friday evening when two police officers had knocked on the door to say that Phil had been seriously injured in a car accident. 'Please wake up.'

She searched his face for any sign of consciousness. He looked gaunt, ashen-faced, vulnerable, with the three-day-old dark stubble covering his usually smooth chin and his short, treacle-brown hair ruffled up like hedgehog spikes. Wires attached him to an assortment of machines that bleeped away in the background. A bandage was wrapped around the top of his right arm where it had been cut in the accident. They said some of his ribs were broken and his legs were badly bruised but he was breathing unaided, which the doctors assured her was a good sign. They were confident he would wake up soon. She prayed he would.

If anything happened to him... If he died... or was brain-damaged, she would never forgive herself. Apparently it was only the side airbags that had saved him from serious injury – or death. His precious BMW, the pride of his life, was a write-off.

'Oh, Phil, why did you have to storm out like that?' she whispered, her eyes resting on the small cut on his forehead for a moment then flicking down to his closed eyes. He looked strangely peaceful, as if he were in a deep sleep. Well, that's what a coma was, she guessed, a deep sleep. She used to love watching him sleep when they were first married, to see his chest rise slowly up and down, his eyes sometimes flickering as he dreamt, marvelling at how lucky she was, what a fairy tale her life had turned out to be. Sometimes he would mumble in his sleep but she could never understand what he was saying; they were unintelligible sounds. She'd give anything to hear them now, to see his eyes open, to know he had suffered no lasting damage.

She squeezed her eyes closed and took a deep breath to calm herself. If only she could turn back time. Back to three days ago. No – to longer ago than that. Back to when they first got married. They had been so happy. It had all been perfect: the wedding, the honeymoon. Perfect. How had it all gone wrong? If only she could change it all.

If it wasn't for her, they would be in Dubai now. Instead, Phil was lying in a hospital bed and she was keeping permanent vigil by his bedside, unable to sleep, to function, consumed by despair and guilt.

It was touch-and-go at first, the doctors had told her. The lorry that Phil had crashed into had pulled his car underneath its carriage. The driver, shaken up and bruised but not severely injured, said that Phil hadn't slowed down at the crossroads, had sped straight into him, that he'd had no time to swerve. Why hadn't Phil seen the lorry? Why hadn't he braked? Was it because he'd been too upset to think straight?

Or did he intend to kill himself?

There it was. The thought that kept nagging her, refusing to go away. Had Phil purposefully driven at the lorry, intending to kill himself? He'd threatened it before, several times, saying that she made him so miserable, so worthless, that he felt like ending it all…

It was her fault. It was always her fault.

'You're too confrontational. Too headstrong. Always so quick to argue.' How many times had her mother said that to her over the years?

'I'm just sticking up for myself,' she'd protested, stung by the criticism. 'I've got a right to stick up for myself. I have an opinion, you know.'

Well, this was where her sticking up for herself had got them: Phil lying in a hospital bed, maybe brain-damaged.

She glanced around as the door opened behind her and her older sister Daisy came into the room. 'Any change?"

'His eyes flickered earlier. The doctor thinks he might come round today,' Freya told her.

'Really? That's great.' Daisy walked over and squeezed Freya's shoulder comfortingly. There were five years between her and Daisy; that and Daisy's rather aloof manner meant that they had never been particularly close, although Freya had idolised her big sister when they were growing up. She was surprised and pleased at how much of a support Daisy had been the last few days. Daisy had come straight to the hospital as soon as Freya, not knowing who else to turn to, had phoned her to tell her about Phil's accident, her voice shaking so much she could barely get her words out. Since then Daisy had barely left Freya's side, comforting her, assuring her that Phil would pull through, keeping her supplied with coffee and sandwiches.

Right after Freya's call, Daisy's husband Mark had sprung into action, dropping the twins off at Daisy and Freya's mother's for the weekend so Daisy could be there for Freya. He'd recently been appointed as regional manager for a large supermarket chain and had to work, but he'd collected the children on Sunday evening. Daisy had also managed to arrange for the other receptionist to cover her morning shift at the dental surgery so she could be with Freya, coming straight to the hospital after dropping the twins off at school.

Meanwhile, Stefan, Freya's boss at IPA Studio, the design agency where she'd worked for the past three years, had insisted on her taking compassionate leave for as long as she needed. Someone else was going to give the important presentation Freya had slaved over for the last few weeks, the one that had caused the row. The row that had resulted in Phil storming out and ending up in this hospital bed.

Not that she gave a damn about the presentation now.

God, she was tired. She rubbed her eyes, blinked furiously a few times in an effort to wake herself up. She desperately needed to sleep, longed to go home, have a shower, something decent to eat, but she didn't want to leave Phil lying here like this. At first she'd been worried that he would die while she was gone, but the doctors said he had stirred in the night when Freya had dozed off in the chair, that they thought he might wake up today, and she wanted to be here when he did. Daisy had offered to fetch her some clean clothes but Freya told her that she had some in a suitcase in the car because they were supposed to be going away that weekend.

It was a lie. They hadn't been going away. She'd packed the case because she'd been planning to leave Phil. She'd just put it in the boot when the police car had pulled up on the drive.

Daisy walked over to the bed and stared at Phil. Her long, dark hair was loose around her shoulders rather than in her usual low ponytail, emphasising the paleness of her face. Her sister looked tired, Freya thought, and no wonder when she'd spent so much time at the hospital this weekend. It was so good of Daisy to keep her company like this, especially when she had the twins to look after, and a part-time job.

She turned to Freya. 'You look exhausted. Why don't you go home? I'll sit with Phil and call you if there's any change. I promise.'

Tears sprang to Freya's eyes. 'Thanks, Daisy. I really appreciate your support,' she said, her voice cracking a bit. 'I don't know what I'd have done without you this weekend.' She took a tissue from her jeans pocket and dabbed her eyes. 'I'll stay a little longer. I want to be here when Phil wakes. I want to make sure he's okay.'

Daisy looked back at Phil. 'Of course you do. I'll fetch us both a drink, shall I? I'm going to have tea, I think. I feel a bit queasy. I think it's the hospital smell.'

'I know what you mean. I feel permanently sick,' Freya told her. Sick with anxiety and worry that Phil wouldn't recover. 'I'll have coffee – make it black, please.' She normally had her coffee white with sugar, but she was so exhausted, every bone in her body ached, and she was hoping that black coffee might wake her up. 'Let me give you the money for the drinks – you can't keep buying them.' She reached for her bag to get her purse and winced as she knocked her right forearm on the chair. It was still tender.

'You're bleeding,' Daisy said sharply.

Freya looked down at the sleeve of her cream jumper and saw a small pool of blood seeping through. 'I grazed it when I was gardening the other day,' she said.

'Do you want a plaster?' Daisy opened her handbag and started to rummage inside. She always had a supply of wipes, tissues and plasters on her in case her six-year-old twins needed them. She took out a wrapped plaster and handed it to Freya, who was scrabbling in her own handbag for her purse.

'Thank you.' Freya opened her purse then handed Daisy a ten-pound note. 'Sorry I don't have the change.'

'It's okay, the machine gives change.' Daisy slipped the note in the front pocket of her bag. 'I won't be long.'

As soon as her sister went out of the room, Freya rolled up the sleeve of her jumper to put the plaster on the cut. The knock on the chair had opened it up again and it was bleeding slowly. She looked over at Phil. How had it come to this? She loved him so much and he loved her too. She was sure he did.

She so desperately wanted him to open his eyes. But when he did, what then? Where did they go from here?

CHAPTER TWO

Three days before

Freya sat on the sofa, her arms wrapped tightly around her knees to try and still the tremors coursing through her body, her tears exhausted now, her eyes fixed on the dirty water stains dripping down the silver-and-white embossed wallpaper. They followed the stains down to the pool of water on the floor, the broken fragments of the crystal vase that had been a wedding present, the beautiful roses it had held now strewn over the light oak tiles: orange and cream petals broken off, stems bent. Only the single white rose remained intact. The first rose Phil had ever given her was a thornless single white rose. He'd told her it meant 'love at first sight' and that he'd fallen in love with her as soon as he'd seen her. She had fallen for him too, immediately charmed by his dark, rugged good looks; come-to-bed, twinkling, ink-blue eyes; quirky smile; soft, lilting voice with just a touch of an Irish accent. When he'd invited her out for a drink she'd instantly agreed. She'd had absolutely no intention of getting serious with anyone, enjoying her freedom after the end of her long-term relationship with a lovable but immature boyfriend a few months earlier. But Phil had sneaked into her heart and taken over her life. She'd accepted his marriage proposal six months later without hesitation, confident of their love for each other. If only she had known then how quickly it would all go wrong.

She loved him so much. So why couldn't she stop this happening? Why couldn't she just be quiet and walk away?

Why couldn't she control herself?

Because she didn't want to be like her mother, dominated by her father, that was why. Her father had never been violent, but he was cold and controlling, and her mother always gave in to him to keep the peace. When she was growing up, Freya had vowed that she would never do that, that she would always stand up for what she believed, for what she wanted to do.

Well, look where that had got her.

She slowly moved her gaze to the door, which Phil – after looking in horror at the broken vase and the cut on her arm – had flown out of a few minutes before, sounding close to tears as he said, 'I can't stand this any more!'

This had to stop. It was too destructive.

She got down on her knees and, taking care to avoid the broken glass, crawled over to the scattered flowers, picking up the heads of an orange then a cream rose – orange for the desire and fascination Phil said he felt for her, cream for her charm and thoughtfulness. Phil had explained the meanings when he'd bought her the first bunch of roses a month after they'd met, when they'd declared their love for each other. Every weekend since he'd bought her a bunch of the same roses. She'd been overwhelmed that Phil thought so much of her and was soon swept off her feet by his devotion and her own heady feelings for him. They had never argued when they were dating, never had a cross word. Phil had so openly adored her; nothing was too much effort for him. Every day they had met, he had been smiling – happy, calm, reliable Phil. And she'd adored him too. He was so sweet, funny, easy-going and generous. He'd showered her with gifts, still did.

Caressing the broken heads of the two roses gently, she closed her eyes, blinking back the tears as their latest argument replayed in her mind.

*

'I've got a surprise for you,' Phil said as soon as he bounced through the door, kicking it shut behind him, one arm full of the sweet-smelling roses, the other holding a carrier bag from the expensive lingerie boutique in town.

'Thank you. You spoil me.' She wrapped her arms around his neck and kissed him, then took the flowers from him and sniffed them. 'They're heavenly.'

'So are these. I can't wait to see you wearing them.' He held open the bag so she could see the glimpse of lacy undies nestling inside. She'd known without looking at them that they would be red. They always were.

She smiled indulgently at him. 'They look gorgeous. Let me put these roses in water then I'll try them on.' She knew they'd fit – Phil was familiar with her size, if not her taste. She preferred cream or black underwear, but she didn't mind wearing red now and again if it kept Phil happy.

Phil followed her as she took the flowers into the kitchen. He leant his back against the white marble worktop, the string handles of the lingerie bag dangling from his fingers, watching as she took the crystal vase down from the shelf, swilled it out under the tap to make sure it was clean and dust-free, then took the container of distilled water out of the black, slimline kitchen cupboard and filled the vase with it before adding two teaspoonfuls of sugar – all tips she'd read on the internet to make cut roses last longer. Phil slid open the drawer by the sink, took out the scissors and handed them to her.

'Thanks.' She carefully unwrapped the roses, got rid of any leaves that would be submerged under the water and cut a forty-five-degree angle in each stem. Then she artistically arranged them in the vase, folded the expensive wrapping paper and put it in the recycling bin. 'They're beautiful. Thank you, darling.' She leant over and kissed Phil again, then carried the vase into the lounge and put it on the light oak wall cabinet, away from direct sunlight. With a bit of luck they should last a week or so now. Phil spent so much on flowers for her, it was ungrateful not to take the best care of them that she could. The first bunch he had bought her had only lasted a few days and he'd been so upset. She'd looked up how to care for them properly after that.

'Now for your second present.' Phil held out the bag of lingerie. Freya smiled brightly as she took out the lacy, almost-not-there scarlet knickers and matching push-up bra. Phil always bought the same style. 'Thank you, darling, this is a pleasant surprise. What's the occasion?' Phil usually bought her underwear for her birthday, Christmas, their anniversary and Valentine's Day. It was the second week of June so none of those occasions fitted.

'Do I need a special day to treat my wife?' he asked, disappointment flicking across his face.

'No, of course not.'

'Good, because I've got another surprise too.' He looked excited, as if he was bursting to tell her, his eyes sparkling, a smile playing on his lips.

What could it be? She cast her mind back to other surprises he'd sprung on her. Maybe it was a weekend away? She had planned on working this weekend but she could work late on Monday if he had arranged something. She didn't want to be unappreciative and ruin the surprise.

'I've booked us a week in a luxury hotel in Dubai,' he announced.

Dubai? They'd been talking about going there – it was a city Freya had wanted to visit for ages. She'd rather have sat down and chosen the hotel together, but she knew that Phil meant well. He loved to surprise her. She smiled. 'That sounds wonderful. When?'

They were pretty busy at the office but she was due some holiday, and once this presentation she was working on was over and the new high-profile account signed and sealed, things would calm down a bit, so she was sure she could manage a week off. Phil worked part-time as a lecturer on the journalism course at the university and had finished his sessions now until September, although of course he still had his articles to write. He freelanced for the local newspaper and several magazines.

'Monday.' He swooped her up in his arms, lifting her up and kissing her. 'So you'd better get packing.'

She swallowed, a vice of anxiety tightening her stomach. 'Monday? This Monday?'

'Yes. Isn't it fantastic? I got a brilliant last-minute deal.'

'Phil. I can't go on Monday. It's Friday evening now! You know I can't take a week off from work with no notice. And *especially* next week. You know I have to do this presentation. I've been working on it for ages and this is an important account.' Her voice sounded like a high-pitched squeak.

He loosened his grip and she almost fell to the floor. 'Surely you can wrangle it. You're owed holiday. Just pass the work on to someone else.' The disappointment on his face made her feel so guilty – and angry. How could he possibly think she could take a week off work just like that? She couldn't let Stefan and the rest of the team down.

'I can't. You should have checked with me before you booked. You're going to have to change the dates—'

'For Christ's sake, Freya, you're not bloody indispensable. Surely you can take a week off.'

Then that was it, they were in the middle of another blazing row, both of them yelling and shouting. Things getting broken.

Then, like always, it got physical.

Finally Phil left, telling her that he couldn't take any more.

She should have handled it better. She could have acted pleased by the surprise. She had Stefan's home number and could have contacted him and explained what had happened, asked if Nadia could take over the presentation.

Stefan might have said no but she could have tried instead of dismissing it out of hand. She was owed the holiday and yes, she had wanted to secure the deal herself, but as long as the company got the new account, what did it matter?

Her mum was always telling her that she was lucky to have Phil, that she shouldn't be so confrontational, that she should learn to back down. She didn't understand that Freya always stood her ground because she was so determined not to be a doormat like her mother had been. Mum had waited on her dad hand and foot, turning a blind eye to his numerous affairs because she wanted to hang on to the big house and comfortable lifestyle. Her father had left eventually, met someone he wanted to make a new life with, and her mother had been devastated. After all the years they'd been together, she ended up bitter that after everything she'd tolerated, her husband had *still* deserted her. Freya didn't want her and Phil's marriage to be like that; she wanted to have a proper partnership, both equals. It was one of the reasons she'd broken up with her ex: he'd been too immature and she'd had to take responsibility for everything.

She suddenly became aware that her forearm was stinging and glanced down at the nasty gash where a chunk of the shattered vase had ricocheted and hit her. Blood was running down from it onto the floor. She got up and staggered into the kitchen, running cold water over the wound to make sure there was no glass in it. God, it stung! When the bleeding ceased a little she carefully inspected the cut. It didn't look like it needed stitches, thank goodness. She took the first-aid kit out of the top cupboard and put a dressing over the wound, then poured herself a glass of water, leaning against the kitchen sink as she drank it, shaking so much that water slopped out of the glass.

Someone could have been seriously hurt today.

She couldn't risk it happening again.

She had to get out. Now.

CHAPTER THREE

Now

Did Phil's eyes just flicker? She was sure she hadn't imagined it. Freya stood up and peered anxiously at her husband's pale face, searching for any sign of movement. There it was again: a light flutter of the eyelids. Was he regaining consciousness? *Oh please, God, let him come round.* She clasped her hand to her mouth, hope rising in her heart, as Phil murmured slightly and his eyelids flickered again. He was! He was coming out of the coma! She pressed the bell to alert the nurse then reached for his hand. 'Phil. Phil. Can you hear me?'

Slowly his eyes opened. 'Freya.' His voice was little more than a whisper.

At that moment the door opened and two nurses and a doctor rushed in.

'He's awake. He said my name,' she exclaimed. 'He recognised me. He said my name.'

'That's wonderful, love. I know you want to stay with your husband but we need you to wait outside while the doctor checks him over,' one of the nurses replied.

'Of course.'

Freya stepped out of the door into the corridor just as Daisy returned with the drinks.

'Phil's regained consciousness. He recognised me!' Freya was almost crying with relief. 'The doctor is with him now.'

Daisy's eyes lit up too. 'Really? Oh wow! That's fantastic, Freya. I'm so pleased.' She handed Freya the coffee. 'Now you can stop worrying. Everything will be fine.' They both sat down on the grey plastic chairs outside the room, drinking the hot liquid in silence. Waiting.

It seemed an eternity before the doctor came out. 'Everything seems to be fine physically, Mrs Keegan. We will follow up shortly with some further tests, but things are looking positive.'

'Oh, thank God. Thank God.' Tears flowed down her cheeks in relief. Things weren't perfect between her and Phil, but if he'd died, she would never have forgiven herself. She threw her arms around Daisy. 'He's going to be okay!'

'I told you he would be.' Daisy gave her a reassuring hug. 'Can we go in and see him?' she asked the doctor.

'Yes, but only for a few minutes, we don't want to tire him out. And it may be best if Mrs Keegan goes in first. Give them a few minutes alone together?' the doctor replied.

Freya desperately wanted to see Phil, to talk to him, but she was nervous too. Scared of what he would say. And of what she should say to him. So much had happened.

Wiping away her tears with a tissue, she took a deep breath and stepped into the room.

Phil was propped up in bed and had some colour in his cheeks now. His face lit up when he saw her. 'Freya, I was wondering if you were here.'

'Of course I am. I've been here all the time.' Not sure what to do, how to act, she hugged him gently, making sure she didn't knock his broken ribs. Then she gave him a peck on the cheek before sitting down on the chair beside the bed. 'How are you feeling?'

'Like I've been run over by a lorry – which apparently I have.' He gave her a wan smile and shook his head weakly. 'I can't

remember a thing about the accident and my head is killing me.'
He nodded ruefully at his bandaged arm. 'This stings a bit, and my
ribs are sore, but the doctor said they should heal in a few weeks.'

'You're lucky you weren't killed.'

He reached out and clasped her hand, holding it tightly in his.
It felt warm, comforting, and she could see the love shining out
of his eyes. 'The doctor said I've been out for nearly three days.
You must have been worried sick.'

'I was.' She bit her lip, tears welling up again. 'Oh Phil, I
thought I'd lost you.'

Then she realised he was staring at her. Was this it, where he
suddenly remembered what had happened?

'You've cut your hair,' he said, the disappointment evident in
his voice.

'What?' For a moment his words stunned her. 'I had it cut a
few months ago,' she reminded him. 'It's almost at my shoulders
again now.' Phil loved her to wear her wavy chestnut hair long and
had been upset when she'd come home with a chin-length bob.
She pushed the memories of that argument out of her mind. She
needed to focus on the here and now.

He looked confused. 'No, you didn't! You've always had long
hair. You had to keep tying it back on our honeymoon because
of the heat.'

She stared at him. What an odd thing to say. 'That was over
two years ago, Phil.'

'What was?'

'Our honeymoon.'

He shook his head vehemently. 'No, it wasn't. We only came
back yesterday. Well, four days ago I should say, as it seems I've
been stuck here for three days,' he corrected himself.

Freya bit her lip apprehensively. He was obviously confused; he
had been out for quite a while though. 'It's been two years since
our wedding, Phil,' she said gently.

'It hasn't! Why are you saying that? We came back from Barbados on Wednesday. I remember it!' His voice rose in panic.

'Phil, it's okay. Calm down.' Freya placed a hand on his arm to reassure him.

The door opened and Daisy came in. 'How's the patient?'

Phil didn't seem to notice her; he was focused on Freya and clearly agitated.

'Your hair was long. I plaited it for you before you went into the sea. That was on Tuesday. Why are you saying it was two years ago?'

Freya tried to keep her voice steady, to talk soothingly despite the anxiety rising within her. 'You've been unconscious, Phil. The doctor said you might be disorientated. It will pass, don't worry.' She glanced over at Daisy. 'Phil seems to have lost his memory; he thinks we've just come back from our honeymoon,' she explained.

'Gosh, really?' Daisy moved over to Freya's side and looked at Phil. 'Do you remember me, Phil?' she asked.

Phil stared at her. 'Yes, you're Daisy, Freya's sister. You've got twins. I think they're about three or four.'

'They're six now and at school,' Freya told him.

'Six?' Phil looked astonished. 'They can't be…'

Seeing the confusion in his eyes, Freya took his hand in hers. 'What's the last thing you remember?'

Phil frowned. 'Stepping off the plane… We'd just come home from our honeymoon…' His voice faded and he was visibly upset. 'Was it really two years ago?'

'Yes, but don't worry, you've only just come round. You'll remember everything more clearly soon.' Freya squeezed his hand reassuringly.

'I think I'd better go and tell the nurse about this,' Daisy said.

Phil closed his eyes and sank his head back into his pillow. He looked weak, vulnerable. And scared. Freya swallowed the lump that had formed in her throat. It must be horrible not to be able to remember things properly.

Daisy returned a few minutes later with a nurse and doctor.

'Can you both wait outside again while we examine Mr Keegan, just so we can assess the situation?' the doctor said. 'And don't worry – a bit of confusion is normal after any sort of traumatic brain injury.'

Freya and Daisy went back out to the corridor.

'Phil looks so frightened,' Freya said, her voice almost a whisper. 'He really can't remember the last two years at all. What if he's got permanent brain damage, Daisy?' Fears were gnawing away at her mind. What if Phil couldn't look after himself? If he was now mentally impaired?

'Try not to worry. Let's wait and see what the doctor says,' Daisy replied, patting her hand. 'He's been in a coma, remember. He's bound to be confused.'

It was ten minutes before the door opened and the doctor came out. Freya jumped to her feet. 'Is he…?'

'He's calmed down and I think it's a good idea if he has some rest now,' she said kindly. 'I think your husband is suffering from what we would call mild retrograde amnesia. In other words, he has lost a specific set of memories. These things can happen.'

'How long will it last? Will he get his memory back?' Daisy asked before Freya could.

The doctor shook her head. 'It's hard to tell. He's lucky, in a way. It is hard to be entirely sure but we've asked him a few questions and it seems like he's probably only lost a couple of years of his memory. Some people lose many years, and in extreme cases they lose their memory completely. As it's only partial it may well come back over a number of days, weeks or years, but we can't say for certain. He might never get those two years back.' She looked sympathetically at Freya. 'I've given him something to help him sleep, so he'll be out now for a while. Why don't you go home and take a rest too? Come back this evening. Things might be clearer in your husband's mind then.'

Freya nodded wordlessly. She was exhausted. And she desperately needed time on her own to think.

'Do you want me to come back with you?' Daisy offered. 'My friend, Lisa, could pick the twins up from school and look after them until Mark comes home.'

'Thank you but I'll be fine, honest. I just want a shower and to get my head down for a bit.' And she didn't want Daisy to see all the broken glass in the lounge. She hadn't had the chance to clear it up after the police had arrived because she'd then been at the hospital all weekend, praying Phil would come out of the coma.

'Phone me if you need anything. Promise?'

'I promise.' She gave her sister a hug. 'Thank you so much for being here.'

'Any time.'

Freya drove home almost on autopilot. She parked her car in the drive and opened the front door. It felt strange to be back home. The house was silent, as if it had been waiting for her return. She walked into the lounge, gazing in despair at the glass vase shattered all over the floor. The crumpled flowers with their broken stems.

She thought about their row. The one Phil couldn't even remember now. And all the other rows he couldn't remember either. She thought about how frightened and vulnerable he had looked lying in that hospital bed.

Should I still leave him?

CHAPTER FOUR

Freya had meant to have a coffee and a bite to eat, take a quick shower, change and then go back to the hospital, but as soon as she sat down on the big comfy sofa with her coffee and sandwich she felt her eyes closing. She was exhausted. Hardly surprising as she had barely slept for the past three days. She placed her mug on the coffee table and rested her head back. *I'll close my eyes for a few minutes*, she decided. *I'll feel better after a power nap.*

The persistent ringing of her mobile awoke her an hour later, her mug of coffee now cold and her sandwich still lying uneaten on the plate. She reached over for her bag where her mobile was still ringing – whoever was calling her wasn't about to give up – and saw that it was her mother. She groaned; she really didn't want to talk to her mum right now. She knew that she was probably just phoning to ask how Phil was, but Freya didn't feel she could deal with her mum's constant questions and her obvious devotion to Phil, who could do no wrong in her eyes. Freya hadn't decided yet what to do about their marriage; her suitcase was still in the car and her mind a messed-up muddle. Just because Phil had had an accident and suffered a partial loss of memory, it didn't mean she should give their marriage another chance.

Because the fact that he didn't remember what had gone on in their marriage didn't necessarily mean that things would be different from now on, did it?

A ping announced an incoming message. Freya opened it up, guessing it was from her mother.

Daisy told me poor darling Phil is awake but suffering from amnesia! How terrible! I hope you are looking after him. Do give him my love.

No 'How are you, Freya?' Just a 'hope you are looking after him', the same words her mother told her every time they saw one another. 'Look after Phil. Men like being looked after.' Well, Freya liked being looked after too, and Phil hadn't exactly looked after her, had he?

She wondered what her mum would think if she knew the truth about Friday evening. About their 'happy' marriage. She'd blame Freya, of course. She was glad her mother had been looking after Daisy and Mark's twins this weekend or she would probably have been over like a shot, wanting to check how Phil was, no doubt trying to move in with Freya until he was recovered. Mum had actually asked Daisy if Mark would bring her back too when he'd picked the twins up but luckily Daisy had managed to persuade her that Freya needed space right now.

Phil was fond of her mother – and no wonder as Mum waited on him hand and foot and hung on his every word – but Freya didn't want to see her until she had made up her mind whether she was going to give her marriage another chance. Besides, if Phil didn't remember the past two years, her mother would be almost a stranger to him – he'd only met her twice before the wedding. Mum had been annoyed that they'd got married abroad and robbed her of her chance to show off to her friends, being mother of the bride and lording over a big wedding. She'd blamed Freya, of course, accused her of being selfish and not thinking of how her family would have liked to celebrate with her.

It hadn't actually been Freya's idea to go off and get married abroad, it had been Phil's, but that didn't matter to her mother. Phil, with his twinkling blue eyes, gorgeous smile and that sexy Irish lilt, had her mother wrapped around his little finger. Women were always like that with Phil. They adored him and he knew it. If they split up, he would tell her, then there would be a queue of women ready to take her place.

Perhaps one of them would make him happier than she did.

She went into the kitchen to make another coffee then sat and drank it slowly, nibbling at her sandwich as she wondered what Phil's family were like. She'd never met them. He didn't even have photos of them. Phil had walked out years ago because he was sick and tired of how they favoured his younger brother, Graham, constantly belittling Phil and putting him down. He'd never gone back and none of his family had attempted to get in touch with him since. She found it strange to be so completely cut off from your family like that.

Had they heard about the car crash, though? It had been on the local news and there had been a big spread in the local paper because Phil wrote for them but she guessed that if his parents didn't live in Birmingham they probably wouldn't have heard about it. She didn't know where they lived, didn't even know their first names. Phil refused to talk about them at all, and she had no way of contacting them to let them know that their son had almost died and was now lying injured in hospital with amnesia. Mind you, Phil would be furious if she did.

What kind of parents are they to not bother with their son for all these years anyway? Freya found herself wondering, not for the first time. Although Freya had a difficult relationship with her father and her mother drove her mad, she couldn't imagine cutting them completely out of her life, or them doing it to her.

Phil had told her how all his life his parents had made him feel worthless, and he'd confessed that Freya made him feel like that sometimes too. Because of the way she didn't trust him, wouldn't let him make any decisions without an argument. She hadn't meant to do that. She admired Phil: he was intelligent, talented, articulate. She'd thought all she was doing was sticking up for herself yet whenever she offered her point of view, Phil said she was argumentative and confrontational. It was like he only wanted his point of view to matter.

Her coffee and sandwich finished, she went upstairs to shower and change. As she walked into their bedroom, the framed photo on the bedside table caught her eye. It was taken on their honeymoon, a beautiful photo of her and Phil, looking madly in love, enjoying a romantic dinner on the beach. They'd been so happy then. What had gone wrong?

Another message pinged on her phone. She glanced at it and saw it was from Daisy. Sitting down on the side of the bed, she opened it up.

What time are you going to the hospital tonight? Do you want me to pick you up? Or meet you there?

It was good of Daisy – she really had been a rock these last few days – but tonight Freya wanted to see Phil alone. She needed to talk to him. To decide what to do.

She sent a quick text back, explaining that she was going back to the hospital soon and was fine on her own, telling Daisy to spend some time with Mark and the twins, thanking her for all her support. Then, remembering her mother's earlier text, she wrote a quick message to her too, saying Phil was still recovering and should be out of hospital soon, promising to keep her updated with his progress.

She glanced back at the photos on the bedside table. Maybe she should take them; they might jog Phil's memory. He remembered their wedding and honeymoon, though; it was later photos she needed. She opened the wardrobe and reached for the plush, light blue photo album she always kept on the top shelf. Across the front in fancy silver script were the words *Our Memory Book*. Phil had bought it the day after she'd accepted his proposal of marriage and painstakingly stuck in photos of their engagement, their honeymoon, trips they'd gone on, evenings out. A record of their perfect married life. Most people didn't print out photos – they left them on their mobile phones or their laptops – but Phil, the master of the selfie or getting other people to take photos of them – always printed out the best ones and stuck them in this album. 'Memories are important,' he said, 'and I want to record all the happy ones so that we never forget how lucky we are to have each other.'

She recalled how those words had really touched her, how lucky she'd felt to be loved so much. If only she'd known then what was ahead.

CHAPTER FIVE

Freya was pleased to see Phil sitting up in bed and with more colour in his cheeks. It had worried her to see him looking so washed out earlier.

'How are you feeling?' She leant over and kissed him on the forehead. 'I've brought you some cheese and chive crisps and a bottle of Coke in case you fancy a snack.' She took them out of her bag and placed them on the cabinet by the side of his bed.

'Thanks. I'm glad to see that they're still my favourites,' he said with a weak smile. 'My headache has eased a bit but I still can't remember anything about the last two years. And I'm dying for a cigarette, so I'm guessing I still smoke.'

Freya pulled a face. She hated Phil smoking and had tried hard to get him to stop when they were first married, before realising that the fallout wasn't worth it. 'Yes, but you shouldn't be smoking now, Phil, not with your broken ribs.'

'Well, I can't in here anyway,' he said ruefully. He patted the side of the bed. 'Sit down. I've been waiting for you to come and see me again because I wanted to ask you something important... And I don't want you to be upset... because I know it's horrible that I don't remember and I'm sorry...but do we have any kids? I feel awful that I can't remember.'

She should have guessed he would ask her that... It'd be a question that would be uppermost in his mind. She ignored the space on the bed he'd suggested she sit on and pulled the chair over instead before answering. 'Don't feel bad, it's not your fault that you've lost some memories. But no, we don't. We decided to wait a while before we start a family.' That wasn't strictly true. Phil was eager to have children, the sooner the better, and had mentioned it regularly since they had got married. It was Freya who wanted to wait. She didn't want to bring a child into the volatile relationship their marriage had become.

He looked disappointed. 'I was hoping, seeing as we've been married two years, that we'd have had a baby. A little son or daughter.' He glanced at her, suddenly awkward. 'Oh God, I haven't put my foot in it, have I? We can have children, can't we? There isn't a problem?'

'No, don't worry. We decided to enjoy a bit of time together first, but it's definitely on the agenda.'

'The doctor asked me some questions about what I could remember, and filled me in a bit on what's been happening in the last two years – still no peace in the Middle East, I see.'

'I wish!' she said. 'I don't think the world has changed that much, Phil. Same old tensions, no miraculous inventions that I can think of.'

He put his hand over hers, his expression intense. 'No, but *my* world changed. We got married and I can't remember any of our marriage. Can you imagine how devastating that is?' Then he looked guilty. 'I'm sorry, it must be horrible for you too, to think I can't remember such precious years.'

She felt uncomfortable under his scrutiny so focused her gaze on his ears rather than his piercing blue eyes – a trick she'd been taught when she went for her first interview. It looked like you were still focused on the person you were talking to but didn't feel so awkward. 'Don't apologise, it isn't your fault. It must be really frustrating for you. The doctor said that your memories will probably come back though.'

He sighed. 'It's crazy. I can remember everything up until two years ago: my childhood in Ireland, moving to Manchester with my family, then to Leeds and going to university, getting a job at Birmingham University and moving there, meeting you in the café that rainy day in Birmingham city centre.' A smile spread over his face at the memory. 'I was smitten right away.'

'So was I,' she admitted. Phil had swept her off her feet so quickly, her feet had hardly touched the ground.

'I remember our wedding and honeymoon. Everything. Until the moment we stepped off the plane.' He rubbed his forehead hard with the base of his palm as if trying to rub away the amnesia. 'It's a total blank from then until I woke up in this hospital bed. Why can't I remember the past two years?' he asked, eyes troubled. 'It's awful not being able to remember anything at all about our married life.'

He looked so distraught that Freya's heart went out to him. Although part of her wished she could forget their married life too and start with a clean slate like Phil was doing.

She reached into the canvas bag she'd brought with her and pulled out the photo album. 'I thought this might help. Do you remember it?' She placed it on the bed beside him.

He nodded, brightening up a little as he traced his hands over the words *Our Memory Book*. 'I remember buying it just after I proposed so we could fill it with photos of our happy memories.'

If only! She wiped the words from her mind. There were some good memories. Lots of them. She cast her mind back to the day Phil had given her the photo album. He'd said, 'We're going to fill this with all the good times we have. Then when we're old we can sit and look through it, remembering all the wonderful things we did, the amazing places we went.'

It wasn't a true record of their marriage though. It only held the good memories. The bad ones would be with her forever, even if Phil had forgotten.

'I'll leave it with you, then you can look through it in your own time. It might jog your memory.'

'I'd like to look through it now, with you. I might remember better that way. And I can ask you questions about anything I can't remember. Do you mind?'

'Sure.' It would be selfish to refuse. There must have been so many questions he wanted to ask, so much he didn't know.

'Come and sit here so we can look through them together,' he said, shuffling over to make room for her to sit on the side of the bed.

She wondered if he sensed how awkward she felt. If he noticed that she was holding back and wondered why she wasn't gushing over him more like a loving wife should do after such a terrible accident. He had no memories of the awful stuff that had happened, the terrible rows, but she did. She knew everything that had happened and she couldn't just forget it all because Phil had almost been killed.

'I don't think the nurses like visitors sitting on the beds,' she said, pulling the chair nearer instead. She leant over as Phil flipped the cover of the album. The first photo was of their engagement: Phil bending down on one knee, holding out the ring, Freya with her hands raised to her face, fingers splayed over her cheeks, an expression of total surprise on her face. When Phil had shown her the photo – secretly taken by one of the waiters – she'd been even more surprised than when he'd proposed. She'd asked what he'd have done if she'd have turned him down and he'd smiled, saying he'd have just deleted the photo but that he'd known she'd accept anyway, because they were meant to be together. He was right to be sure of her acceptance; she hadn't hesitated in her reply.

Freya bit her lip, her mind in turmoil as Phil slowly turned the pages: photos of them on day trips out, holding hands, kissing, looking so happy. They both laughed at the photo of them in fancy dress for a 1920s-themed party the Christmas before they got married, Phil looking like a gangster with his dinner suit, spats and pencil-thin moustache, Freya with her silver flapper dress, blonde curly wig and white feather boa.

'I remember this!' Phil said, chuckling. 'It was the university Christmas do. Fergus came as a woman with bright red hair and a short dress, stockings and suspenders.' Fergus was another lecturer at the university.

'That's right. And one of his suspenders broke and his stocking kept rolling down to reveal his hairy leg,' added Freya. It had been a fun night.

'I could never look at him the same again.' A big grin spread over Phil's face. 'Every time I saw him I kept thinking of that red wig and his stocking rolled down to his ankle.'

He turned to Freya and kissed her on the cheek, his eyes shining. 'I might not remember everything, Freya, but I do remember how happy we are and how much I love you.'

Phil's eyes were on her and she could feel the expectancy in the air. He was waiting for her to state her love too. She couldn't say the words he wanted to hear, knowing that she had been about to leave him, but she didn't want to tell him what a terrible mess their marriage had become either. If he didn't know, couldn't remember any of it, then maybe there was a chance they could make a fresh start. If she wanted to, that was.

'I'm glad you remember that,' she said softly. She turned over to the next page. Photos of their wedding: Freya in her pretty, Bohemian-style wedding dress, with the full-length embroidered veil that loosely framed her face, Phil in his white suit that made him look even more handsome. Photos of their honeymoon: them both lying on the beach in Barbados, their luxury suite, their romantic dinner on the beach, paddling in the sea, dancing – the waiters had always been willing to take photos for them. It had been such a lovely time. The memory of how happy they had been then flooded back to her and a tight knot formed in her throat.

'I remember all of this,' Phil said softly, the emotion raw in his voice. He turned the page over and gazed at the photo of him carrying Freya over the threshold into their new home, both laughing, looking so happy. They'd bought the house six weeks before their wedding and had spent days decorating it, but Phil hadn't wanted Freya to move in until they were married. 'Call me old-fashioned but I don't want us to live together until you're my wife,' he'd said, holding her hand and looking so deeply into her eyes that she'd felt powerless to refuse him. Besides, she'd had to give a month's notice on the flat she was renting, so what did it matter? Phil's flat was already under offer – it had been on the market when they'd met. He'd bought it because it was conveniently close to the university but decided to sell it because it was too noisy in the middle of the town. When they'd got engaged, they had looked for a house together, within easy commuting distance to both of their places of work. The sale of Phil's flat had gone through, so he had moved into the new house, wanting to get it ready for Freya to move into the day they got back from their honeymoon.

She watched as Phil turned the pages, photos showing them both out and about. Phil wrote articles for several magazines so they often spent weekends looking around stately homes, visiting quaint villages or attending exhibitions or events.

'It's no good. I can't remember any of it! It's like looking through someone else's photos.' There was a catch in Phil's voice and the glisten of tears in his eyes as he closed the album.

'I'm sorry, maybe I shouldn't have brought it…'

'Yes, you should have! It was a lovely idea, it's just so upsetting that I don't have any memory of it all. I started this book because I didn't want to forget any bit of our life together and now I've forgotten it all.' He placed his hand on hers again and squeezed it tenderly. 'How could I forget the two most important years of our lives?'

It must be so confusing and frustrating for him, she thought sympathetically. 'Be patient – you only gained consciousness this morning. Shall I leave the photo album with you? Then you can look over it again?'

They both turned as the door opened and Daisy walked in. She paused for a moment, her eyes going to the closed photo album and then to Phil and Freya, their heads huddled together, Phil's hands clasped around Freya's.

'I'm not disturbing you, am I? I know you said you'd be fine on your own, Freya, but Mark came home early so I thought I'd pop in anyway.' Her eyes rested on Phil. 'Well, you look a lot brighter than you did this morning.'

'We're looking through our photo album. I thought it might jog Phil's memory,' Freya told her.

Daisy nodded. 'Good idea. Has there been any improvement?' Her eyes were still on Phil.

'Nope. The last two years are still a complete blank,' he replied.

'Well, it's early days yet.' Daisy walked over to Freya. 'Mum is desperate for me to pick her up so she can come and visit Phil but I've managed to hold her off. I thought you two might appreciate the time together, especially with Phil's memory loss.'

'Thanks. I'm not sure Phil's up to many visitors. Are you?'

Phil shook his head. 'I don't mean to sound ungrateful – it's nice that people care – but I don't really remember your mum. I feel too confused to chat to people who are almost strangers to me right now.'

'That's okay. You only met my family a couple of times before the wedding so of course you wouldn't recall them much,' Freya pointed out. Whereas she hadn't met Phil's family at all. She wondered again whether to ask if he wanted his family to be informed about the accident but decided he'd mention it if he did.

Daisy turned away and started rummaging through her bag, pulled out her phone and glanced at the screen. 'Of course. I'll talk to Mum later tonight and tell her to leave it until you feel a bit stronger.'

'Perhaps she could visit when I go home,' suggested Phil. 'I might remember things more clearly once I'm back in familiar surroundings.'

'I'm sure you will,' agreed Freya, trying not to panic at the thought of Phil coming home. He looked so vulnerable with his bandaged arm and broken ribs and she instinctively wanted to look after him.

But was that a risk worth taking?

*

So, he's alive. And I'm relieved. I didn't expect to be – I thought I wanted him dead, but when I saw the ambulance and the police all over the scene, watched them carry his body on a stretcher, I knew that I hadn't really wanted him to die. My anger had consumed me and all I could think of was making him suffer, like he'd made me suffer, but I don't want him dead. That would make me a murderer. I could have been locked up. I still could be if anyone finds out what I did.

I still want him to suffer, though. I want him to realise what he's done, to be sorry. He's evil: a cruel, callous bully. He can't get away with that. I'm not going to let him. This isn't over yet.

CHAPTER SIX

Tuesday

Knowing that Phil was out of danger was such a relief that Freya slept soundly all night, only waking when her mobile rang the next morning. She sighed when she saw that it was a call from her mother.

'Hello, Mum.'

'I didn't wake you, did I? I thought you would be too worried about Phil to sleep in late…'

There it was, the usual thinly veiled criticism: if her mother didn't actually voice her opinion that Freya wasn't a good wife to Phil, she always hinted at it.

'He's out of danger now, Mum, and I was exhausted. It's been a stressful few days.'

'Which is exactly why I wanted to come over and help you look after Phil, but Daisy said it would be too much for him. That he doesn't remember me.' She sounded hurt.

'He's got amnesia, Mum. He can't remember the last two years. The doctors said his memory will probably come back, though. And no, it isn't a good time to visit at the moment. It'd be best to leave it for a while.'

'What about when Phil comes out of hospital? You'll need help then, won't you? You'll be taking time off work to look after him, I hope.'

'I'm on compassionate leave this week, Mum. I'm not sure about next week. I'll see how Phil is.'

'For goodness' sake, how can you even think of going back to work and leaving Phil to cope?'

'I'm sorry, Mum, I have to go, there's another call coming in.' It was a lie but she needed to get her mother off the phone before she went into a full-blown lecture on how Freya should look after Phil.

'All right, dear. Well, give darling Phil my love and let me know when I can come and see him.'

'I will. Bye, Mum.'

Freya sat up, cross-legged, tapping her chin with the phone. Honestly, her mother drove her mad. Phil could do no wrong in her eyes. No wonder Freya couldn't confide in her. She needed to talk to someone, though. Her head felt fit to burst. On Friday evening she had been sure their marriage was over. But now…

She'd have a shower and go and see Daisy. She wasn't working today and the twins were at school. Daisy wasn't someone she normally turned to but she'd been so supportive the past few days and Freya felt that they'd grown closer. She was sure her sister would listen and give her some good advice.

Freya took her time in the shower, letting the warm water cascade over her, washing away the stress. Finally, hair shampooed and conditioned, and feeling a lot more relaxed, she reached for the fluffy white bath towel hanging over the nearby rail. As she rubbed herself dry she caught the cut on her right forearm again and winced. It was healing now but still tender. She shut her eyes tight at the memory of the vase hurling across the room and shattering, pieces scattering everywhere, one searing into her arm, another hitting Phil's forehead. He'd been furious.

'You always do this! Every time I try to do something nice you turn it into an argument and then this happens!'

Freya hadn't replied; she'd simply stood there, shaking as she looked at the blood trickling out of the cut on her arm and down Phil's forehead.

'I can't deal with this any more. I'm going!' Phil looked anguished, his voice trembling.

She'd wanted him to go. She couldn't cope any longer either. She'd wanted Phil to go and never come back.

As he'd slammed the door, her legs had finally given out underneath her and she'd crumpled to the floor. She had to get away. Phil would come back; he always did. Well, she wouldn't be here when he came back. She'd had enough. She wanted a divorce.

Now Phil couldn't remember any of that fight, or any of their other terrible arguments. All he remembered were the happy times when they were dating, their wedding and honeymoon. He thought they were happily married. If only.

Freya pulled a colourful, thin, long-sleeved top out of the wardrobe, and a pair of white cropped trousers. It was a sunny day, though not as hot as it would have been in Dubai. She bit her lip as she ran her brush through her hair, wishing they were there now, sunning themselves on a soft, sandy beach. Instead Phil was lying in a hospital bed.

Was it her fault? Had she been the one who'd raised her voice first, angry that once again he thought her work wasn't important and expected her to fall in with his wishes?

She made a cup of coffee and half-heartedly nibbled at a piece of toast, deep in thought, the clatter of the letterbox startling her for a moment. Toast in hand, she got up and stepped out into the hall to see a magazine lying on the mat. She picked it up: the *Climate Changer*. Phil had it delivered every month – he had been trying to get something accepted by them for months and had been jubilant when a few weeks ago they had finally accepted one of his articles. She'd take the magazine to the hospital with her today, give him something to read.

She took her coffee out into the garden and sat down at the table. She loved this garden – they'd spent ages planning it, getting it right when they'd first moved in. Well, Phil had. The university where he worked part-time always closed for the summer, which meant he had weeks at home. Yes, he was writing, as he was constantly at pains to tell Freya, but he spent a lot of time doing the house and garden too. Freya envied him his time off in the summer and had sometimes told him so. 'You could work from home too if you went self-employed,' he'd told her. In fact, he'd asked her to several times since they'd been married, wanting her to give up her job at IPA Studio and work part-time as a freelancer, but she'd refused. She'd freelanced for a few years before she got the job at IPA, but the income was too irregular and she enjoyed her job even if it was hectic. She liked going to work, meeting people. Besides, she wasn't sure if it would be a good idea for her and Phil to be rattling around the house together every day; they'd probably get on each other's nerves. And Phil was so impulsive, he'd suggest going out whenever he wasn't working and expect Freya to drop everything and go with him – then there would be a fight if she refused.

Like with the holiday.

Her coffee finished, she walked slowly into the kitchen. She loved this house. And she loved Phil. The nice Phil. The Phil who made her laugh so much she literally had a pain in her side, the Phil who had swept her off her feet that very first date, who bought her flowers, chocolate, presents, who hugged her, told her she was the most beautiful woman in the world. All her friends thought he was wonderful too, told her how lucky she was. Everyone thought they were the perfect pair and had a wonderful marriage. There was a dark side to their marriage, though, one she had never told anyone about.

Phil insisted that it wasn't him, it was her. 'You make me like this. You're so bloody argumentative and stubborn,' he often told her.

She picked up her car keys and bag and set off to see Daisy. Maybe a chat with her sister would help her sort out what to do.

CHAPTER SEVEN

'Hello, Freya. Good to see you,' Mark said as he opened the door. 'Daisy said Phil is on the mend now. I'm so pleased. It must have been such a worrying time for you.'

'Yes, he is, thank goodness.' Freya hovered on the step. 'I'm sorry, I didn't realise you were home, Mark. I should have sent a text instead of turning up like this. I wanted to talk to Daisy, but I can come back if it's an inconvenient time. Or phone?'

'It's not a problem, I'm leaving for work soon. Daisy will be delighted to see you. She's in the kitchen.' Mark pulled the door open wider for Freya to walk through. 'Go on in.'

Freya headed for the kitchen, where she found Daisy looking pale and tired, half-heartedly eating a bowl of muesli. When she saw Freya, Daisy's eyes widened, and she put the dish down.

'Freya. Have you had news? Has Phil's memory come back?'

'No, but I wanted to talk to you… Are you all right?' she asked as the colour drained from her sister's face. Daisy jumped up and went running past Mark, who had just followed Freya in. Freya heard the downstairs toilet door slam shut and the sound of retching.

'She was like that yesterday morning too.' Mark looked concerned.

'Has she got a tummy bug?' Freya asked. 'She mentioned that she was feeling a bit queasy at the hospital yesterday.'

'That's what we thought but it cleared up by midday. Now she's been sick this morning too. God, it reminds me of…' Realisation dawned in his eyes; he turned away, went over to the sink and filled a glass with cold water.

Is he thinking that Daisy could be pregnant?

They both turned as Daisy came back in and Mark handed her the glass of water.

'Thanks.' She gulped it down.

'That's the second morning you've been sick. You don't think…' Mark paused, his forehead creased with worry.

Daisy's hand shook as she lowered the glass, panic all over her face. It looked like the idea hadn't even occurred to her. Her eyes rested on Mark's face but she couldn't seem to find the words to reply.

'Hey, I didn't mean to worry you. I'm sure you're not. And if you are, it'll be fine.' He squeezed her shoulder reassuringly. 'Take it easy today and we'll talk tonight. I'm sorry but I have to dash now.' He kissed her on the cheek and was off.

Daisy looked as if her legs were going to give way. She sat down at the table and chewed her bottom lip as she stared down into her glass.

'Are you okay, Daisy?' Freya was concerned at how troubled her sister looked.

'I was just remembering, there was that time we had a curry and both had an upset stomach the next day. The doctor said that the pill didn't work so well when you had an upset stomach.' She raised her eyes to Freya, looking utterly distraught. 'Oh, Freya, I could be pregnant!'

'Would it be such a bad thing if you are?' Freya asked, sitting down beside her.

Daisy's eyes clouded over. 'It will be a disaster,' she said simply.

The tone of her voice worried Freya; she had thought that Daisy and Mark's marriage was rock-solid. *No one knows what goes on behind closed doors*, she reminded herself. *Look at me and Phil.* Well, her sister had been a support and comfort for the worst few days of Freya's life, and Freya was determined to return the favour. She got up. 'Let me make us both a cup of coffee then we'll talk about it.'

'Tea for me, please. I can't stomach coffee first thing now,' Daisy told her.

Freya sat, sipping her drink, as her sister poured out how she had struggled when the twins were born, barely sleeping, going days without finding time for a shower or a decent meal. 'A baby is the last thing we need. Molly and Max are at school now, off our hands. Mark and I finally have time to breathe, have the occasional night out – when he isn't working all the hours under the sun, that is.' She wiped away the tears that spilt out of her eyes with the back of her hand. 'It was a really hard time when they were both little, Freya. It's only really got easier since they've started school.'

Freya reached out and squeezed her sister's hand. 'Look, you might not even be pregnant. Take a test and find out. You could be worrying over nothing.'

'I will. I'll get one today. But what if I am? Oh God, what if it's twins again? I can't go through all that again. I can't.'

'The odds are that if you are pregnant, it will probably only be one baby this time. And I'll help you out. I'm sure Mark will be amazing too. He is so supportive.'

'That's the trouble. Mark's kind, supportive… and boring. The spark's pretty much gone out of our marriage. We're both so busy we're like ships passing in the night. We hardly make love any more, we're both too tired to do more than have a quick cuddle. Even Mum noticed. She insisted on having Molly and Max overnight a couple of months ago, saying that we needed some quality time together.' She told Freya how she and Mark had gone out for a curry then both had an upset stomach so their plans for a romantic weekend had been scuppered. Then Mark had instigated a quick love-making session on the Sunday morning. 'If I am pregnant, it must have been then,' she said. 'Which means I'm a couple of months gone.'

She looked so panic-stricken that Freya impulsively gave her a hug, not knowing what to say. She had never seen her sister look so upset.

Daisy sniffed, reached over and grabbed a tissue from the box on the table, and blew her nose. 'Take no notice of me, I'm being emotional. Like you said it could be a false alarm. Now, tell me what brings you here. Is it Phil?'

'Yes, but don't worry, he hasn't had a relapse or anything.' Freya took a deep breath. She'd never confided in anyone about this but she desperately needed advice. 'The thing is, we haven't been getting on great either, Daisy. We have terrible arguments. We had one the night of the accident.'

'How terrible?' Daisy asked, her eyes fixed on Freya's face.

'Violent,' Freya admitted. Then she paused, choosing her words carefully. 'Phil throws things. He lashes out, hits me.' She swallowed. 'I was leaving him the night of the accident. That's why I had a suitcase in my car. I don't know what to do now.'

She could see the shock in Daisy's eyes. 'Phil hits you,' she repeated slowly. 'Phil? He seems so easy-going and—'

'I know that's what everyone thinks. The truth is he has a terrible temper. Friday night he threw a vase of flowers up the wall. He was throwing it at me but I moved just in time. A chunk of glass cut my arm, though.' She pointed to the cut on her arm. 'I pretended that I grazed it gardening – it was the same broken glass ricocheting that cut Phil's forehead too. Then he stormed out. He was so angry, too angry to drive carefully – I'm sure that's why he crashed the car.'

Daisy stared at her, stunned. For a moment it seemed as if she was lost for words. Then she said firmly, 'Freya, if Phil is violent, you absolutely shouldn't go back to him.'

CHAPTER EIGHT

Freya thought about Daisy's words as she drove to the hospital. She knew she would say the same to her sister if she'd told her Mark was abusive and that it was the sensible thing to do in normal circumstances. These weren't normal circumstances, though. Phil had been in a traumatic road accident and now had amnesia – it seemed callous to leave him for something he couldn't even remember he'd done. And if he could remember nothing since returning from their honeymoon, a period of time when they had been really happy together, she couldn't help hoping that maybe that would mean he would revert to the person he'd been before they had got married.

'Freya!' Phil smiled as she walked in. He looked a lot brighter today.

'Hello, Phil. How are you?' Freya bent over and kissed him on the cheek, seeing the puzzlement on his face because she hadn't kissed him on the lips like she always used to do before they were married. She couldn't bring herself to do that; she was still hurt by his actions, still unsure of whether they had a future together.

'I'm feeling good. The headaches have eased and I've been down to the canteen for lunch and then had a wander in the garden. How are you? This must have been such a worrying time for you.' His eyes were full of concern.

'It has been, but it's good to see that you're getting better.' She reached into her bag and took out the magazine, placing it on the bed beside him. 'I brought you this – it was delivered today. I thought you might like to read it. I'm sure it's boring being stuck in here.'

'It is a bit.' He glanced at the magazine. 'Thanks. I might as well put my time in here to use and see if I can come up with an article idea that they might finally accept.'

Of course, he didn't remember that he'd already had one published in there. 'You sold them an article a few weeks ago.' She pulled up a chair to sit beside the bed.

Phil looked surprised. 'Did I? What article?' He clapped his hand to his forehead in exasperation. 'I hate this! The biggest moment of my writing career and I can't even remember it!'

'It was about the reality of climate change. You were really pleased. We went out to celebrate.' Only the night had ended in another row but he wouldn't remember that. 'Do you want me to look for it in your study? I could bring you a notebook and pen too.' She had no idea where he'd keep it; she rarely went into Phil's study. They respected each other's private space.

'It's okay, I'll read it when I get home. The nurse gave me my notebook and pen, and my watch, phone and wallet. She said my clothes were ruined and had to be dumped.' He sighed. 'I can't even remember what I was wearing. I feel so hopeless, Freya. Like a part of my life is missing.'

Freya reached for his hand and squeezed it reassuringly. 'It's early days yet. Your memory could come back to you any time.'

'I hope so. How many rejections did I have before they accepted my article?'

How could she answer that? Phil was always so secretive about his work, never telling her what he was working on until he had it accepted. She could always tell when he'd had a rejection, though – he'd be moody, on edge – but the few times she'd tried to talk to him he'd been snappy so she hadn't pressed it. It was because he was insecure, she knew that. He'd told her how his parents had always favoured his younger brother, Graham, how they'd always made Phil feel second best. Graham had been doing a law degree, planning on being a barrister, and was the apple of his parents' eyes. Whereas Phil wanted to be a journalist, which his father thought was a complete waste of time so refused to fund his university education. That was why Phil didn't see his parents. He couldn't keep taking the comparison, the rejection, the way they made him feel that he was a failure.

'I don't know, you never told me. But I'm sure it wasn't many.'

'How did we celebrate?' he asked. 'Did we go to Dulcie's?'

Their favourite restaurant. The one Phil had taken her to when he'd proposed. 'Yes, you even ordered a bottle of champagne. It was a lovely evening.'

It had been too. They'd had some happy times together, her and Phil. Could they put the bad times behind them and start again?

'What about my fortieth? I saw the party pictures in the album and some pictures of us in Rome. Did we go there for my birthday?'

'Yes, we went for a long weekend.'

His eyes clouded. 'I've moved into another decade, visited the city I wanted to go to most in the world, and I can't remember it. What did we do there?'

So she told him how they'd visited the Colosseum, tossed a coin in the Trevi Fountain, visited the Altar of the Fatherland, the Spanish Steps.

'Did we go to the Vatican too and see the Sistine Chapel?' he asked eagerly.

'No, we didn't have time but we made a promise we'd go again.'

He looked at her with eyes so sad that her heart melted. 'All those beautiful memories and I've forgotten them.' He raised her hand to his lips. 'We'll have to make more,' he said softly. 'Lots more.'

They both turned towards the door as it opened and two police officers came in.

'Mr Keegan?' the female officer asked.

Phil nodded. 'That's me.'

'And I'm Freya, his wife.' Freya stood up. What were the police doing here? 'How can we help you?'

'We'd like to talk to you about the accident. We've received some new evidence.' The officer looked grave. Freya felt uneasy. Were they going to charge Phil with dangerous driving? He must have been speeding down that hill not to be able to brake in time.

'What evidence?' Phil shot Freya a worried glance.

The police officers moved closer and this time it was the man who spoke. 'The insurance company ordered some standard investigations and have reported to us that the accident happened because your brakes failed, Mr Keegan.'

'There can't have been anything wrong with the brakes. Phil only recently had his car serviced,' Freya butted in. 'It sailed through, no problems.'

The police officer's next words shook Freya to the core. 'I'm afraid that the insurance company have evidence to suggest that the brakes were tampered with.'

CHAPTER NINE

The police officer's words kept going round and round in Freya's mind as she drove home. The police had questioned Phil, wanting to know what he could remember about the accident, but his mind was a total blank and she could see that he was getting distressed trying to recall it. He got in such a state that the doctor, who had come in to check on him, then suggested that they all leave and allow him to rest.

'We'll leave it a few days until we have more information,' the female police officer told Freya when they were outside Phil's room. 'Mr Keegan may have remembered more by then.'

A honk on the horn pulled Freya out of her thoughts. She should have been paying more attention to the road – look what had happened to Phil!

He could have died. She could have lost him forever. And yes, Friday evening she had been so upset that she had never wanted to see Phil again, but that didn't mean she wanted him to die.

The police thought that somebody did, though. Or at least, they wanted him seriously injured. That had really shaken her up.

She pushed the thought from her mind. She had to concentrate on her driving; she'd think about everything else once she was safely home.

*

She headed straight for the kitchen, where she flicked on first the light then the kettle. She really needed a cup of coffee. And she was starving. She turned on the oven, knowing there were plenty of ready meals in the freezer, her mind whirring with the enormity of her dilemma. Should she leave Phil, as she had planned, or give him another chance?

She could imagine how shocked everyone would be if she left. Her family and their friends thought that she and Phil were the perfect couple, so happily married. The stunned look on Daisy's face when Freya had confided in her today proved that. Daisy had believed Freya, though, and had told her to leave Phil.

That's exactly what she was doing on Friday night but things were different now. The accident changed everything.

She took a frozen lasagne out of the freezer, peeled off the film top, placed it on a baking tray and slid it into the now-warm oven. Phil hated ready meals but they were a good standby when they were both out at work all day. 'If you went freelance and worked from home, you could cut down your hours and have more time to prepare healthier meals,' Phil had told her a few times. She'd pointed out that when he worked from home he rarely cooked from scratch. That hadn't gone down too well; he'd accused her of not taking his writing seriously and another row had followed.

Freya was tired of fighting her corner. It was always one rule for Phil and another for her, and whenever she tried to stick up for herself, a huge row ensued. She squeezed her eyes tight to block out the consequences of some of those rows. Phil had been so easy-going, so pleasant and understanding before they got married. 'It's you who has made me this way. You start these fights. And you know just what buttons to push,' Phil repeatedly told her.

She'd seen the love shining out of his eyes today when he'd told her that he loved her. Could they get it back? That heart-thumping, overwhelming, nothing-else-mattered love that they'd once had for each other?

She made the coffee and sat down at the kitchen table. She wanted Phil back so much. The lovely, caring, supportive partner he used to be.

It was as if fate had given them a second chance. All Phil remembered was the love they had shared – he had forgotten all the bad stuff. Could she forget it too?

She closed her eyes, breathing in slowly, imagining how she would have felt if Phil had been killed, imagining a life without him. After all, hadn't she – more than once – wished for exactly that?

CHAPTER TEN

Wednesday

When she arrived at the hospital the next morning, Phil was sitting up in bed, looking a lot brighter. 'The doctor said I'm making good progress and can go home on Friday,' he told her. 'I'll have to come back for a check-up in a month's time, though.'

Two days away. Even though she had been expecting it, the reality threw her. She had two days to decide if she wanted to make another go of their marriage or not. To decide if it was safe to stay with Phil.

'That's really good news,' she agreed, pulling up the usual chair to sit beside him. 'Have any more memories come back?'

'No, and I still can't remember anything about the accident. I keep thinking about what the police said…'

'Don't. The insurance company must have made a mistake. The police said they were still conducting tests,' Freya reminded him.

'I know, but it's such a shock.' He rubbed his forehead. 'I've got this huge void in my mind and so many questions. I've written a couple down and I was hoping you could answer them for me – do you mind?'

'Of course not. Fire away.'

He took a notebook off the bedside cabinet and flicked the pages over. 'Here we are.' He shot her an embarrassed glance. 'Sorry if any of these are awkward.'

'It's fine,' she replied although inwardly she was bracing herself, wondering what he was going to ask.

'First, do we have any pets? I'm guessing not as there are no photos of any in the album.'

'No, we've talked about getting a dog at some point but at the moment we're both busy working.' *Gosh, this feels a bit odd.* She could feel herself tensing up, wondering what was coming next.

Phil looked awkward too. 'Are you still working at IPA? I remember that we had discussed you quitting and working freelance when we got married.'

'Yes, I am. We decided it was better for me to continue working at IPA for a while. It's a good regular wage and gives us the opportunity to save for a family.' Another lie. She hated taking advantage of his amnesia like this, but why cause upset when she didn't have to?

He looked down at his notepad then back up at her. 'Do I still work at Birmingham University? And write for the local *Telegraph*?'

'Yes, and you've had lots of features published in various magazines too. You're in demand!' she told him, trying to lighten the mood a little. She knew it was only natural he would have questions, but this felt so stiff and formal, as if she was being interviewed for a job.

'Let's hope I can remember if I've got any deadlines. I don't want to be letting people down and losing work. It's not good for my professional reputation.'

'The staff at the *Telegraph* and university already know about the accident. They've both sent good wishes and told me to tell you not to worry about anything, to just concentrate on getting better,' she reassured him. 'And it's mid-June now, and you only work there part-time, so your teaching sessions are finished until September. As for anything else, you'll have written it down in your calendar – you always keep records.'

'That's good. I've been worrying about work. Thanks so much for answering my questions. All this can't be pleasant for you.'

'It's fine. I don't mind.'

He reached for the album that was lying on the side of the bed. 'I've been looking at the photos again, hoping something will jog my memory, but it's all still a blank. What if I never get my memory back? Those two years will be lost forever.'

'The doctor said that it's likely your memory will come back in time,' she reminded him. 'And you might remember more when you're back home, in familiar surroundings.'

Suddenly, Phil grabbed her hand and leant forward, his eyes worried. 'You won't go straight back to work and leave me on my own all day, will you, Freya? I feel so weak and vulnerable. I'm scared I might collapse, or a memory might come flooding back that shakes me up.'

Freya hesitated. With the news that he was fit enough to come home, she'd assumed that, if she did decide to give their marriage another chance, she could go back to work on Monday, thinking that after the weekend Phil would be fine to look after himself. He could take it easy, sit out in the garden perhaps, and she really needed to get on with the new client. But if he felt that vulnerable, maybe she should think about doing flexi-time…

'I can't not go into work at all, Phil. And I can't do all my job online. But I'll talk to Stefan and see if I can work from home a couple of days a week for a while, until you feel stronger.'

'Thank you. I really appreciate it.' He leant back into his pillow. 'I feel so tired now.'

'You rest. I'll visit you again later,' she said, leaning forward and kissing him on the cheek, but he wrapped his arm around her neck, gently pulled her closer and – taking her completely by surprise – kissed her on the mouth. Her first instinct was to push him away but she hesitated, not wanting to hurt him. Then his kiss deepened and she gave in to it and had to admit that it felt good. Maybe the love was still there.

But she needed more than love. She needed to know that she was safe.

Perhaps she was. As long as Phil didn't remember what had happened before.

CHAPTER ELEVEN

Daisy hadn't come to the hospital since Monday but Freya wasn't surprised about that. She knew that Phil was recovering, and anyway, she had enough on her hands. She wondered if Daisy had taken a pregnancy test yet and – if so – what the results were. She dialled her sister's number, ready to offer her support if needed.

'Hello, Freya. How's Phil? Any new memories?' Daisy asked.

'No, but he looks a lot brighter. He's coming home on Friday.'

'And you're okay with that? You're giving him another chance?'

'I'm still trying to make up my mind. Part of me wants to give it another go. The accident has changed Phil. He's kinder, softer, more like he used to be. And it feels a bit cruel to abandon him when he's so weak and vulnerable.' She paused. 'But I don't know whether to risk it. It's such early days.'

'Take your time. Make sure you think it through. He's not that badly injured, he could cope. And, if you do decide to stay, just make sure that you have an escape route if things go wrong.'

'I will.' The same thought had occurred to Freya. She probably wouldn't know if Phil had changed until he came home and she spent more time with him. But that could be dangerous. Right now, she didn't know what to do. Then she remembered that her sister had her own problems. 'Anyway, how are you feeling now? Did you take a pregnancy test?'

There was a long silence then Daisy replied in a voice so quiet that Freya could barely hear her. 'Yes. And it was positive. I'm pregnant.'

'Oh, Daisy. Are you okay?'

'I'm fine, I just have to get used to the idea, that's all. And Mark is being so lovely. Don't worry about me – concentrate on you and Phil.'

'If you ever need to talk…'

'I'm okay, honestly, I was having a wobble yesterday, that's all. I have to go now, Freya, I need to go to the shops before I pick up the twins.' And with a muffled goodbye she was gone.

Poor Daisy. The news of her unexpected pregnancy had clearly really floored her, but Freya was sure she would soon bounce back. Daisy was strong. It was Daisy who had held the family together when their father had upped and left, who had kept everything going while their mother fell apart, encouraging her to make a new life for herself, and pushing Freya into still going to university. Daisy was a coper. Freya was sure that once her sister adjusted to the shock of being pregnant, she would be pleased at this new addition to their family. She remembered what Daisy had said about her and Mark drifting apart. Well, it sounded like he was being supportive now, so maybe this baby would bring them both together again. She hoped so. All marriages went through bad patches, after all. Maybe Phil's accident would bring her and Phil together again too. Then she remembered that she hadn't told Daisy about the police visiting the hospital. *It's only a suspicion at the moment*, she thought, resolving not to tell anyone until the police were sure whether the brakes definitely had been tampered with or not.

She stopped off at the supermarket to get some supplies, then set off home. Her colleague Nadia phoned as Freya parked up in the drive. She'd already texted a couple of times this week, as had Stefan.

'Hello, Nadia.'

'Hi, hun, just checking that you're okay. How's Phil?'

'Recovering well – the doctor said he can come home in a couple of days. He still can't remember the last two years, though.'

'It'll come back. And if it doesn't, losing two years of your memory isn't that bad, is it? Better than losing it all. Or dying.'

She was right. 'Too true. Now, how did the Kada presentation go?' she asked, wanting to change the subject and guessing that was the main reason that Nadia had phoned. The presentation had been scheduled for earlier this afternoon.

'Perfect! And… drum roll, please! We got the contract. Obviously I'll hand it all back over to you as soon as you're able to come back to work, but I thought you'd want to know sooner.'

'That's amazing news! I can't wait to be back. Though I'm hoping Stefan will let me work from home a couple of days a week so I don't have to leave Phil on his own too much. He's feeling a bit vulnerable what with his amnesia and broken ribs.'

'I'm sure he will – Stefan's always flexible like that and it's perfectly reasonable that you want to be at home to keep an eye on Phil.'

They chatted for a while about work-related stuff then Nadia announced she had to go as her supper was ready. 'Take care of yourself and call me if I can do anything.'

'Thank you.' As she ended the call, Freya thought how lucky she was to work for such a friendly, supportive company. That was one of the reasons she hadn't wanted to leave and work freelance from home, as Phil had kept asking her to do.

If she did give their marriage another chance and worked from home until Phil was fully recovered, would he make it difficult for her to go back to work, beg her to work from home all the time? Would she have to fight with him about that again?

Phil seemed to have reverted back to the easy-going Phil she had once loved so much. But how could she know if he would remain that way?

CHAPTER TWELVE

Thursday

It had taken a great deal of thought and soul-searching but by the next morning Freya had made her decision. Phil was really looking forward to coming home tomorrow and it would be cruel to tell him that she was leaving him, leaving him alone to cope with his injuries and memory loss from the accident. *I'm sure he has changed but any sign of him being abusive and I'll get out right away*, she promised herself. She had to give Phil a chance. She owed him that much. He could have been killed. And however bad things had got between them, there was a part of her that still loved him, and wanted him to revert to the man he had once been.

First, though, she needed to go into work to talk to Stefan. She was sure she could sort out a flexi-time agreement that would allow her to spend time with Phil and continue working but didn't want to discuss that over the phone – it was better done face to face. And she wanted to see everyone again, talk about the new project, make sure she wasn't completely out of the loop. She'd worked hard on the Kada account and didn't want to lose it. Phil might still be a bit fragile, but he didn't need her home all day, every day. And it would be good for them to have a bit of space from each other.

'Freya, honey, how good to see you!' Julia, Stefan's secretary, jumped up from her chair and across the room to give Freya a big hug. 'How are you? And how's that gorgeous husband of yours?' She stood back and scanned Freya's face. 'You look tired, but that's only to be expected.'

'I am tired, but I'm feeling a lot better today. I've come to see Stefan, ask if I can arrange some flexible working.'

'I'm sure he won't mind at all. He and Nadia are in a meeting but I'll tell him you're here as he might want to include you.' She picked up the phone.

I hope it's about the Kada contract, Freya thought, eying the door of Stefan's office. She couldn't wait to hear all about it.

'He said to go straight in,' Julia announced, putting down the phone.

'Thanks.' Freya gave a polite knock on the door then walked in.

Stefan stood up as soon as she entered. 'Freya, good to see you. How's Phil?'

'Fine – apart from some memory loss, a few broken ribs and an injured arm. He's coming home tomorrow.'

'That's good news.' Stefan sat back down and indicated for her to sit in the empty seat next to Nadia. 'Now, how are you fixed about coming back to work?'

She was pleased that he'd raised the subject; it made it easier for her. 'I was wondering if I could work flexibly for the foreseeable? Even though he's making a good recovery, I don't want to leave Phil at home by himself all day, not just yet. So if I could work from home a couple of days a week…'

'No problem, we'll have a talk and sort that out. But first, let me bring you up to speed with the Kada deal.' He beamed. 'Kada absolutely love your ideas – you did a great job there. Well done.'

Freya was chuffed. Stefan was a good boss but he didn't give praise lightly, so his comments meant a lot to her. She listened as he filled her in with what had happened at the meeting, the deal they had signed, and what the company wanted. As he outlined everything, Freya felt herself relax. It was good to be back at work again and have something else to think about. She loved her job and the design team she worked with.

'So now let's talk about your flexi-hours because we definitely want you to be Kada's first point of contact.'

They discussed various options, finally deciding that for the next month Freya would come into the office to work on Mondays and Fridays, then work the rest of the week at home, and try to arrange any necessary face-to-face meetings with clients during her 'work in the office' days.

'I also know you still have several days' holiday due to you, so if you need to take the odd day off to look after Phil without needing to do any work, just email and let me know,' Stefan told her.

Freya was relieved; it sounded like a perfect arrangement. After going for a coffee break with Nadia and some other members of the team, she set off to do a supermarket shop before going to visit Phil again; she'd only picked up a couple of items last night and needed more supplies for when Phil came home. She'd blitz the house too after the afternoon visit.

Phil's eyes lit up when she walked in. He was obviously so happy about the thought of coming home the next day that Freya gave him a hug and spontaneously kissed him quickly on the lips. Phil's eyes sparkled.

'How are you feeling today?' she asked as she sat down.

'Better. Not so achy. Bloody frustrated, though! I'm getting stir-crazy lying here,' he told her. 'Although at least I've thought of a few ideas for articles. I'll write them up when I get home, even if it'll be a bit slow – my arm is still aching.'

'You've got some speech recognition software on your computer,' Freya told him. 'You use it a lot because you get RSI in your fingers.'

'Do I? There's such a lot I can't remember.' His face clouded over.

'It'll come back to you, I'm sure, once you get back in familiar surroundings.' Freya squeezed his hand, though part of her secretly hoped that some memories of their fraught relationship would never come back. 'At least you still remember me, and that we're married, and our home. Imagine if you couldn't remember that.'

She'd been thinking about that last night. It would have been terrible if Phil had lost his memory completely or had no memory of her at all. They had to be grateful that it was only the last two years he'd forgotten.

'Tell me what you've been doing today,' he urged.

'Well, I went into work to arrange flexi-hours.' She told him what she'd arranged with Stefan. 'I can't work from home every day, but you'll be fine on your own Mondays and Fridays, won't you?'

'I'll manage… At least it's either side of the weekend.' He frowned. 'I know you said my courses at the uni are finished for the summer but I wonder if I should be doing some marking or planning next year's course? Do they know about my accident?'

'Yes, Tom read about it in the newspaper and phoned to ask how you are. Remember I told you? The editor of the *Telegraph* phoned too. You can contact them in a week or so when you feel stronger.' She'd only told him this yesterday; she hoped he hadn't got short-term memory loss too.

They chatted for a while, easily, just like they used to do. And when she was about to go, Phil reached for her and pulled her to him. 'How about another kiss goodbye?'

'Now you're being greedy.' She bent down, lowering her lips to his. Then his arm was around her neck, gently pulling her closer, deepening the kiss, and she remembered just how much she loved him. They loved each other.

They were going to be happy this time. She'd make sure of it. Phil was so weak and vulnerable, she would have the upper hand now.

CHAPTER THIRTEEN

Phil

Friday

'Here we are. Home.' Freya's voice was bright and breezy as she pulled up in the drive outside a semi-detached house in a cul-de-sac, which Phil immediately recognised as their home. From the outside it was pretty much as he remembered: a dark green door with a polished brass letterbox, knocker and number 9, large drive with a lawn to the left and paved driveway alongside the single garage on the right, large bay window. He was relieved that it felt so familiar. A memory suddenly flashed across his mind of them getting out of a taxi; they'd just returned from their honeymoon.

'I remember us coming home from honeymoon… and I carried you over the threshold!' he said, excited as the image of them both laughing as he swept Freya off her feet came into his mind. 'Maybe I'll remember more things now I'm home.'

He saw something – was it apprehension? – in Freya's eyes but then she smiled. 'I hope so.'

She got out of the car, walked around the bonnet and opened the passenger door for him. 'This is the wrong way round. I should open the door for you,' he said as he carefully eased himself out, mindful of his still-painful ribs.

'Just be glad that you're alive. I am,' she told him, kissing him on the cheek. She locked the car then took his arm, and they both walked over to the front door.

It's strange to lose part of my memory yet remember so much, Phil thought as Freya opened the door and they stepped inside. This house was so familiar to him, yet he had lost the two years since the day he had opened this very same door and carried Freya over the threshold. Would it be the same inside? he wondered. Had they decorated? So many questions were floating around in his mind as he walked in the hall.

'Does it look how you remember it?' Freya asked as she closed the door behind them. 'Does it feel like home?'

Phil took in the silver-grey carpet that covered the hall and stairs, the silver-and-white embossed wallpaper, the large framed mirror on the wall. 'This looks the same.' Then he turned to the left and walked into the lounge, scanning the room: the same wallpaper, but light oak tiles instead of carpet, the grey rug he'd remembered was replaced by a cream one, cream pleated curtains, a new cream soft leather suite – they'd had the black leather one from his flat, he remembered. What else was new? He frowned as he searched the room. The cream leather pouffe and the sleek light oak coffee table.

'We've had quite a bit of new stuff in here. It looks great.'

'Yes, we got the sofa last year, and bought the new curtains and rug to match. Oh, and the coffee table to match the unit.'

Phil walked over to the light oak unit running along the right wall – their wedding photo was in pride of place, and there were various ornaments scattered about. His gaze paused. There was something else that should be there. What was it? He searched through the fog in his mind and then it came to him, piercing through the mist like the sun's rays through a cloud. The crystal vase that his department at the university had clubbed together to buy them as a wedding present. It was a beautiful vase. They'd put it on the lower shelf of the unit just before they'd gone on honeymoon and he'd promised to always fill it with roses for Freya. Roses were a symbol of their love for each other.

'Where's the vase?' he asked.

He saw something flicker across Freya's face again, an emotion he couldn't quite catch before it was gone.

'The crystal one? I'm afraid it got broken.'

'That's a shame. I loved that vase.'

'Me too. Fancy a cup of coffee and a sandwich?' she asked. 'I've got steak and mushrooms for tonight but thought you'd prefer something lighter for now.'

'Please. I'll just have a wander around while you make it. See what I can remember.'

He walked from room to room slowly, trying hard to remember the last two years of living here. These walls must hold so many memories, if only they could speak to him. Freya was already in the kitchen – a long kitchen with the white marble worktops and sleek black cupboards that he remembered, and an alcove leading to the dining area with the familiar light oak table with a black marble top and four light oak chairs. Nothing much had changed here then.

He walked up the stairs and saw a door on the left and two doors on the right. The bathroom was the door on the left, and the first door on the right was going to be the spare room and a study. They hadn't decided yet whose study it would be – well, they hadn't when they'd come back from honeymoon. He opened the door, taking in the single bed with the white lace bedcover, the white desk and chair, the artwork on the wall, and knew that it was Freya's room. So he had the converted garage room – he was pleased about that; it was the one he'd wanted, he remembered.

He was the one who worked from home the most so needed the bigger, more accessible room. He opened the door to their bedroom, his eyes skimming over the king-size bed with the cream padded headboard and footboard, the lilac and white bedspread, the floor-length, lilac, pleated-top curtains at the window – the bedspread and curtains were both new but the rest was the same as he remembered. Slowly he walked over to the wall-to-wall white wardrobes, opening the door on the right, which he'd remembered as his. Rows of shirts, trousers and jackets hung there. He opened the next door. Here were casual clothes, jeans, T-shirts, jumpers. He moved along to the next wardrobe, opening it to reveal Freya's clothes, not as neatly sorted out as his, but then Freya was untidy, he remembered that. Her flat had always been a mess – organised chaos, she'd laughingly called it. It had driven him mad although he had never shown it. Did it still drive him mad now or had he learnt to tolerate it?

'Lunch is ready!' Freya called.

Slowly he turned and walked out, down the stairs and into the kitchen. Two plates of wholemeal bread and ham sandwiches and a bowl of mixed salad were on the worktop, and two cups of coffee. 'How was it? I don't think we've changed that much in the last two years, have we?'

'It doesn't seem so – except the bedspread and curtains,' he remarked.

'We changed the colour scheme a couple of months ago. Want to eat at the table?'

'Sure.' Using his left hand he helped her carry the things over to the dining table – his right arm was still painful although it was healing now. They sat and ate, chatting a bit awkwardly at first but then somehow they managed to relax, and they ended up sitting out in the garden, relaxing in the sunshine, reminiscing over their honeymoon, things they had done, with Phil asking Freya questions which she patiently answered.

He didn't ask her where he'd been driving to last Friday on his own, though, and she didn't mention it either. He had a feeling they both had things they wanted to forget.

That night, in bed, they snuggled up to each other, said they loved each other, kissed just like they used to do, but Phil couldn't shake the niggling feeling that something was wrong and he sensed that Freya was tense too. Finally, he fell asleep on his left side, cuddled up to Freya, his arm wrapped around her waist like they always used to do. He was home, with his wife.

In the middle of the night he woke with a start. Something had disturbed him. Then it came to him. A dream. Something thrown against the wall, shattering glass everywhere. He touched his forehead – the glass had hit him, he was sure it had. The cut on his forehead hadn't been caused by the car crash. Someone had thrown something glass against a wall and it had bounced back and hit him.

He looked down at Freya sleeping beside him. What had happened? What had he forgotten?

CHAPTER FOURTEEN

Saturday

Sunlight was streaming through the bedroom window when Phil
opened his eyes. For a moment he lay there, enjoying the close-
ness of Freya's body against his. It was so good to be back home.
Even though he had been in a side ward by himself, he'd found
it difficult to relax with all the hustle and bustle of the hospital.
He glanced at the digital clock on his bedside table: eight thirty.
Freya was still soundly sleeping; she must have been exhausted.
He lay still for a moment, recalling the strange dream he'd had
of shards of glass shooting everywhere, one of them hitting his
forehead. Was it a memory or a dream? He probed his mind for
memories of things that had happened after they'd returned from
their honeymoon but there were none. It was all a blank. How
could he forget two years of his life when he could remember so
clearly the day he and Freya had first met? He'd fallen in love with
Freya as soon as he'd seen her. The memory of that day flooded
back into his mind.

*

Phil paid for his coffee and glanced around at the bustling café.
It looked like he'd be drinking this standing up. Great. He really
wanted to sit for a few minutes and jot down some notes; his

article for the *Telegraph* was due tomorrow. Out of the corner of his eye, he spotted two women getting up from a small table in the corner and quickly legged it over there before someone else could grab it. He plonked himself in the seat just as an elderly couple headed over to the table, disappointment registering on their faces before they turned away. If Phil hadn't been so desperate for a few quiet minutes to work, he might have given up his table to the old couple. As it was, he put his briefcase down on the empty seat next to him, hoping it would deter a stranger from sitting there and trying to engage him in idle conversation. He hated pointless chatter with people he had never met, and usually avoided crowded cafés like this, but it was raining and he'd just missed his train due to the meeting running over. It had gone well, though – he'd got a commission for a monthly magazine article. He took a sip of his coffee, pulled his notebook out of his briefcase and started to write.

'Excuse me, is that seat taken?'

Damn, just what I need. And it was a woman too – she was bound to want to chat. He looked up resignedly then his breath caught in his throat at the vision in front of him: vibrant jade-green eyes, cheeks flushed, her bright red lips curved in a smile, raindrops sparkling on her long chestnut waves, the promise of a stunning figure underneath the electric-blue raincoat and knee-length black boots, her black-leather gloved hand holding a mug of coffee. She was early thirties, he guessed, beautiful, and she looked so *alive.*

'No.' He reached across to move his briefcase. 'Please sit down.'

'Thanks.'

She placed the mug of what he could now see was cappuccino down on the table in front of her and eased herself into the seat as Phil closed his notebook. 'Please, don't let me disturb you. You carry on.'

He didn't want to carry on with his writing. He wanted to talk to her, find out more about her, make a connection so that she didn't just finish her coffee, get up and walk out of his life. He watched transfixed as she rolled off her gloves then picked up the sachet of sugar, the dark blue varnish on her short fingernails very slightly chipped. She ripped the corner of the sachet and emptied it into the foamy coffee, then gently stirred it round before taking out the spoon and licking the froth off the back of it. He wondered if she realised how seductive she looked, licking the spoon like that. She glanced up, as if suddenly aware that he was staring at her. Their eyes locked for a second and he felt a shiver of desire. Not just desire. Love. He suddenly knew for certain that he wanted to spend the rest of his life with this gorgeous woman.

'Rubbish weather, isn't it?' It was a safe comment to make – the British always talked about the weather.

She nodded and smiled back. 'Do I detect an Irish accent?'

He grinned. 'I thought I might have got rid of it by now. It's been years since I lived in Ireland. I'm from Omagh.'

'There's still a lilt to your voice.' She tilted her head to one side, the smile still playing on her lips. 'It's nice. My grandmother was Northern Irish. She lived in Ballyclare – I loved to visit her when I was a child.' She glanced at the closed notebook. 'Are you a writer?'

'Yes, I've a regular feature in the *Telegraph*. I was just jotting down notes for my next article.'

'Impressive.' She sounded as if she meant it.

'Not really, it's the local *Telegraph* not the London one,' he confessed although he secretly hoped she was impressed. 'I'm a part-time lecturer at Birmingham University too.' He sipped the last of his coffee and leant back slightly in his chair. 'What do you do?'

'I'm a marketing consultant,' she told him. 'I work for a graphic design agency called IPA.'

He had actually heard of IPA. They had a brilliant reputation, dealing with lots of high-street retailers and popular companies. 'Now it's my turn to be impressed.'

She grinned. 'I have to admit that I'm dead chuffed. I only landed the job a few months ago – I was freelancing until then. The freedom of working for yourself is nice but I decided that it was even nicer to have a regular pay packet.'

'I know that feeling,' he admitted. It was one of the reasons he had applied for the position of part-time lecturer on the journalism course at Birmingham University all those years ago. Freelance work paid well but it was difficult to earn a regular income from it. 'I'm Phil, by the way.' He waved his hand in greeting; shaking hands seemed too formal. 'Phil Keegan.'

'Hi, Phil, I'm Freya. Freya Swinton.' She gave him a little finger wave. She was so at ease, confident, vivacious. He couldn't let her just walk out of his life. Had she got a husband, he wondered, or a boyfriend? He hoped she hadn't.

They chatted away easily, Freya telling him about how she'd gone to the University of Worcester with dreams of being a graphic artist and ended up working as a consultant instead. 'I enjoy it, though, more than I thought I would.' He told her how he'd gone to the University of Leeds, with dreams of being a hotshot journalist on one of the London newspapers. 'The local *Telegraph* is as far as I've got,' he admitted. 'I have a regular column with them – and contribute to a few magazines. I'm still working on breaking into one of the broadsheets, though.'

'Hey, having your own column is an achievement to be proud of.' She took a slow sip of her coffee. 'But do keep on trying with the broadsheets – you should never give up on your dream.'

'I won't. I'm stubborn like that,' he told her.

'Determined, not stubborn,' she corrected lightly. 'Determined is a good trait; stubborn isn't always.'

'And are you… determined too?'

'Oh no, I'm stubborn. That's how I know it isn't a good trait.' Her eyes twinkled and he wondered if she was jesting or not.

She glanced at her watch. 'I'm afraid I have to go – my train is due in ten minutes and I don't want to miss it. The trains don't run that frequently to Worcester.' She grabbed her bag and stood up. 'It's been nice talking to you, Phil. Thanks for letting me share your table.'

He stood up too. 'Maybe we could do it again sometime… if you're free and want to, that is.'

She nodded. 'I am free and yes, I'd love to.'

So they exchanged numbers, agreed to meet up in Birmingham city centre at the weekend and Freya hurried off.

They met the following Saturday evening, had a drink then went for dinner, chatting away easily as if they had known each other for years. It was as if they belonged together. When Phil presented Freya with a single white thornless rose, she seemed genuinely touched. He gave her one for every date, and it was only after the fourth date she asked him what the significance of the white rose was.

'It's always a single white rose with no thorns,' she told him, sniffing it appreciatively. 'Most people give red roses. Are white roses your favourite?'

'Red roses are a cop-out; they require no thought. Don't you know the language of roses? What the colours mean?' he asked her softly.

Her beautiful green eyes met his, transfixed as he told her that a single white rose symbolised love at first sight. 'I fell in love with you as soon as I looked up and saw you standing by my table in the café,' he confessed. He saw shock and then pleasure register on her face. He lifted his hand and gently traced the outline of her lips with his thumb. 'I didn't want to tell you before, in case you thought I was coming on too strong. I didn't want to frighten you off. But now…' He hesitated, his voice breaking slightly, then composed himself. 'I have to tell you because I need to know if you feel the same way. If you don't, then I'm afraid that I have to walk away before I get too hurt because every time I see you I fall in love with you even more.'

'You love me?' Her voice was little more than a whisper, her eyes still holding his.

He nodded. 'I do.' He wrapped an arm around her waist, his eyes never leaving her face. 'What I need to know is do you love me?'

She hesitated and he held his breath. Had he been too hasty telling her how he felt? To his relief and delight, she nodded emphatically. 'Yes, I do. I do.'

They made love that night, and from then on they were inseparable. Within six months they were married.

They had a wonderful wedding on the beach in Barbados, where they were staying in a five-star hotel. They'd taken long moonlit walks along the seashore, made love every day, been so happy. He had known then that he'd been right to marry Freya. She was the one for him.

This time it would be okay.

CHAPTER FIFTEEN

Freya stirred and opened her eyes. 'Morning. Have you been awake long?'

'Ten minutes or so,' he told her. 'I was thinking about the day we first met. I'm glad I can remember that.'

'Me too.' She edged up on her arm and kissed him on the cheek. 'Sleep well?'

'Mostly. I had this weird dream. Well, I'm not sure it was a dream. It felt real, more like a memory.'

'Oh?' She looked curious. 'What about?'

He frowned. 'I can only remember a bit of it. Shards of glass shooting everywhere, one of them hitting my forehead.' He touched the cut. 'I thought I was remembering the accident at first but then I realised that the glass had been thrown against a wall.' He turned anxious eyes to her. 'Did we have a row? Did one of us throw a glass against a wall?'

She hesitated then nodded slowly. 'Yes. We had a row the night you had the accident. You threw the vase – the crystal one – against the wall. It broke. Some glass hit you and some hit me.' She held out her forearm so he could see the almost-healed cut.

Phil was stunned. 'I threw the vase? Why?'

Freya swallowed. 'You'd booked us a surprise holiday to Dubai – we were supposed to be there this week – but I had to work. I'd been working on the presentation for the Kada account. I said I couldn't go away at such short notice and you… lost your temper.'

Phil was shocked at her words. Had he really done this? He couldn't believe it. 'Oh my God, Freya! That's really awful. I just can't believe I would act like that. I'm so sorry.' He cupped his hands over his face, stunned and ashamed.

She reached out and touched his shoulders. 'It doesn't matter now. It's not important.'

He lowered his hands, hardly able to meet her eyes. 'It's appalling behaviour. I'm so sorry. No wonder you were a bit… awkward at the hospital. You were upset with me.'

'You stormed out. I thought we were over…' Her eyes clouded over.

Oh God, this was awful! She must have been so hurt, and angry too, yet she'd still come and visited him, sat by his side. No wonder she hadn't wanted to kiss him at first. He took her hand in his, his eyes holding hers. 'I'm sorry, truly I am. I don't know how I could do such an awful thing. You should have told me when I asked about the vase.'

'I didn't want to upset you by mentioning it. It was just a stupid row.'

'I hurt you!' Horrified, Phil's eyes rested on her cut. Then back to her face. 'I haven't done anything like that before, have I?'

He knew by the expression on her face that he had. 'Freya? Please tell me the truth. Don't try and protect me.'

'A few times,' she admitted softly.

Her answer left him reeling. What kind of person was he? 'I can't remember this at all. Was it after we got married?' He was confused, hardly believing her words. 'How could I have when I love you so much?'

'It's okay. It doesn't matter. It's in the past. Things can be different now. *You* can be different.' She wrapped her arms around him and they hugged each other tight.

'I'm so sorry. And so ashamed,' he whispered, bewildered. How could he have done this to Freya? He loved her; he had thought they were happy. Now it turned out he had hurt her? He didn't know how to deal with this.

Freya looked at him sympathetically. 'It was awful but it's in the past. We're making a fresh start,' she replied. 'I'll go and make us a cup of coffee. You rest here awhile.' She slipped out of bed.

'Let's drink it in the garden,' Phil told her. 'I'll come down too in a minute.'

He wanted a few minutes to gather his thoughts and deal with this shocking revelation. How could he have acted in such an appalling way – and have no memory of it? And how could Freya forgive him for it? Was there more to it than she had said, something she was keeping from him? Should he ask her to tell him exactly what had happened?

Thinking about it gave him a headache. He pulled his jeans on over his boxers and went down to join Freya. To his surprise, she was standing by the open back door and there was no sign of the coffee machine bubbling.

'What's up?' he asked.

She turned to him, troubled. 'When I came down the back door was open.'

'What? Has someone broken in? Is anything missing?'

'I've checked and nothing seems to be. You didn't get up in the night for a smoke and forget to shut the door, did you?'

Did he? 'No. I'm sure I didn't. I can't remember,' he said, confused. 'I'm sorry.'

'It's okay, don't stress. It doesn't matter. There's no harm done,' Freya said reassuringly. 'You do sleepwalk sometimes when you're stressed.'

So he had started sleepwalking again since he and Freya had got married? Why? It was something he'd only done when he was stressed, and he couldn't remember doing it for years, well before he met Freya. But what had he been stressed about?

CHAPTER SIXTEEN

Sunday

It was a bright June day; white clouds scattered across a light blue sky. As they both sat out in the garden, the sun warm on their arms, Phil gazed around at the colourful flowers in pots dotted here and there, the small pond and rockery, the neat lawn. It had just been a lawn when they'd bought the house. They'd certainly worked hard on it over the past two years. His gaze rested on the big pot of red geraniums and he paused, a memory niggling away at the back of his mind. He stared at them, concentrating, but nothing came. Perhaps he was remembering the trip to the garden centre to get them.

'We've really transformed this garden. I only remember the lawn and a couple of flower beds,' he said.

'Yes, we spent lots of weekends out here brightening it up. It's gorgeous, isn't it? We usually eat out here in the summer – we work outside a lot too.'

It sounded as if they were happy together. Yet apparently he had got so angry over a last-minute holiday that he'd hurt Freya and just because she couldn't take time off work to go. He was ashamed that he had been so selfish and cruel. Okay, yes, it would have cost a lot of money and he wouldn't have wanted to waste that, but what the hell had he been thinking of, booking a holiday without checking with Freya? And it was no excuse for such disgusting behaviour.

Thinking about the holiday, he realised he ought to find out the details and alert their insurers. It must have cost a fortune and they couldn't afford to lose that much money. He had no idea who he had booked it through and didn't want to mention it to Freya because it would mean bringing up that terrible argument again. There was bound to be some information about it on his desk or computer – he'd go and have a mooch in a bit, see what he could find.

'Why don't we go for a drive this afternoon?' Freya's voice cut through his thoughts. 'We could go to the Mill Pond, sit outside with a soft drink and watch the boats go by on the canal. Do you fancy it?'

He remembered the Mill Pond, a picturesque pub by the river. It had been one of their favourite weekend haunts when they were dating, and he was pleased that they still frequented it.

'Sounds good to me,' he said. 'I could do with getting out for a bit, after being in hospital all week. We could have lunch there?'

'Yes, let's. About twelve thirty?'

'Perfect.' Phil finished off the last of his croissant, chewing it thoughtfully for a moment. 'I think I'll pop into my study for a bit and familiarise myself with what I've been doing over the past two years.'

Freya said she wanted to potter about in the garden for a while, so when they'd finished their breakfast, Phil made his way to his study in the converted garage – they obviously left both their cars parked in the drive. He looked around and saw that he'd partitioned off the front half of the garage, with a door leading into it, where he kept garden tools and other bits and bobs; he could also have easy access to it from outside by lifting the garage door. He'd made a neat job of it too, he thought approvingly. He closed the door again and went over to his desk, sitting down and starting up the laptop. The screen sprang to life. Then a blank box appeared, prompting him to put his password in. Damn, he'd forgotten it was password-protected. He hoped he hadn't changed his password over the last couple of years. He typed it in only for a message to flash up telling him that the password he had entered was incorrect. Bugger. What would he have changed it to? Would he have kept a record of it somewhere? He pulled open the top drawer of his desk and rummaged through for a notebook. Then the next drawer, and the next. By the time he got to the bottom drawer, he had found several notebooks but none with passwords in them. Had he committed the password solely to memory? How stupid of him! Though he wasn't to know he would lose his memory, was he?

The computer screen was blank now, gone into hibernation. He booted it up again, staring at the blank space for his password. Then he noticed the words underneath: *Forgotten your password?* Ah, he'd do that, as long as he could answer the security questions. And this time he'd write it down.

Finally, he was in. Various folders were scattered over his screen – he always put things in folders; he liked things to be tidy. A quick glance showed they all seemed to be articles he was working on or university-related stuff. He clicked on the folder marked 'Uni Course' to see what he was teaching now; surely it was pretty much the same stuff. He glanced through the lesson plans – he was still teaching journalism, and yes, it was things he was familiar with. Thank goodness.

There was no folder marked 'Holiday', so he scrolled through the documents. Ah, here it was, a folder called 'Hols'. He clicked on it. There were folders labelled 'Rome', 'Venice' and 'Egypt'. He opened them up one by one and read the details, trying to imagine the hotels they'd stayed in, him and Freya sunbathing on the beach, sightseeing, walking along the beach at midnight like they had done on their honeymoon. How could he forget two years of his life?

His head started to throb. God, he wished he could turn back the clock to the evening of the crash, that he had never gone storming out as Freya told him he had done. He still couldn't believe that he'd acted like that, that he'd booked a holiday without checking that she wasn't working first, then gone mental at her and smashed that lovely vase.

You've only got Freya's word for that. As the words floated into his mind, he paused to fleetingly consider them then pushed them back out again. Freya wouldn't make up something like that.

After an hour of fruitless searching, he still hadn't found any mention of a holiday in Dubai. He'd run a search on 'Dubai' just to make sure, but nothing came up, and he had thoroughly checked his emails – thank goodness the password was saved to his computer – in case he hadn't yet saved the details to the 'Hols' folder. Nothing there. Maybe he hadn't booked it online. Maybe he had seen a late deal in a travel agent's instead? That would explain why he had booked it without checking with Freya first, because it had been a bargain, and he'd obviously believed she could take the time off work. He wouldn't have booked it if he hadn't believed she could get away, would he? He searched through all the desk drawers once more, then the trays on his desk, getting more and more frustrated.

There was no record of the holiday being booked.

What was going on? Surely there would be a record of it? And someone must have been wondering why they hadn't arrived. Wouldn't they phone or email him? Reluctant as he was to ask Freya, it was the only thing left for him to do.

She was still out in the garden, watering the pots. She turned around as he came out. 'Everything okay? You look a bit stressed.'

'I thought I'd better alert the insurance people about the missed holiday, get our money back, but I can't find the details anywhere,' he confessed. 'I've had all my desk out, checked my email. Zilch. Do you know who I booked with?'

He saw a cloud pass over her face and guessed she was thinking back to that awful night. He wished he hadn't had to ask her, that he could have quietly cancelled without bringing it all up again.

'You didn't tell me anything about it, Phil. You just said you'd booked us a holiday as a surprise but when I said I couldn't get away that week, we ended up rowing and you stormed out.'

A dull pain was forming across his brows, and he massaged his forehead with his fingers. 'How can I cancel when I don't know anything about it? I should have some record of it. A receipt, an email.'

'Maybe it was in the car.'

She could be right, and they'd said the car was a write-off. If the holiday details had been in there, then they were probably destroyed. He rubbed his forehead again. 'I hate this, not being able to remember anything.'

She smiled brightly. 'Don't worry, you're bound to feel confused. It must be horrible not remembering stuff. Forget about the holiday for now. We have months to tell the insurance company about your accident. Just concentrate on getting better.'

He couldn't forget about it – it was the damn holiday that had caused the argument. It must have been very important to him – maybe that was why he'd got so angry. He'd planned to spoil Freya and maybe she'd dismissed it without even discussing it, shut him down right away. Even so, it was inexcusable for him to throw the vase and then storm out.

If that's what he had done.

Maybe it had been *Freya* who threw the vase, and that was why he'd stormed out. He couldn't make sense of it all.

Freya walked over and gave him a hug. 'Come on, let's go to the Mill Pond now. It'll do us good to get out for a bit.'

As her arms wrapped around him and she nestled her head on his shoulder, he relaxed. She was right: he had to forget about the damn holiday and the awful row – the important thing was that he and Freya loved each other. All couples had rows, and okay, it sounded like this one had got out of hand, but it was in the past. He had to make sure it never happened again.

CHAPTER SEVENTEEN

Monday

'Daisy!' Phil was surprised to see his sister-in-law standing on the doorstep. He'd actually thought twice about answering the door when the bell rang, and if he'd seen it was Daisy, he probably wouldn't have – he was tired and his ribs were aching, and he really didn't want to talk to anyone right now. 'Freya's at work today – didn't she tell you?'

Daisy looked a bit awkward. 'Yes, but well… I need to speak to you.'

He stared at her, uncomprehending. Why did she want to speak to him? And why had she come when she knew Freya wasn't at home? He didn't like the sound of this.

'Can I come in for a few minutes?' she asked. 'It's a bit private to discuss on the doorstep.'

That sounded ominous. 'Sure.' He stepped back, opening the door wide.

'Thanks.' She walked in then along the hall into the lounge. Phil followed her through, closing the door behind him.

'What's this about?' he asked. He didn't feel like being sociable, especially with someone he barely knew and had never particularly liked.

Daisy was standing with her back to the doorway, almost as if she was ready to make a quick exit if things got uncomfortable. Phil walked past her, stood facing her.

'How are you feeling?' she asked.

'My ribs are still pretty sore, and this is a bind.' Phil nodded at his bandaged arm. 'Otherwise I'm okay. Thanks for asking. Has Freya asked you to pop in to make sure I'm coping okay?' He couldn't think of any other reason why she would be here.

She ignored the question, her eyes resting on his face as if trying to assess his reaction. 'What about your memory? Have you remembered anything from the last two years? Anything at all?'

Ah, was this about the argument the night of the accident? Had Freya told her about it? He guessed she was bound to – as sisters they must be close. He shook his head. 'Nothing at all. Freya told me about our argument, if that's what you came to talk to me about. I'm really ashamed about that. I can't believe I acted so badly just because she couldn't ditch everything and go on a last-minute holiday with me. I'm sorry, truly I am.'

'Well, it's good to know that you're actually admitting it instead of pretending that Freya was the one at fault.'

'What do you mean?' He shook his head, bewildered. He had no idea what Daisy was talking about and could see that she was really annoyed about something. What else had he done that he couldn't remember?

It took her a long time to answer, and when she finally did, her words stunned him.

'You phoned me on Friday night. You sounded really upset and said that Freya had thrown the vase and it had cut your forehead. You said you were leaving her. You're a good actor – you had me convinced!'

Phil scratched his head. 'I don't understand… Why would I say that?' Then something else occurred to him. 'And why would I phone you?'

Daisy went pale. 'I'm sorry, I need to sit down.' She placed a hand on the arm of the sofa and eased herself down, looking so queasy Phil thought she was going to throw up.

'Are you ill? Do you need a drink?'

'A glass of water, please,' she whispered.

Phil fetched it, using the ice dispenser in the fridge to make sure the water was cold. He watched in concern as Daisy took the glass from him and sipped it. Why was she here, and was what she'd said true? None of it made sense. He waited impatiently for her to compose herself.

'Why have you come here? What did you want to speak to me about?' he asked.

'Nothing. It was a mistake.' She took a long gulp of water, put the glass down on the coffee table in front of her and got to her feet. 'I think it's best if I go.'

She took a few steps towards the door but Phil reached out and grabbed her shoulder to stop her.

'Please don't walk out on me after dropping a bombshell like that. You said I phoned you to say Freya had hurt me and I was leaving her. You came to talk to me when you knew Freya would be at work. And you seem angry with me. You obviously wanted to talk to me about something I've done – what is it?'

She turned to him and he saw the panic in her eyes. What was she keeping from him? Was Freya lying when she said he was the one who threw the vase?

'Tell me the truth, Daisy,' he pleaded. 'Did I really phone you and say that about Freya? Why? Why would I confide in *you*? I barely know you.'

She flinched as if he had slapped her across the face, then she raised her chin defiantly, her eyes meeting his. 'Because we've been having an affair over the past few months, Phil. You were leaving Freya on the night of the accident. We were going away together.'

CHAPTER EIGHTEEN

Phil's shock was quickly replaced by anger. How could Daisy tell a lie this big? Was she trying to cause trouble for him and Freya? 'You're lying!' he shouted furiously. 'I would never have an affair with you. Never! I don't even fancy you! And I love Freya. You're a bloody liar!'

Daisy backed away, visibly shaking. Then she laughed, a scornful, mocking laugh. 'Of course I'm lying,' she scoffed. 'I was testing you, Phil, checking to see if you can control your anger now and making sure that you aren't conning my sister into believing that you've lost your memory so that she'll give you another chance. You always blamed Freya for the rows and the violence, even though you were the abusive one.'

Phil gasped at her words, his mind spinning. He didn't like Daisy, could only remember meeting her a couple of times. Why would he tell her lies about Freya? He couldn't understand why she was here and saying these things.

'She thinks that you've changed, that because you say you've lost your memories of the last two years you can both start again and be happy, that you won't be violent any more. Well, you might have forgotten, and Freya might believe you have changed, but I don't. I know what you did, how you've treated my sister, and I've come to tell you that I'll be watching you.'

Phil stared at her, eyes blazing, fists clenched tight. He wanted to yell at Daisy to stop telling her lies and to get out, but he was in turmoil, not knowing if they *were* lies. Was he really such an awful person?

'I don't trust you, Phil. You're a liar and a bully. You'd better not hurt my sister again or I'll call the police on you.'

She turned and walked out of the lounge, along the hall, towards the front door, but Phil suddenly charged after her, wanting – needing – more answers. He seized her shoulder, spun her around, anger now taking over from bewilderment.

'Why did you say we had an affair? And pretend that I'd been confiding in you?'

'I wanted to see how you'd react. To see if you were still so quick to lose your temper. And it worked. Look at you!' She wriggled out of his grasp, contempt written all over her face. 'Freya must be mad to give you another chance. And you had better treat her right. Like I said, I'll be watching you.'

She turned around before he could answer and walked out of the front door, leaving Phil shaking.

He went out into the garden and lit a cigarette. Freya hated him smoking so he tried to restrict how many cigarettes he had and always smoked outside. At least he thought he did – he couldn't remember the last two years. And he'd been warned not to smoke with his injured ribs, but sometimes it was the only thing that calmed him down, and right now he felt really agitated. What the hell had all that been about?

His first instinct was to phone Freya and tell her what had happened but he stopped himself.

Daisy had said he'd told her that Freya was abusing him. Yes, she'd taken it back, like she'd taken back that they were having an affair. But it was a strange thing to say just to provoke him and see if he would lose his temper.

People were always provoking him. Graham, his parents, Marianne. Was Freya? Did she push and provoke until he finally saw red and lashed out?

He hated this, not being able to remember. Anyone could tell him anything they wanted about the last two years and he wouldn't know if they were lying.

How could he know for sure: was it him or was it Freya who lashed out?

*

The house is in darkness when I approach. It's easy to get in. Just like last time, they've left the top kitchen window open – lots of people do that in the summer. They don't realise how easy it is to slip your hand through, grab the side window latch and turn it, then you've got the window open and you're in.

*Last time I chickened out when I got inside. I was scared someone would hear me so I looked around downstairs a bit then I left – out of the back door, leaving it open a bit to let him know someone had been in. I wanted **him** to be scared for once, instead of scaring other people.*

This time I want to let him know that someone is on to him, is watching him. So I leave him a note in his study. Then, I can't resist it, I creep up the stairs. The bedroom door is open so I peer in and see them sleeping, him cuddled up to her, his bandaged arm resting on top of the duvet. They look all cosy, like they are really in love. Are they? Maybe she is, but him… Is he even capable of loving anyone?

I want to wake her, warn her about what he is capable of, but I don't. I turn away and go back down the stairs. I leave the back door open again, though, to let him know that I've been, but this time I take the spare back door key with me – there's a whole bunch of keys hanging on a rack in the kitchen… Stupid or what? It didn't take me long to find the right one. I'll have a copy done so I can get in easier next time, and return it before they even notice it's gone.

I wonder what he'll think when he sees my note. There's no way he'll even think it's from me. It's like he's forgotten all about me. But I haven't forgotten. I'll never forget what he did. And I won't rest until he's paid for it.

CHAPTER NINETEEN

Tuesday

He'd been dreaming again. This time it was a hazy dream of him sitting in a field, on a blanket, having a picnic. A woman was talking to him and he'd turned to answer, but before he could see her face he'd woken up. He lay awake now, his eyes still closed, trying to recollect and make sense of his dream. Was it Freya he'd been with? He tried to cast his mind back to relationships he'd had before Freya. Had he ever been on a picnic with one of them? Or maybe it was just a meaningless dream, brought on by Daisy's words yesterday, pretending they'd had an affair. It was a sick thing to say and it had troubled him. He couldn't fathom out why she had come to see him and why she would say such a thing.

It was no wonder he'd got angry though he wished he hadn't. He'd played right into her hands, failed the 'test' she had set him. As if he would believe that he'd had an affair with her. Daisy didn't attract him in the slightest – she was pretty enough, he guessed, but her expression was always hard and she was waspish with her tongue. He didn't know how her husband – Mark, that was it – put up with her.

He yawned and rubbed his eyes. He shouldn't have got so angry with Daisy. She'd been frightened – he could tell even though she'd tried to pretend that she wasn't. Well, she'd got the reaction from him that she'd wanted. A dull ache throbbed across his forehead. He closed his eyes and tried to block out the questions whirring in his mind.

'How are you feeling?' Sunlight blasted into the room as Freya opened the curtains.

Phil blinked and stared at her, surprised for a moment to see that she was dressed in denim shorts and a white T-shirt, then remembered that she was working from home today. She looked gorgeous, with that honey tan and the shorts hugging her butt really tight. He wanted to ask her to come back to bed but his ribs were still tender.

'Okay… a bit heavy-headed.' He propped up the pillow, sat up, reached for his coffee. 'You're up and about early. I didn't hear you get up.'

She smiled. 'I might be working from home but I still have to be at my desk at nine, and it's almost that now.'

'Is it?' He glanced at the clock beside him and saw that she was right, it was five minutes to nine. 'I think I've been out like a log.'

'Not all night. You must have gone downstairs at some point, maybe for a drink?'

Phil frowned. 'Really? I can't remember that. How do you know – did I wake you?'

Freya sat down on the end of the bed. 'No, but when I got up this morning, the back door was slightly open again.' She paused. 'I don't want to worry you, Phil, but… well, that's twice now, and we don't want someone sneaking in while we're sleeping and taking our stuff.'

He shook his head. 'I didn't get out of bed. I'm sure I didn't.'

She placed her hand on his, reassuring him. 'Don't stress. The painkillers you're on are pretty strong. You were probably half-asleep.'

'Maybe.' That worried him. It was bad enough losing the past two years of his life without going out into the garden in the middle of the night and not remembering it, then forgetting to close and lock the door behind him. Had he been sleepwalking again? If so, it was the first time he'd done it since he was a child – aside from the night before. Mind you, he had gone through a traumatic accident. Was he talking in his sleep too? He'd been told he did that when he was stressed. He felt a bit nauseous at what he might have been saying after Daisy's visit.

'I was dreaming a bit last night. I hope I didn't disturb you, muttering and fidgeting.'

She smiled at him. 'You were a bit restless but it was fine.'

'So I didn't say anything?'

'Not that I heard. I was flat out, though – I didn't even hear you go downstairs.'

'Sorry. I hope I don't make a habit of that. Maybe you should take the key out of the back door when we go to bed so I can't get out.'

Freya looked thoughtful. 'That's a good idea – I'll hang it on the key rack. If you're sleepwalking, you might not bother to search for the key and decide to come back to bed instead.' She bent over and kissed him on the forehead. 'Stay in bed, rest for a while. I need to start work now but I'm only next door if you need anything.'

'Okay. Thanks for the coffee.' He sat up straighter and sipped the hot black liquid as Freya walked out of the room. He heard her go into the bedroom next door, where he guessed she'd already put her coffee on her desk. It was nice to have her working from home instead of in the office; he liked knowing that she was around. He felt a bit vulnerable with this deep void in his mind, especially if he was doing things he couldn't remember.

As Freya was home, hopefully Daisy wouldn't come calling again. She was the last person he wanted to see right now. In fact, he never wanted to see her again; it was horrible to try and trick him like that. And saying all that stuff she'd said about him hurting

Freya. He would never hurt Freya. He loved her. Throwing that vase was a one-off, surely? He wouldn't have meant it to hit Freya. Although Freya had mentioned that there had been a couple of other occasions he'd been abusive. He was ashamed of that – if it was true. Daisy's visit had made him question that.

Part of him wanted to tell Freya about Daisy's visit, let her know how poisonous her sister was, but a bigger part was frightened to, in case there was some truth in Daisy's words. He was wondering now if she had come to see him because she didn't know who to believe, because for some unknown reason he had told her that *Freya* was abusing *him*. Was she saying that Freya was one of those women who went berserk if you upset them, threw things, got aggressive? If she was, maybe he'd phoned Daisy in desperation, needing someone to confide in and thinking her sister might be the best person to advise him. Apparently when he'd been in hospital, Freya had told Daisy it was him who had thrown the vase, and obviously she now believed her sister. Surely Freya wasn't like that? He couldn't believe it. Yet why would he tell Daisy she was? The trouble was he couldn't remember so had no way of knowing what was true. He had to be careful, just in case. Especially as he was still feeling weak and vulnerable.

He finished his coffee, went for a quick shower and got dressed. The holiday booking was still bothering him. Yes, as Freya had pointed out, they had plenty of time to claim on the insurance and get their money back, but it was this holiday that had caused the big argument that had resulted in the car accident and him losing his memory. It was important to him that he find some details of it, something concrete that he could see for himself instead of having to take Freya's word for it. Even if, as Freya had theorised, he'd had the details with him in the car and they'd got damaged or lost in the accident, there should still be some trace of the booking somewhere. He'd have kept details of the travel insurance – he always made a photocopy of documents like that in case he lost the original. He liked to be prepared. Did his bank or home insurance provide travel cover too? he wondered. If so, it would be easier to track down. He'd start with them first.

Feeling more positive now, he picked up his empty cup, ready for a refill before going down to search his office again, intending to go through it methodically, one drawer, one file at a time. As he passed the spare bedroom, he heard Freya on the phone; she sounded bright and businesslike. 'That's ten thirty on Friday then,' he heard her say. He guessed it was something to do with this new account she'd taken on. She was working in the office Mondays and Fridays, she'd told him; she must have been arranging a meeting. Not wanting to disturb her to ask if she wanted a drink too, he carried on down into the kitchen, made himself a strong, black coffee and took it to his study.

He pushed open the door and headed straight for his desk, spotting his black planner in the right corner. Why hadn't he checked that before? He might have written some details in that. He reached for the planner and a piece of paper fell out, floating to the floor. That could be what he was looking for. Maybe he'd scribbled a reference number on it, some details of the holiday. He bent down, picked it up and froze. It was a short, typed note that said in bold black letters:

I'M WATCHING YOU. YOU WON'T GET AWAY WITH IT.

He suddenly remembered what Freya had said about the back door being open again when she got up. Had someone been in, left this note for him?

He scanned the study. Nothing seemed to be missing. The laptop would have been the obvious thing to take but it was still there. He hurried out into the hall, checked the lounge. Nothing missing. Freya surely would have checked when she noticed that the back door was open anyway.

What did it mean? Who had written it and put it on his desk? What wouldn't he get away with?

His first instinct was to tell Freya about the note but he thought better of it. She would want to tell the police. He had to be careful about involving them, or Freya before he knew exactly what was going on. He had to find out why someone had broken into their house and left him a note. What had he done?

Then he remembered Daisy's parting words: 'I'll be watching you.'

CHAPTER TWENTY

Freya looked up from the computer screen as Phil opened the door. She swivelled her chair around to face him when she saw his expression. 'What's up?'

'It's this bloody holiday! I can't understand why I can't find anything about it.'

'I wish you'd stop fretting over this, Phil. I've told you we've got plenty of time to sort out the travel insurance. Give yourself time to recover first.'

'I need to find it, Freya! It's important!'

He hadn't meant to sound so agitated. She shot him a surprised look. 'Remember I suggested that you might have had it in the car and it got lost in the crash? It's the only logical explanation. You hadn't been in the house long enough to put the details away anywhere.'

'What about the travel insurance, though? I always buy travel insurance and always make a photocopy and I would have left it on my desk. There's no sign of that either. It's almost as if I never booked a holiday.'

Freya sighed. 'I think you only booked the holiday the afternoon of the accident, Phil – you didn't tell me about it until you came home that night. I doubt you would have had time to make a photocopy of anything.'

'It doesn't make sense. There must be some kind of record somewhere. How did I pay for it?'

'You usually put holidays on the credit card, as extra protection if something goes wrong,' she told him. 'Have you checked your bank and credit card statements? They will show who the payment was to, then you can phone the insurance company and explain what's happened.'

Phil slapped his forehead. 'Why didn't I think of that? I still have the same bank account, don't I? Halifax? Is my credit card with them?'

'Yes, I think so. We both have our own accounts and credit cards. I know that you bank online, though, so you should be able to get the details up. Actually, you bought me some new underwear too, and some roses. Have you found the receipts for those?'

'Did I? Good to know that I'm not all bad.' She could have told him this before. He'd spent the last few days thinking what a total bastard he was.

'Of course you aren't. We haven't really discussed that evening much, have we? So it slipped my mind. Anyway, I'm not sure it will be of any help if you do find the receipts, apart from telling you what shopping centre you were in. I think the best course of action is to check your credit card statement. I just need to send an email then I'll come and see how you're getting on. Okay?'

'Sure. I don't want to interrupt you while you're working.' It was obvious she was low on his list of priorities right now.

Freya had clearly picked up on the peeved undercurrent in his voice because she shot him another look and turned back to the screen. He had to stop being so snappy. It was just so frustrating to not be able to remember anything.

Shortly after, Freya brought two mugs of coffee into the garage, where Phil was bent over his laptop. He looked up as she came in and saw her glance at the mess around him. Various papers and files had been strewn over the floor as he'd searched in frustration for any documentation connected to the holiday.

'I can't find my bloody banking password,' he groaned. 'I was hoping I'd written it down but I've looked everywhere and I can't find it. Do you know it?'

She shook her head. 'Sorry, but we each have our own bank accounts and we don't go onto each other's computers. We respect each other's privacy.' She passed over his mug of coffee. 'I've been thinking – once we get our money back from the insurers, why don't we rebook the holiday for a bit later, a couple of weeks before you go back to teaching at the university perhaps? Give you time to recover and I can give work enough notice for someone to fill in for me.'

He took a long sip of his coffee. 'Yeah, that sounds good. I just need to find the perishing holiday details. I wish I could remember my password.'

'Why don't you click the "forgotten your sign-in details"? They'll go through some security with you, but they'll get you back online.'

'I was worried that I might not remember the security details, that's why. It was bad enough logging onto my computer when I couldn't remember the password.'

'Well, I'll stay here while you do it, then I might be able to help if you can't remember. If you can't get on, I'll phone up and explain to them what's happened.'

'Okay, I'll give it a go.' Phil put his mug down and clicked the link. Luckily the security questions were ones he remembered and he was soon back online. As he signed into his bank account with his new log-in and password, Freya peered over his shoulder, which made him feel a bit uncomfortable. She'd said they valued each other's privacy and now she was looking at his bank account; it felt as if she was spying on him. He was glad when her phone rang and she turned away to answer it. 'I'm sorry, Phil, I have to take this, it's Stefan. Will you be okay now?'

He nodded. 'Sure, all I have to do now is check the bank and credit card statements for any payments to a holiday or insurance firm.'

Phil stared at the screen. There was no record of a payment to a holiday company over the past couple of weeks – Freya had said that it was a last-minute booking but the accident was over a week ago, so the transaction should be showing now. He went back over the last couple of months in case he had booked it earlier and only just told Freya – although God knows why he would do that! There were some cash withdrawals of a few hundred pounds but he was sure a holiday for two to Dubai would be a couple of thousand pounds, so he couldn't even explain it away by saying he'd paid cash. He signed out, sat back in the soft black leather desk chair and closed his eyes wearily. What was going on? If only he could remember.

He thought back to the strange conversation with Daisy, when she'd said that Phil had told her Freya was abusing him. Could he have been telling Daisy the truth? Was this part of Freya's act? Pretending that he'd told her he'd booked a last-minute holiday, then got angry because she couldn't take time off work and stormed out, almost getting killed. When actually she had caused a massive row over something and thrown the vase against the wall, cutting his forehead in the process?

He tried to probe back into his mind for the memories buried deep in there but they eluded him. There was nothing. Not even the whisper of a half-memory.

Freya didn't seem that bothered about finding the holiday details either. She hadn't bothered to look for them all the time he was in hospital. Was that because she hadn't left his bedside? Or because there had never been a holiday at all?

CHAPTER TWENTY-ONE

The ringing of the doorbell interrupted his thoughts. Who was that now? He was tempted to leave Freya to answer it, then decided against it in case it was bloody Daisy again. He had to deal with it, whatever it was. He couldn't stand being weak, having no control over his life.

He opened the door and caught his breath when he saw the two police officers who had visited him in hospital standing on the doorstep.

'Sorry to trouble you, Mr Keegan, but we'd like to talk to you about the accident again, if you have a few moments to spare,' the female office said.

'Of course. Come in.' Phil heard Freya's footsteps on the stairs as he stepped aside to let the police officers in.

They all walked into the lounge, Freya and Phil taking seats on the sofa, together but not touching, while the officers remained standing.

'The insurance company have conducted further investigations and have reported to us that there is no doubt that the brakes of your vehicle were tampered with, Mr Keegan.' It was the male officer who spoke now.

A band of tension started to form around Phil's head. So it was true. Someone had tampered with his brakes. Someone wanted him dead. He'd thought he'd caused the accident by driving too fast. That he'd stormed out, got into his car and sped off, consumed – if Freya's account was true – with red rage, without a thought for his or anyone else's safety. But he hadn't. Someone had sneaked up to his car and made sure that the next time he drove it he wouldn't be able to stop. He couldn't take it in. Who would want him dead? It couldn't be true.

The policeman's eyes rested on Freya's face. 'Did you ever drive the car, Mrs Keegan?'

She nodded. 'Yes, we both share the cars. I have a Ford Fiesta and use that for work, while Phil uses the BMW, but if we're nipping out, we'll use whatever car is parked first in the drive.'

'In that case we can't presume that whoever tampered with the brakes intended to cause harm to Mr Keegan. They could equally have intended to harm you. But let's go with that premise for now. Do you know anyone who would want to harm you, sir? Do you have any enemies?'

Phil stared at them, the band of tension tightening so much that he felt like his brain would pop out of his head. Obviously he did have an enemy, a dangerous enemy, the threatening note proved that but he had no idea who it could be. He couldn't bloody remember. He shook his head wordlessly.

'I'm afraid that Phil has amnesia as a result of the accident and can't remember the past two years so would have no idea if someone had a grudge against him.' Freya reached out for Phil's hand. 'But to my knowledge there is no one who would want to harm Phil. Are you sure that the brakes didn't simply fail?'

'The insurance company are certain,' the officer told her. 'Their investigation showed that the nuts to the brake fluid pipes had definitely been loosened, causing a leak of the brake fluids resulting in brake failure. Someone wanted to injure or kill whoever drove that car next.'

CHAPTER TWENTY-TWO

'I don't understand it, Freya. Why would anyone want to kill me?' Phil said when the police officers had left after warning them both to be careful and to let them know if they remembered anything or if anything suspicious happened.

'Neither do I.' Freya looked worried. 'Remember I said that I found the back door open on Saturday and this morning?' She swallowed then continued. 'What if it wasn't you? What if someone broke in? If they're watching you... us. Maybe we should have told the police about that?'

He thought of the note and felt sick with fear. He didn't want to tell the police; he was scared what he'd done to make someone hate him like this. It must be bad if someone wanted him dead. 'I don't understand what's happening, Freya. I feel like I'm in some sort of bloody nightmare.' He thumped the side of his forehead with his balled fist. 'I wish I could remember. I hate not knowing what's happened. It's doing my head in. Why would someone want to kill me?'

Freya touched his arm gently. 'Let's try and think about this logically. Do you think you would remember if you got out of bed in the middle of the night and went out into the garden?'

He massaged the base of his neck with his hand. He was sure he would remember but he had to convince Freya he had left the back door open or she'd be phoning the police. 'I don't know. Maybe not if I was fast asleep. I used to sleepwalk when I was a kid.'

'You've sleepwalked a few times since we've been married, Phil, but I usually hear you get up.'

'But nothing's been taken. There's no sign that anyone has been in the house.' *Apart from the note on my desk.*

'I know – but the back door was left open. What if that was done deliberately because someone wants us to know that they can get into the house? That they can get to us whenever they want?' She looked shaken.

'I don't see why anyone would want to do that.'

'Neither do I but we can't get away from the fact that the police are sure the brakes of the BMW were tampered with. Knowing that someone might have sneaked into our house while we were sleeping makes me really nervous. I think we should tell the police about the break-ins.'

Phil shook his head adamantly. 'But they're not break-ins, are they? There was no forced entry and nothing got taken.'

Freya looked at him incredulously. 'Phil, we could both be in danger.'

'I'm sure it was me sleepwalking. Who would bother to break into a house and not take anything? We'd just be wasting the police's time.'

'I guess you're right, but if it happens again, we'll tell them. Okay? We can't risk it, Phil – whoever tampered with the brakes of your car is dangerous.'

'I know. I still can't get my head around it. I'm going out for a cigarette – and don't remind me I shouldn't smoke with my ribs like this!' he retorted as he walked out into the hall. He needed something to de-stress; he felt like his head would explode.

He paced around the garden, puffing on his cigarette. Someone was trying to mess with his mind and he was determined to find out who it was.

CHAPTER TWENTY-THREE

Wednesday

Someone wanted him dead.

The knowledge ate away at him like a rat gnawing at his brain, preventing him from sleeping. Someone had tampered with the brakes of his car. The crash wasn't an accident. Someone had wanted to kill him. And someone was creeping into his house late at night, had left him a note saying they were watching him. Was it the same person? Were they waiting for another chance to kill him?

It was still dark and the glowing numbers on the clock told him that it was just gone three. He was too restless to try to go back to sleep now. Freya was still sleeping soundly beside him so he carefully got out of bed so as not to disturb her, grabbed his jeans and went downstairs for a drink and a cigarette.

He pulled on his jeans when he reached the bottom of the stairs and went into the lounge, poured himself a small tumbler of whisky, picked up his packet of cigarettes and quietly opened the back door then stepped out into the garden. He didn't want to wake Freya, and he needed time to think. Alone. He sat down at the table, took a cigarette out of the packet, lit it and inhaled slowly. He had to try and make sense of what was happening. If only he could remember the events of the evening he'd had the accident.

He took another drag of his cigarette and closed his eyes, trying to remember. Where was he planning on going when he'd got in the car? A car screeched in the distance as it took the corner too fast and suddenly an image flashed across Phil's mind, hazy around the edges at first as if it was out of focus then zooming in sharper. It was as if he was watching it on a TV screen in his head. He was in his car, speeding down the hill towards the crossroads at the bottom; a lorry was coming out of the side road so he pressed the brake pedal. Nothing happened. Fuck! He blasted his horn, practically stood on his brakes but he couldn't slow down. He was nearly on top of the lorry. *Crash!* Then darkness.

Sweat poured off him as the image faded. The insurance company were right: his brakes had been tampered with. He had tried to stop the car and hadn't been able to.

Someone definitely wanted him dead.

Who? Why?

He thought over Daisy's words. What if by some remote chance he'd lost leave of his senses and they had been having an affair, then Mark found out? Could he have tampered with the brakes for revenge? From what he remembered of Mark, he seemed easy-going, but you never knew how people would react when they were up against it.

Or Daisy herself? He shook his head. She wouldn't want him dead if they were having an affair, would she?

Could it be Freya? The thought struck him with a jolt. He mulled it over. It was possible that she found out about his affair with Daisy and wanted revenge. That could have been what the row was about.

Then he remembered how close Daisy and Freya had been at the hospital. If she had found out he and Daisy were having an affair, surely Freya would have had it out with her and banned her from coming to the hospital?

He shook his head; none of it made sense.

Who else could it be? A colleague? His head was throbbing as if it would explode any minute. He had to remember. He had to. Someone was out to get him and he had to figure out who it was before they did him serious harm. Killed him, even.

He took a mouthful of whisky, coughing as it hit the back of his throat, the liquid burning as it slid down. He wanted to down the bottle, to drink himself into oblivion so he wouldn't have to try and fathom it all out, but what was the use of doing that when he would still have to face it tomorrow?

The back door opened and Freya stumbled out, looking half-asleep, still dressed in the cute shorts and vest she wore to bed. Her hair was mussed up – she must have woken up, found him gone and come down to find him. How he longed to confide in her, to ask her all the questions that were churning around in his mind, to tell her what Daisy had said and about the note he'd found on his desk, but how could he when he didn't know what the hell he had done to upset someone so much?

'Are you okay, Phil? Couldn't you sleep?' she asked softly, sitting down beside him.

'I just kept thinking about what that police officer said, that someone tried to kill me. Then I had a flash of memory about the crash – I remembered trying to brake and I couldn't.' He related his vision to her, his eyes fixed on her face, now lit up by the porch light, wanting to see her reaction. 'Why would someone want to kill me, Freya? Why?'

She shook her head, putting a comforting hand on his arm. 'I don't know. Maybe the insurance company have got it wrong. Maybe the brakes just failed.'

'They have to have some evidence to back it up, surely? The police will be investigating now.' His eyes held hers. 'Please be honest with me, Freya, even if you think it might hurt me. You're the only one I can trust. You said I… hit you.' He swallowed. 'Was it bad? Did I ever really hurt you?'

She clenched her hands in her lap and looked down at them, her voice trembling a little. 'It was frightening, and I had some bruises, a cut lip, but nothing that needed treatment if that's what you mean.'

Bruises! A cut lip! What the hell had their marriage been like? 'I'm so sorry.' He squeezed her hand. 'I can't believe I could have done that to you. I love you so much. I'm really, really sorry.'

'I know you are. It's okay. It's in the past,' she told him, not quite meeting his gaze. He didn't deserve her. She was the best thing that had ever happened to him – how could he treat her like that? How could he risk losing someone as wonderful as Freya?

'Do you know anyone who might have a grudge against me?'

He scrutinised her expression. He had to know if she was lying, hiding something from him. She shook her head. 'I'm as flummoxed as you are, Phil. I have no idea why anyone would mess with the brakes of your car.'

'And…' He wasn't sure whether to ask her this, didn't want to put the doubt in her mind, but if she knew, then he would see it in her eyes. 'I didn't cheat on you, did I?' He licked his lips. 'I mean, I'm sure I didn't, but I need to know so I can put things right between us.'

He saw the shock in her eyes and realised that this was something she had never considered. She shook her head vehemently. 'Of course not. We love each other. Yes, you have… had… a bad temper but you would never do that. You told me how much it hurt you when your first wife cheated on you and you learned that the son you loved so much wasn't yours, and we both swore that we would always be completely loyal to each other.'

He thought back to Marianne, his first wife. He hadn't seen her for nearly eleven years. They hadn't exactly parted amicably, and he had been devastated when he found out that Danny – the child he'd been raising – wasn't really his son. He'd tried to put the whole terrible business out of his mind and swore that he would never get married again. Then he'd met Freya…

'Why did you ask that? Why would you even think it?' Freya's voice broke through his thoughts. She looked worried and he wished he could take back the words. The last thing he wanted to do was to make her suspicious. Daisy was lying. He was sure of it. He didn't even fancy her – why would he have an affair with her?

'I'm sorry. I needed to make sure. I can't remember anything of the last two years and it scares me. I'm trying to think of any reason someone would want to kill me, dreading what might come out of the woodwork, what a terrible person I might have become.'

Freya looked at him warily. 'Look, maybe it's a mistake. I'm sure you haven't done anything awful.'

She didn't sound sure. Was she worried what he'd done too? 'Then why did someone tamper with my brakes? Who wants me dead?' he asked. It was the question that was burning in his head. He had to find out. His life was in danger. He couldn't trust anyone. Except Freya. He could trust her, couldn't he?

Then he remembered what the police had said: that whoever had messed with the brakes had intended to harm the driver. They had all presumed that someone was after Phil as it was his car, and he was driving it that night, but Freya drove the BMW too. It could be Freya they were after. Maybe the note had been meant for Freya too; whoever had sneaked in might have thought it was her study.

It could be Freya who had upset someone, not him.

Because she could tell him anything she liked, knowing he couldn't remember.

*

I see them just in time and step back from the gate, standing in the shadows for a while, watching them. He's got his arm around her, gazing at her as if he really loves her. If only she knew what he's really like. The danger she's in. She'll find out soon – he won't be able to keep up the act. I'm surprised he's kept it up this long. Or maybe she does know but won't let herself believe it. Maybe she's taken in by that charming smile, those twinkling eyes, the Irish charm of him, and thinks it must be her at fault. She's not the only one to be taken in, to think it's her. It's time he paid for what he did, but I can't do anything now. I don't want to frighten her. I'll be back, though, when he's on his own. I'll wait for her to go to work and sneak in. But I won't let him see me, not at first, not until he's really scared. Then I'll confront him. Remind him what he did.

CHAPTER TWENTY-FOUR

Freya

Two years ago

The sound of a pop song interrupted her sleep that day. It took her a moment to register that it was the radio alarm clock and another couple of minutes to remember that they were back home. They'd returned late last night from their wonderful wedding and honeymoon in Barbados and were both due in work this morning. She kept her eyes closed for a moment, holding on to the memory of lying on the sugary white sand, paddling in the turquoise sea, walking hand in hand under the moonlight. It had been a perfect two weeks; how she wished they hadn't had to come home. She opened one eye and looked at the red numbers on the digital clock in front of her. Three minutes past six. She didn't have to be in work until nine but Phil had an early start. He had a meeting with an editor in London today and was hoping to get a regular feature in one of the high-street magazines.

'It's not six already, is it?' Phil mumbled, his voice still thick with sleep.

Freya turned around and he wrapped his arms around her. 'I wish we had another couple of hours in bed,' he said, nuzzling her neck.

'I'll go and make coffee while you shower and get ready,' she told him.

'Thank you, gorgeous.' They kissed then Freya rolled back over and out of bed, reaching for her black silk dressing gown that was draped over the chair, and wriggling into it. Phil yawned and rubbed his eyes. She smiled at him. She loved him so much, she thought as she made her way downstairs into the kitchen.

She made two cups of coffee, adding milk and sugar to hers, then carried them back upstairs. The bed was empty and she could hear the shower in the en suite running. She hoped the meeting went well – it would be such a good start to their married life if Phil got a regular feature, she thought as she sat on the bed, sipping her coffee.

Phil came out of the shower, rubbing his hair with the towel. 'Could you grab me my hair gel out of the case, please?' he asked.

Phil was really particular about his hair. He kept it short and spiked up. It really suited him. She let her eyes roam over his naked, lean body. He would be forty next year but had the body of a man ten years younger. He kept himself really fit.

'Freya.'

'Sure.' She put her cup down and went over to the two suitcases standing underneath the window. They'd got back so late last night they hadn't bothered to unpack. She laid Phil's silver case down flat and unzipped it. Everything was packed neatly inside. She unzipped the covered half and took out his black toiletry bag, opening it up to get the gel. There was no sign of it. Then she remembered, she'd checked the hotel bathroom at the last minute, spotted Phil's hair gel and her hairspray by the side of the sink and slipped them both into her washbag. She moved over to her case, opened it and took out her gold washbag, frowning when she realised it was sticky. Something had leaked. Opening it up, she groaned when she saw everything covered in a sticky goo – Phil's hair gel. 'Damn, the top mustn't have been put on properly and it's leaked everywhere,' she told him, taking the bottle out of the bag and holding it by the neck so he could see. 'Just look at it! It's all over my stuff!'

She grabbed a wipe and started to clean the bottle but Phil snatched it from her.

'Bloody hell, Freya! Why didn't you check that the lid was on correctly?'

Her check! That was charming when he was the one who'd left the bottle in the bathroom and hadn't closed the lid correctly.

He turned it upside down into his hand. A drizzle came out. 'It's fucking empty!'

Freya spun around in surprise. She'd never heard Phil shout or even swear before. He looked furious as he kept shaking the bottle to try and make more gel come out.

'Why the fucking hell didn't you check the lid? I've got no more gel. Now I'm going to go to the meeting looking like a freak.'

She got to her feet. How dare he blame her? 'It's your hair gel. Why didn't you check it?' she pointed out. 'I was the one who found it in the bathroom where you'd left it!'

'Fucking hell, Freya! You were the one who did the fucking packing. Are you thick or something? Anyone with any common sense would check that the lid was on tight.' He threw the bottle across the room. It hit her make-up bag, knocking it over and spilling the contents onto the floor.

'Now look what you've done!' Freya yelled at him, a slither of fear crawling inside her. She had never seen Phil like this. 'Calm down for goodness' sake. It's only hair gel.'

Phil stormed over to her, eyes bulging, the vein on his forehead pulsing. She instinctively stepped back, her mouth suddenly dry, her heart pounding like a drum. 'Don't you tell me to fucking calm down. You know how important this meeting is to me. Are you deliberately trying to mess it up?'

She swallowed, her eyes fixed on his face, not daring to answer. He shoved past her and into the bathroom.

Freya stood there shaking as she heard water running, guessing he was dampening his hair. She was totally stunned and freaked out by his behaviour and didn't intend to be there when he came out of the bathroom, so she went down into the garden, waiting until she heard Phil's car start before she went back inside. Tears stung her eyes; they'd just come back from a perfect wedding and honeymoon, where they hadn't had one cross word, and now, it was as if Phil had turned into a stranger. She would never have dreamt that he could act in such a terrible way. She had actually felt frightened of him for a few moments.

She ran over the scene in her mind, trying to pinpoint what would have caused the mild-mannered Phil that she knew and loved to snap like that. She could understand that he was upset that he couldn't gel his hair, like she would be upset if she had to go to an interview and had run out of mascara, but that didn't excuse his behaviour. Nothing excused his behaviour.

She made herself another cup of coffee to calm her nerves and took it upstairs. When she stepped into the bedroom, she gasped at the scene in front of her. Phil had pulled all his clothes out of his wardrobe and tossed them onto the bed. The empty bottle of hair gel still lay on the floor by the wardrobe, her make-up still scattered everywhere. It was a total mess. It was as if a toddler had had a tantrum in there. She bit her lip and fought back the tears. Well, she wasn't going to tidy up his mess.

She drank her coffee then picked up her make-up and got ready for work.

Phil's actions were on her mind all day and she found it difficult to concentrate. Mid-afternoon a text came in from him.

I am so sorry, darling. I don't know what came over me. It's just I really wanted to make a good impression and you know how I am about my hair. Will you forgive me?

Freya read the message but didn't reply. His behaviour was inexcusable. If he thought she was going to message right back saying she forgave him, he had another think coming.

Half a dozen sorry messages later, each more contrite than the last, she finally texted back and said that she forgave him but hoped he would never do it again.

I promise you I won't. I love you.

She replied:

I love you too.

When she got home, Phil had a delicious dinner cooking, had cleared up all the mess in the bedroom and presented her with a bunch of roses: fifteen red ones instead of the usual cream, orange and white. 'Fifteen roses means I'm sorry, and red for undying love,' he told her as he wrapped his arms around her. 'Will you forgive me? Please? I can't live without you.'

She nodded, wanting to forget all about it and for them to return to their easy, loving relationship, excusing his behaviour as stress.

Little did she know then that there was worse to come.

CHAPTER TWENTY-FIVE

Now

Why had Phil asked her if he'd been unfaithful? Freya couldn't get the question out of her mind. Did he think he had been? Was a memory coming back to him? Or was he simply clutching at straws, trying to find a reason why someone wanted to harm him?

She tried to imagine not being able to remember the last two years. It would be awful, but it wasn't that long a period of time, not long enough to change your whole personality, to think that you might have had an affair. They were still in the early years of their marriage, for goodness' sake. Why would he think he'd cheated on her?

Unless he had been planning to?

She shook her head. Phil's last memory was of returning from their honeymoon, where they had spent a wonderful two weeks in the sun, lounging on the beach, making love in the afternoons, sitting in the hotel bar sipping cocktails and watching the entertainment in the evenings. They had been so happy. Phil had been the one who had been eager to get married, who had pushed for it, swept her off her feet with his love. Why would he do that if he'd been planning on cheating with someone else? It didn't make sense.

Maybe he'd cheated before, when he was with someone else, and thought he might have reverted to form. Maybe he was the one who had cheated in his previous marriage, not his ex-wife?

She'd been so surprised when Phil had confessed before their ceremony in Barbados that he was divorced; she'd had no idea that he'd been married before. It was years ago, he assured her, and he didn't like to talk about it because his ex had cheated on him; he'd even found out that the child he had adored wasn't his son, which had broken his heart. He'd pushed it to the back of his mind, pretended it hadn't happened. Was it the full story? She sighed. What did it matter? It was all a long time ago.

What was more important to her was figuring out if she could trust Phil, whether the amnesia was real or if he was he faking it to trick her into staying with him. It was a convenient way of getting her to forgive him for his abuse, or of covering up something she hadn't found out about yet, something that someone wanted to kill him for.

She had been planning on phoning Daisy today, checking that she was okay. She'd left it a few days to give her and Mark a chance to talk things through. Hopefully Daisy would have adjusted to the shock news about her pregnancy now. She was a good mother and Freya was certain she would soon be excited about a new baby. She also wanted to tell her sister what had been happening and ask her advice. She didn't really want to talk about her fears over the phone, though, not when Phil was in and could possibly overhear. He was fast asleep in their bedroom next door now, worn out after his disturbed night. She could see that his ribs were still so painful and he complained of bad headaches. She was tired too, but her mind was far too buzzy to sleep. She would phone Daisy later. If Phil went into his study or the garden, maybe she'd be able to talk undisturbed then.

She'd been immersed in her work for a couple of hours when she heard Phil get up. He popped his head around her door half an hour later, his hair still damp from the shower. 'Can you take a break and have a cuppa with me?'

She really could do with finishing the task she was working on, but she didn't want to refuse. The whole point of her doing flexi-time was so that she could spend more time with Phil while he was recovering.

She smiled at him. 'Sure. I'll be down in a few minutes.'

She heard him go down the stairs and into the kitchen, and quickly finished writing her email. She reread it to make sure there were no typos then pressed send and went downstairs.

Standing in the doorway of the kitchen, she gaped at the scene in front of her. Phil was taking tins and boxes out of the cupboard and piling them on the worktop, obviously looking for something. One of the tins fell to the floor and Phil swore.

Unease gnawed at her belly. Phil liked everything to be in its place. What hadn't she stacked away correctly? She swallowed the feeling of panic and asked steadily, 'What are you looking for, Phil?'

'The bloody coffee! Surely we have another jar?'

Don't bite! she reminded herself. *He's just out of hospital, still feeling confused. Be calm.* She wasn't going to make the mistakes of the past. 'We do. I got one last week. Here, let me look for it.'

She squeezed past him, and as she did, her elbow knocked a jar of marmalade onto the floor. It cracked open and the marmalade trickled out all over the tiles.

'Bloody hell, Freya!' Phil exploded.

Freya bit back the retort that if he hadn't piled everything on top of each other it would never have happened. She didn't want a row.

'Sorry. I'll clean it up in a minute. Let me find the coffee for you first.' Trying to quell the tremble that was coursing through her body, she rummaged through the cupboards and finally found the coffee jar in the cereal cupboard. Of course, she'd unpacked in a hurry when she came back from shopping last week; she'd barely had time to grab a sandwich before she had to go back to the hospital to visit Phil.

'What's it doing there?' Phil grumbled as he took it from her, opened it and spooned instant coffee into two mugs.

'I guess I must have got distracted when I was putting away the shopping,' she said. 'Why don't you take your coffee outside and I'll clean up this mess then come and join you.'

'Okay, thanks.'

As soon as Phil had gone out into the garden, Freya took some deep breaths and tried to relax now the fraught moment had passed. It was hard to hold her tongue but she would do it… for now anyway. Phil was struggling with pain and the amnesia; she had to be patient with him. She was feeling quite fragile herself too. The last thing either of them needed was an argument.

She looked at all the tins and packets laid out on the worktop, the broken glass and marmalade spilt over the kitchen tiles. It wasn't fair that she should have to clean up all this mess. Phil always got in such a state when something wasn't in the place he thought it should be, blaming her for being lazy, not bothering to do things correctly. And in the past she had always stood her corner, telling him it was no more her responsibility than his.

She closed her eyes as memories of one of their really bad rows flashed back into her mind. They were about to eat dinner, a delicious meal of roast chicken, roast potatoes, greens and stuffing that she had made while Phil had been painting the fence in the garden – something he hated doing. Actually he hated doing any DIY jobs but they couldn't afford to pay someone so they had to do it themselves. She'd tried to help him with the jobs but never seemed able to do it the way he wanted her to, and it always ended up in a row, so that day she'd left him to it and cooked a dinner instead. He came in from the garden looking hot and flustered but his eyes lit up when he saw the dinner, and he washed his hands then reached for the salt and pepper. The pepper pot was almost empty. She'd forgotten to buy more – she never used pepper herself, but Phil put it on most meals. She could see that he was getting more and more annoyed as he shook the pot over his dinner.

'It's empty,' he snapped. 'Where's the new one?'

'Er, we haven't got one. I didn't realise it was empty,' she replied.

'You know I can't eat my dinner without bloody pepper!' he snarled. 'Why didn't you check?'

Annoyed at his attitude, she retorted, 'Why didn't you tell me? I never use pepper. How am I supposed to know?'

The next minute Phil threw the dinner up the wall, screaming at her that he couldn't eat it without pepper. She screamed at him that he was a selfish pig, then they were in a full-blown row which ended with Phil slamming her against the wall and storming out, saying he was going out for a decent meal.

It was her fault, he told her later – she was always so mouthy, always nagging, always confrontational, always pushing his buttons.

Maybe he was right. She'd backed down now, hadn't she? Pacified him and a row had been prevented. *But why should I have to back down all the time?* a little voice nagged in her head. She refused to listen to it. She had to forget about the past arguments, push them out of her mind and concentrate on the future. She wanted them both to be happy. They'd been given another chance to make their marriage work and she desperately wanted to succeed.

CHAPTER TWENTY-SIX

'Look, I'm sorry. I didn't mean to get ratty. I've just found out someone tampered with the brakes of my car and tried to kill me,' Phil said when Freya joined him in the garden. 'What have I done that's so awful someone wants me dead?'

Freya had been asking herself the same question.

Phil could get so angry, and although he always blamed her, telling her that she 'pushed his buttons', and she had believed it, she wondered if it was true. Perhaps he'd lost his temper with someone else, hurt them, and now they were out for revenge? She hadn't mentioned Phil's anger to the police officers but wondered if she should have done. Whoever was doing this was unhinged, and the police needed all the information possible to help them catch him. Or her.

'Frey? Please forgive me.'

She glanced at him. He looked really contrite. And anxious.

'It's okay, I understand,' she replied. She did, too; it was only natural Phil would be feeling upset, worried about what the police had told him. She was too. But she couldn't help thinking that it was more than that, that Phil was concealing something from her. Did he suspect who wanted to harm him? Was it one of the students at the university? There had been that student when they had been going out together, who had got too close to him, messaging him at home, trying to catch him alone to talk. Freya had persuaded Phil to report her in the end, pointing out that the girl could accuse him of all sorts and he could lose his job. He hadn't wanted to do it but had agreed it made sense. Maybe something like that had happened again?

'Why don't you talk to Tom, see if he can shine a light on anything. Sometimes the students get upset if they don't get the grades they want, and there was a student who had a bit of a crush on you once. She made a real nuisance of herself.'

'Did she? What happened?'

Freya filled him in briefly. 'It all got sorted out okay, and I'm not saying it is a student doing this. I'm just suggesting talking to Tom as he's your closest friend.' She didn't say 'only friend' even though it was true. 'And you work together too. He might know something.'

'I will. It would be good to talk to someone else about this.'

Freya glanced at her watch. She still had a lot of work to get through, but it was lunchtime now. She'd go and check if she had any messages that needed answering urgently then suggest that they go out for a drive – that might take Phil's mind off things. She could carry on with the project later.

She went upstairs to check her mail and retrieve her phone, which she'd left on her desk. There was a missed call from Daisy. She'd wanted to talk to her sister about what the police had told them, but if she phoned Daisy back now, they'd get chatting, and she really wanted to make lunch and get Phil out of the house for a few hours. It was such a lovely day, the fresh air would do him good. She sent a quick message saying that everything was fine and she would phone her later then went down to put the kettle on. Phil was pacing around the garden now, smoking. She sighed. He'd been warned not to smoke but what could she say? Nagging him wouldn't help. And to be fair he must feel really stressed about everything. She couldn't imagine not remembering the last two years of her life. Thank goodness she hadn't been in the car with him.

The thought jolted into her mind that she could have been the one to drive off in the BMW – she often used Phil's car if she was going for a quick trip to the shops. Then she'd be the one who was injured, perhaps with no memory of the last two years.

And no memory of Phil's abuse. Maybe that would be a good thing. Try as she might, she couldn't completely empty her mind of it, feeling jumpy every time he looked agitated. In a way, Phil was lucky not to remember: he could start afresh.

CHAPTER TWENTY-SEVEN

She had a Facebook message request from an Aileen Keegan.

Hello, Freya, I'm Philip's mother, your mother-in-law.

Freya stared at the opening words of the message, reading them again in astonishment. Phil's mother had messaged her.

She sat back in her chair, leaving the message unopened for a moment as she wondered what this woman, a total stranger to Freya, wanted. Perhaps she'd read about the accident in the newspaper, regretted that she'd had nothing to do with her son for all these years and decided to contact him again. Knowing that he could have died would have really shaken his mother and probably made her realise that she could have lost Phil forever, without having the chance to make amends. Phil wasn't on Facebook, or any other social media, so tracking down Freya might have been her easiest option to make contact. It wouldn't have been difficult to do: the newspaper article had mentioned Freya by name, shown a photo of her and Phil together.

Freya clicked on the message to see what it said, knowing that Aileen wouldn't be able to tell that it had been read unless Freya replied.

I hope you don't mind me contacting you in this way, but I read about Philip's accident and wanted to check how he was. And how you are too – this must have been so awful and stressful for you. I phoned the hospital and they said he had been discharged so I'm presuming that he isn't severely injured.

I've thought a lot about Philip over the years. I'm so pleased to hear that he is married, and I have a new daughter-in-law. I'm so sorry that we haven't met yet and really miss Philip. I had hoped so much that he would get in touch with us when things calmed down. When I read the newspaper article, learnt how Philip nearly died, I knew I had to try to contact him. He's my son, when all is said and done, and twenty years have gone by since we last saw each other. The past is all water under the bridge as far as I'm concerned. Please let me know how he is, give him my love and tell him that I would like to see him again, and to meet you too. I do hope you will reply and let me know how you both are.

With love,
Aileen

Freya read it over again. Twenty years. She hadn't realised it had been that long. It must have been heartbreaking not to have contact with her son for all that time and then to find out that he had been involved in a serious accident. She said she regretted what had happened too. Perhaps Phil's parents hadn't meant to favour his brother, and now they were older, they'd looked back, realised what they'd done and wanted to make amends. Sometimes you don't realise how things affect other people until years later.

Phil never talked about his family; he always dismissed any questions she asked by saying he hadn't seen them for years and that was the way he liked it. He had been adamant that he wasn't inviting his parents to their wedding, much as she'd tried to coax him. How would he take it if she told him his mother had got in touch, wanted to see him now?

He might be pleased, especially as his mother had made the first move. Maybe almost dying in the accident would make him think about his parents, make him want to see them again. She was sure he must miss his family after all this time but was probably too proud – or too stubborn – to contact them. She'd show him the message right away.

She went downstairs to Phil's study, knocking on the door before opening it. Phil was busy typing away. 'Have you got a minute, Phil?'

He glanced up. 'Sure.'

She walked over and sat down on the edge of the desk. 'I've had a Facebook message. From your mum. She said that she was really upset when she read about the accident, and that she's worried about you and wants to see you again.'

Phil looked stunned. 'What?'

Freya opened the Messenger app on her phone and showed him the message. He read it stony-faced. 'Well, I don't want to see her.'

Freya was shocked by the coldness in his voice. 'Phil, she's your mum, she misses you and is worried about you. Surely you miss her too?'

'No, I don't. And where's the apology for how they all treated me? The years of rubbishing me, of making me feel inadequate while Graham could do no wrong? They haven't tried to contact me all this time, so they needn't bother now just because they've read that I had a bad accident and their consciences are pricking them a bit. I want nothing to do with any one of them.' He slammed his fist down on his desk. 'Delete that message and block her!' he ordered.

'What?' She was bewildered at his reaction. 'Phil, think about this. Your parents must be getting on in age now. They just want to see you again while they can. Look, read the message again! She said that she regrets what happened.'

'Well, it's taken her long enough, and it still isn't a sorry, is it? That message is from my mum, not my dad or goody-goody brother. They obviously don't want to see me and I don't want to see them. Not after how they treated me. My mum chose her side and she can stick with it. Like I said, I want you to delete the message and block her.' She gasped and he glared at her. 'I mean it, Freya. This is my bloody family not yours, and I don't want you to have anything to do with them. Give me your phone.'

She bit back the refusal that sprang to her lips. He was right, this was his family. She had no idea what had gone on for him to walk out on them all those years ago and never look back. If he didn't want to see them, then that was up to him.

'I'll do it,' she said but he snatched her phone from her, tapped away then handed it back. 'There. I've done it.'

How bloody high-handed of him. She wanted to yell at him that she would have done it, that he had no right to tamper with her phone, but she didn't – he looked so angry and she was scared that the wrong word would start off one of their rows, so she simply glared back at him.

Then his face softened. He reached out and pulled her to him. 'Look, I'm sorry. I normally wouldn't mess with your phone, but I need to know that you've blocked her, Frey. I don't want my family contacting you. They're poison.' He held her tight, his hand gently caressing her back. 'You do understand, don't you?'

'Yes, of course. It's fine,' she assured him, her emotions a mix of anger and relief that Phil had calmed down.

'I'll just finish this article, then maybe we can have something to eat,' he said, smiling now. It always astonished her how quickly he could change his moods.

'Sure. I've got some work to do. Shall we say an hour?'

He kissed her on the forehead. 'Perfect.'

As she walked up the stairs, Freya was still pretty shaken up by what had just happened. Phil had looked so angry; it had unnerved her and he had no right to snatch her phone like that and block his mother. It was her account. It was up to her who she blocked. She would never dream of taking Phil's phone from him and blocking someone on it.

She understood that Phil had been upset when he was growing up that his parents favoured his brother, but that was twenty years ago. And maybe they hadn't meant to favour Graham, they simply had more in common with him, like her mum with Daisy? Freya always rubbed her mum up the wrong way whereas Daisy got on well with her, but she would never consider cutting her mum out of her life. It felt like a shame that Phil wouldn't even listen to his mum, hear what she had to say.

She sat down at her desk, feeling a little angry herself, wishing she had stood up to Phil a bit. What was the point of causing an argument, though? Things were difficult enough at the moment. She moved the mouse so that the computer screen flicked to life, showing that she was still logged into her Facebook account. For a moment she hesitated then resolutely clicked onto settings and unblocked Aileen. It was cruel to treat her this way when she had reached out to Phil – he was her son. Perhaps if Freya kept contact open, giving Phil a little more time to think about his mother's message, she could help reunite her husband with his family.

She typed in the reply box.

Hello, Mrs Keegan.

Then she hesitated. That sounded so formal, and Phil's mother had signed off as 'Aileen', so she altered it.

Hello, Aileen, thank you for getting in touch. It was kind of you to think of us and contact me. We are both okay, thank you. Phil suffered broken ribs and bruising but is otherwise unhurt. He also has some amnesia, having forgotten the past two years of his life – our whole married life. We are hoping this is temporary. I'm afraid that he isn't ready to meet you yet. I'm so sorry. Perhaps he will when he feels a little better.

She paused, wondering how to sign off, then settled for 'all the best, Freya'. Before she had time for second thoughts, she hit send.

CHAPTER TWENTY-EIGHT

Phil

Damn. Why had his mother decided to get in touch after all these years? That was the last thing he wanted, dragging all that up again. As far as he was concerned, his family was dead to him. He never wanted to see or hear from them again. They had never cared about him, had wiped him out of their lives. Now, just because he'd had a bad accident, they thought they could come back into it as if nothing had happened. Well, there was no chance of that. His mother had a bloody cheek messaging Freya. Was she trying to poison his wife against him? He hadn't liked taking Freya's phone from her and blocking his mother but he'd had to do it. There was no other choice if he wanted him and Freya to be happy together. If he allowed his family back into his life, he knew without any doubt that they would cause trouble and ruin things for them. Especially his brother Graham. He hated Graham with a vengeance and was sure that the feeling was mutual. Graham had ruined his childhood – he thought he was so clever, sucking up to his parents all the while. Little golden boy. And they'd shown who they preferred, hadn't they?

Memories of that last day flashed across his mind: the anger, the violence, the blood on his cheek. He hadn't meant it to go that way but Graham was always prodding, pushing, taunting, smirking because he got better grades at school, showing off. They'd both got into university – Phil first, going to Leeds to study journalism, then two years later Graham had got into Oxford to study law. They were both home for the week, to celebrate their father's birthday. Graham had bought him a new set of personalised golf clubs, whereas Phil had grabbed a present at the last minute, a cream cashmere scarf. It was a nice scarf, but it didn't compare with personalised golf clubs in a leather holdall. Goodness knew where Graham had got the money from. Their father had been delighted with Graham's present and tried to conceal his disappointment when he'd opened Phil's, but they'd all seen it, especially Graham, who had looked at the scarf disdainfully and said, 'Pushed the boat out, haven't you?'

'Robbed a bank, have you?' Phil shot back.

'I saved up. I wanted to buy Dad something special,' Graham told him. 'You should try it.'

Before Phil could retort, their father butted in. 'Now, boys, it's the thought that counts. I love both presents.'

But Graham wouldn't let it go. He spent the whole week needling Phil, boasting about the internship he'd got with a local law firm, how he was going to be a barrister. Their parents had been all over him, so proud. None of them had wanted Phil to study journalism – it wasn't a 'proper career' like Graham's, and his father never stopped trying to persuade him to transfer to a business studies course instead. Phil had tried his best to ignore them all, to keep a smile on his face, not to rise. Until the night he went out with his mates, came home late, stumbling and crashing into the coat stand in the hall as he let himself in and found Graham waiting for him. Graham laid into him, demanding what time he thought this was to come home, accusing Phil of being selfish and waking their parents, and suddenly they were scuffling. Their parents, woken by the commotion, came down just as Phil punched Graham full in the face, knocking him flat on his back. His father shouted at Phil, prodding him, telling him how ashamed he was of him, and before Phil knew what he was doing, he had punched his father in the chest. He hadn't meant to. It was as if all the years of feeling inferior to Graham, of living in his shadow, had finally broken him. His father clutched his chest, gasping for breath, and all hell broke loose. An ambulance was called for his father, and his mother told Phil to get out. Phil hastily packed and left.

The next day Phil returned, contrite and worried sick about his dad. Graham had been waiting for him again. Smirking, he said his dad would be okay, no thanks to Phil, and that their parents never wanted to see Phil again. When Phil tried to protest, Graham told him that if he ever showed his face again, both his father and Graham would have him charged with assault. They'd taken photos of the bruises that Phil was responsible for. So Phil left and never went back.

Anger at the injustice of it had bubbled inside him, growing into a festering wound over the years. He hadn't meant to hurt his father but they had pushed him, all of them, until he couldn't take any more. Why did everyone do that to him? Marianne had done it too, nagging, pushing, prodding – it was like a million pinpricks in his skin until one day it was a pinprick too much. He didn't want his parents turning up now, ruining things. They were out of his life and he wanted it left that way.

He shut his eyes. He wished he'd forgotten those years instead of the two precious years he'd had with Freya. He loved her so much, had been over the moon when she'd agreed to marry him. Had they been happy these past two years or had she pushed him too? He wished he could remember. She was so cagey around him, as if she was hiding something.

He put his hand to his throbbing head. He wished he could rip it open and see what secrets were locked in there.

CHAPTER TWENTY-NINE

Freya

Phil was quiet and seemed on edge all evening. He barely spoke, his attention fixed on the TV but obviously not watching the detective drama that was playing out on the screen. Freya was quiet too. The message from his mother that morning, and Phil's over-the-top reaction to it, hung between them even though he had apologised. Freya was troubled at how aggressively he'd reacted – and although she was trying not to show it, she was really furious about how he'd taken her phone. She couldn't help but start to wonder if something else had happened between Phil and his family, something he hadn't told her about, that had caused the fallout. And it had to be something massive for it to last all this time, for Phil to not even invite them to their wedding. Whatever it was, Phil was still angry and upset about it but obviously had no intention of discussing it with her. It was a strained, miserable evening, not helped by the fact that it started to rain so she couldn't even sit in the garden and relax.

She lay awake half the night, listening to the rain pattering against the window and Phil snoring softly beside her. She couldn't stop thinking about the events of the last few days, and whether she could trust Phil. He had been so angry when he had seen his mother's message and she had seriously feared that he would be abusive again. Had she been right to take him back and give him another chance? Was he a danger to her? She felt like she was living with a stranger now that Phil had no memory of their married life together, and she had no idea how he would react to anything. She'd been about to leave him the night of the accident. And had almost left him a couple of months ago.

Memories of that day flooded back into her mind. They'd been out shopping, bought some pots and plants and had spent the afternoon putting the plants into the tubs and placing them around the small garden. Then their friends Jenna and Craig had phoned and asked them out for a meal; another couple were joining them too. Phil had been reluctant to go but Freya had talked him into it – she loved to socialise and they hadn't been out for a few weeks. So they'd got changed and met Jenna and Craig at the Indian restaurant. It had been a fantastic evening, lots of wine, delicious curry, and the other couple, Soraya and Ishan, were really easy to get on with. Ishan was sitting opposite Freya, and when he and Jenna, who was a PR consultant, discovered that she worked in marketing, they soon all got into a conversation about different marketing strategies. The conversation was buzzing and Freya was really enjoying herself. Phil seemed to be enjoying himself too, chatting away to Soraya and Craig about some of the articles he'd had published, but when they got into the taxi she saw that he was stony-faced. *What the hell have I done now?* she thought, annoyed. It had been such a lovely evening; why did Phil have to spoil it? 'What's the matter?' she asked.

'What do you think?' he replied.

She replayed the evening, wondering what on earth had upset Phil. Had someone said something to him that she hadn't heard? He could be a bit touchy, always thinking people were getting at him, or going over conversations looking for hidden meanings and insults.

'I don't know. I didn't hear all the conversation,' she said.

'I don't think you heard any of it – you only had eyes for Ishan.'

Oh God, here we go again. He was jealous because she had talked to Ishan – and Jenna – yet he had talked to Soraya and Craig all evening.

She decided not to say anything else until they got home, not wanting to have a row in the back of the taxi.

As soon as they got into the house, Phil threw his keys down on the table and poured himself a glass of whisky.

Uh-oh.

'Don't I get one?' she asked.

He narrowed his eyes, glaring at her over the glass. 'I think you've had enough, don't you?'

'I've had a couple of glasses of wine, and so have you!' she retorted. 'Don't spoil the evening by being petty.'

'Spoil the evening!' He practically spat the words out. 'You've already done that! Showing me up by looking all doe-eyed at Ishan and hanging on to his every word. Everyone noticed!'

'Don't be silly, I did no such thing. I was talking to Jenna too and we were all discussing—'

'I know what I saw!' He slammed the glass down on the table, slopping whisky everywhere.

'Look, Phil, everyone was talking to everyone tonight. It's what you do when you go out with friends. You were chatting away happily to Soraya and Craig.'

'That's because you, my wife, couldn't be bothered to talk to me. I wasn't going to let everyone know how much that upset me, was I?'

She was so mad at him then. He always did this. They went out with friends, had a lovely evening together, and when they came home he'd start moaning about something someone said or did – or even worse, something *she'd* said or done. She was sick of it.

'I am allowed to talk to people, you know. You don't own me!' she screamed at him.

He moved so quick he was standing in front of her before she realised he'd even moved, his face so close to hers they were almost touching noses. 'You're my wife! Is it too much to expect you not to flirt with other men?'

The drink made her brave. 'I was not flirting! I was bloody talking. Just like you were!' she screamed, stepping back. 'I'm not listening to this any longer. I'm going to bed.'

'Don't you dare walk out on me when I'm talking to you!'

She held up her hand. 'Not listening.' And she carried on walking over to the door.

Then she felt a sharp pain in her arm as Phil grabbed it and pulled her back. 'I'm fucking talking to you and you had better listen.'

The sight of his bulging eyes, tell-tale vein throbbing in his forehead and red face snarling soon sobered her up. *Shit.*

'Get off me!' she shouted as bravely as she could.

Phil snarled and hurled her over to the other side of the room with such force that she fell against the wall, hitting her head. Everything went hazy. She was vaguely aware of Phil storming out of the kitchen and going up to bed. She crept over to the sofa, sobbing, wanting to get away but knowing that she wasn't sober enough to drive. *I'll leave tomorrow. I'll pack my bags and go as soon as I'm fit to drive*, she promised herself, wrapping the throw around her and finally drifting off to sleep. The next morning, she woke up to find that she had an ugly bruise on her arm and the side of her face where she'd hit the wall.

That's it. I've had enough, she decided, staring in the mirror at the bruise. She went upstairs to pack a case, fully intending to walk out, but Phil was full of remorse. Crying, he told her that he'd only meant to pull her back, to stop her walking off, but had slipped and accidentally hurled her across the room. He hadn't realised she'd hit her head. He'd gone to bed as he didn't want them to argue any more. He was so upset, so apologetic that somehow he convinced Freya that it was her fault, that she had spent most of the evening chatting to Ishan, totally ignoring everyone else, that Phil had tried to speak to her a few times and she hadn't even acknowledged him. He'd felt shown up, he told her, sadly. He understood that Freya had had a drink and didn't realise how much she'd been flirting. But all she'd had to do was apologise instead of arguing back and storming out of the room. He hugged her, said he was sorry, he loved her and would never, ever hurt her intentionally, but she had to stop antagonising him. It wasn't fair to provoke him like that. He hated being left out – it was what his parents used to do.

She remembered feeling guilty then. She should have realised that when Phil felt that people were favouring her, felt that she was ignoring him, that it made his old insecurity rise up again. She should have included him, should have understood how rejected he would feel. So she apologised, unpacked her case, promised never to do it again. Phil apologised too, assured her of how much he loved her, promised he would never get angry with her again…

But he did, didn't he? And already he was showing signs of anger again. Had she been right to give their marriage another chance? Was she in danger?

CHAPTER THIRTY

Freya

Freya woke the next morning with a heavy head. The rain had stopped, thankfully, and the sun was now shining again, but she didn't really feel like working, so she had a lukewarm shower and made her coffee extra strong, in an attempt to liven herself up.

When Phil went into the shower, Freya quickly checked her phone, her hand shaking when she saw that she had another message from Phil's mother.

Hello, Freya. Thank you for your reply, I appreciate it. I had hoped that Philip would agree to talk to me but I know how stubborn my son can be, and I doubt if that has changed in the twenty years since I last saw him. It is a big ask but would you meet me? I really would love to meet you, my new daughter-in-law. And there is something I would like to talk to you about – I didn't want to put this in writing, preferring to tell Philip face to face. But his father, Charles, has cancer and I'm afraid it's terminal. Although Charles is as stubborn as Philip, I know he would dearly like to see our son again, as would I. I don't know if Philip has talked to you about that dreadful day when our family was blasted apart but I suspect not. I don't want to write details in a message. Would you meet me so we can talk and see if we can find a way to reunite my family?

Please. It would mean so much to me and especially Charles, who has such a limited time left, to see Philip again.

With love,
Aileen x

Freya read it again, slowly. Aileen sounded genuine, and desperate. Her husband, Phil's father, was dying. How could she refuse the poor woman's request to meet? And she had to admit that she was curious to meet Phil's mother, and to learn more about Phil's childhood. All she knew was that he had grown up in Northern Ireland. She had no idea when he had come to live in England or where his parents lived. Although they could well have moved since Phil left home. She wanted to know more about the row too, wondering if Phil had told her everything that had happened twenty years ago, and if there was some way she could reunite the family before his father died. She sat on the edge of the bed, mulling it over. With Phil not at work, and herself working from home most of the week, it was going to be difficult to meet his mother if she had to travel far, unless she pretended she had an urgent meeting to attend. She felt guilty about leaving Phil home alone at the moment – he looked so tired and vulnerable and complained that his ribs were still sore and that he had frequent headaches – but she was relieved that she would be back in work tomorrow and Monday. She was desperate to get out of the house. The atmosphere was so charged, she felt that if she said anything wrong, it would lead to a massive row. She'd ask Aileen if she could meet her one afternoon next week; she could book it as a day's holiday – she was owed enough.

The bathroom door opened and Freya closed the message down quickly, not wanting Phil to see it. He came out towel-drying his hair. 'Are you starting work already?' he asked.

'I'm afraid so. I've got a few emails to answer and a graphic to design. I'll do a couple of hours then we can sit in the garden and have a coffee if you want?'

'That'd be good.' He leant over and kissed her. 'Love you.'

'Love you too,' she replied automatically, her spirits lifting. Phil looked a lot happier today.

As her laptop booted up she thought about Aileen's message. She knew that Phil would be furious if he found out that she had gone against his wishes – make that instructions! – unblocked his mother and replied to her. But she was determined to meet Aileen and try to help her reconcile Phil and his father. She had to. She would never forgive herself if Phil's father died and she hadn't tried to help. And Phil, when he calmed down, would probably be glad that she had done so. He was trying to be a better man now, and twenty years was a long time to bear a grudge. She'd message Aileen later and arrange something.

She sat down at her desk and started work. The next couple of hours flew by and it wasn't until Phil shouted up the stairs that he'd made her a coffee that she realised it was eleven thirty. She'd promised to join him for a coffee in the garden, she reminded herself. She was so engrossed in her work she could sit at the desk all day, but Phil needed company too – she had to stop and take a couple of breaks with him.

'I'm taking it out into the garden,' Phil shouted.

'Great idea. I'll be down in a sec.'

A few minutes later she joined Phil outside, where he was seated at the wooden table, sipping his mug of coffee. A tray with another mug of coffee and a plate of assorted biscuits rested on the table. Freya picked up the mug and reached for a Bourbon cream. 'Thank you,' she said, sitting down. 'Lovely day, isn't it?'

Phil nodded. 'I thought I might get out for a bit, go for a walk.'

Freya cast a glance at his face: he looked tired, troubled. 'I could take a break if you want me to join you?'

He shook his head and reached out to touch her hand. 'That's kind of you but I know how important this new account is. You get back to work and I'll have a stroll on my own. I promise to take it easy and I'll only be an hour or so.'

It was a lovely, sunny day, ideal for a walk. She guessed Phil needed a bit of time to himself. Besides, he was right, she did need to work. She didn't want Stefan to think she couldn't handle the extra work and pass it on to Nadia. Also it would give her a chance to contact Aileen without worrying that Phil would come in and catch her. And to call Daisy too.

'Okay, but don't overdo it,' she agreed. 'And if you get too tired to walk back, phone me and I'll come and pick you up.'

'Don't worry, I won't go far,' he promised.

She swallowed the last of her coffee and grabbed another biscuit. 'See you in a bit then.' She kissed him on the forehead and went back upstairs. A few emails had come in while she was away from her desk so she dealt with them, shouting goodbye to Phil as he called to say he was going now, then opened Messenger to reply to Aileen.

I'm so sorry that Phil isn't ready to meet you yet, Aileen, but I would love to. Where would you like to meet? We live just outside Worcester, so if you live more than an hour's drive away, perhaps we can meet somewhere halfway? Would Birmingham city centre suit you? Afternoons about four would be best for me. Any day except for Mondays and Fridays as I work in the office then.

Phil will thank me for this, she told herself. She knew that if she'd fallen out with her parents, she'd be devasted if either of them died before she had the chance to make up with them.

She called Daisy but it went to answerphone so she sent a quick message asking Daisy to phone her back. Then she clicked on the Kada folder on the screen of her laptop and was soon engrossed in a new design for Kada's header. So engrossed that when her phone rang it made her jump. She glanced at the screen. Nadia. She'd had a couple of texts from her in the week, asking how Phil was. She'd been so supportive helping out with the Kada account when Phil had been in hospital, and Freya felt that they'd grown closer as a result.

'Hi, Freya, how are things?' Nadia asked cheerily. 'How's the patient?'

'He's gone for a walk, actually. He seems in good spirits but he's struggling with this memory loss,' Freya told her. 'And it's really bugging him that he can't find the travel insurance or the receipt for the holiday he'd booked for us – he wants to tell them what happened and get his money back.'

'There should be some record of it, surely?'

'He can't find one. And he didn't tell me any details of the holiday so I can't help.'

'That's weird. Still, I guess it doesn't really matter. The important thing is that Phil is okay and home again.'

'Yes, that's what I keep trying to tell him.'

She wondered whether to tell Nadia about the police saying that someone had tampered with the brakes on Phil's car but decided against it – best keep that to themselves until they had more information. So she moved the conversation on to talking about the project, planning a roller banner for the website and a Facebook advertising campaign, so that Freya could work on some ideas to show at the meeting tomorrow. They chatted away for a while then Freya heard the front door open.

'I'd better go, Phil's back,' she said. 'I'll see you tomorrow, Nadia.'

She heard Phil go into the kitchen and then shout out. She raced down the stairs and stopped at the kitchen door, aghast at the scene in front of her. Water was pouring out of the tap over the sink and onto the kitchen floor, and there was now a thin film of water across the kitchen. How the hell had that happened?

'You left the bloody tap on!' Phil accused, splashing through the water to turn off the tap. Then he pulled the plug out of the sink.

'I didn't. I haven't been downstairs since you went out,' she told him. 'You must have done it.' She couldn't understand it. They rarely even put the plug in the sink – they had a dishwasher, and when they washed up the odd item, they used the bowl.

'When?' Phil demanded. 'I've only just walked through the door.'

Freya shot an anxious glance at him; his jaw was set and the vein on his forehead was throbbing. *He's angry*, she realised, her stomach tightening a little. 'Phil, I promise I haven't been downstairs since you went out,' she said as calmly as she could. He had obviously washed a cup or something in the sink before he went out and not turned the tap off completely. She was worried how forgetful he was becoming. Could it be connected to the accident? He never used to be so forgetful. She didn't want to make a big thing of it but would have to keep an eye on him. What if he left something cooking on the stove?

'You must have forgotten. Don't worry, it doesn't matter. I'll clear it up. It won't take long.' She squeezed the top of his arm as she walked past him to get the mop bucket. Phil turned to her and for a moment she thought she saw panic in his eyes. 'It's okay, Phil. Leave it to me,' she reassured him.

By the time she'd mopped up the water in the kitchen, Phil was in his study, bent over some papers.

What should I do? she thought as she stood watching him. *I've no idea what's going to happen next.*

As if sensing her presence, he glanced up.

'Are you ready for lunch yet?' she asked. 'It's gone one.'

'Not yet. Another hour maybe,' he replied. 'Is that okay with you?'

'Sure.'

He turned his attention back to his papers and Freya made her way back upstairs.

His anger had disappeared as quickly as it had come, and it was almost as if he'd forgotten about the flood in the kitchen, she thought worriedly. Was the amnesia more serious than the doctors realised?

CHAPTER THIRTY-ONE

Phil

Phil waited until he heard Freya going back upstairs then pulled out the piece of notepaper he'd just shoved in his drawer. It had been lying on his desk, waiting for him when he came back from his walk. Typed in the same bold capitals as the previous note. He held it out and read it again.

YOU CAN'T ESCAPE FROM ME.

Short, typed, unsigned and meant to frighten him. Someone had sneaked into their house in the middle of the day with Freya working upstairs, walked through the kitchen, down the hall and into the garage room and placed the threatening note on his desk, wanting to let Phil know how easily they could come and go. So it hadn't been Freya who'd left the tap running. He had so hoped it was her. He couldn't stand knowing that someone was sneaking into their house whenever they wanted to. It was almost as if they had a key.

He took the big dictionary down and pulled out the other note, laying them both side by side.

I'M WATCHING YOU. YOU WON'T GET AWAY WITH IT.

Both notes were short, threatening, anonymous. He wondered if Freya had been right and the sender was a former student at the university, someone who had a crush on him. It happened to the lecturers sometimes – although breaking into his house and leaving notes was a bit too unhinged.

The only thing he could think of doing was going through his diary and online calendar and seeing if he could find a clue there; he'd always been meticulous about keeping records of meetings and work deadlines. He liked to be organised. Hopefully he'd find something that could shed a light on this. He slipped both notes between the front cover and first page of the dictionary then put it back on the shelf. He didn't want Freya to find out about the notes until he'd worked out who had a grudge against him. Then he flicked through his desk diary. It was mainly university stuff: tutorials with students, deadlines for when assignments had to be marked, and restaurant bookings for his and Freya's birthdays and their anniversary. There was no mention of a holiday in Dubai, he noticed, but then Freya had said he'd booked it at the last minute, so he guessed he hadn't had time to put it in his diary.

He checked his online calendar, which seemed to be a record of his freelance writing work: when he'd delivered articles, meetings with editors, exhibitions and events he was going to. There were a couple of meetings with the editor of the local *Telegraph*, a couple with magazine editors or people he was interviewing. Nothing out of the ordinary.

Then something caught his eye. According to the calendar on the screen, he met someone called Billy every Tuesday at lunchtime at a place called Benbows. Who the hell was Billy?

Maybe he was an editor of a magazine, or someone he was writing a regular article for. Phil picked up his phone and scrolled down his contacts, stopping at the name Billy. There were no details for him, just a number. Whoever this Billy was had obviously not read or heard about Phil's accident as there was no text from him wishing him a speedy recovery, like there were from many of his contacts. That would suggest he wasn't a close friend, so yes, maybe someone he was working with. He typed 'Billy' into the search bar of his email but nothing came up, which didn't mean anything as people's email addresses didn't always reflect their names. Maybe he should call Billy, tell him he'd lost his memory and ask him if he would mind reminding Phil what they were working on. It could be a bunch of articles and he didn't want to lose work. After a few minutes' hesitation, he dialled the number. No reply.

Phil tapped his chin with the phone. Should he leave a message? He'd been meeting this person regularly for months apart from the last two weeks before his accident. Did that mean whatever project he had been working on was finished? He turned back to his laptop and searched through his work files for anything he'd recently completed. Nothing. On the off chance, he checked his list of students at the university. There was no Billy among them.

Frowning, he dialled the number again, rehearsing what he'd say as he listened to the dial tone.

There was no answer.

He didn't want to make a nuisance of himself. Billy was obviously busy and would have Phil's number in his phone if they met so regularly, so perhaps he would get back to him.

As he put the phone down on his desk, he heard the ping of an incoming message so slid the screen to read it. It was Billy.

What do you want, Phil?

Phil frowned. He'd expected a 'Sorry, mate, I'm busy, I'll phone you in a bit' or even a 'Good to hear from you, hope you're okay' but this message sounded curt. As if he'd upset Billy for some reason.

He texted back:

I need to talk to you when you have a few minutes to spare.

A few minutes later the phone rang, the name 'Billy' flashing across his screen. Phil felt a bit anxious as he answered the call, wondering if he would recognise the voice. The doctor had told him anything could trigger his memory.

'Why are you phoning me?'

Phil almost dropped the phone in shock. He recognised the voice all right. It was Daisy.

CHAPTER THIRTY-TWO

Daisy

Oh God, he must have remembered the affair. Daisy placed a shaking hand over her stomach, her other hand still holding the phone. That was the only credible explanation for Phil to phone her then end the call as soon as she answered. She had to talk to him, to tell him to keep quiet, let him know that she and Mark were going to make a go of their marriage. She was sure that Phil wouldn't want Freya to find out, so they both had to make a pact to never tell a soul what had happened between them.

Unless… what if Phil had phoned because he remembered how much they loved each other and wanted her back? She shook her head. She wouldn't – couldn't – continue seeing Phil. Not now. Not after how he'd reacted when she'd told him about their affair. The scorn, the anger, as if the very idea of having an affair with her was loathsome to him. And the way he'd dumped her so callously before the accident too – because she wouldn't leave Molly and Max. He was the one who had chased her, asked her to run off with him, and she'd been ready to until he'd made it clear he didn't want her children too. 'I don't want to be looking after your kids; I want my own kids,' he'd told her. She would never forgive him for that.

And then there was the way he had lied to her, manipulated her into believing that it was Freya who was abusing him. She wanted to warn Freya, but how could she without revealing that she'd had an affair with Phil?

She paced around the kitchen wondering what to do. If Mark found out, he would leave her, she knew he would, and it would destroy her relationship with Freya. What had she been thinking of to be swept away by Phil's good looks, his charm, his soft words as he'd unburdened himself to her, shown her the scars of his fights with Freya? How could she have been so taken in that she'd betrayed both her husband and her sister?

She'd been feeling lonely, unloved, that was why. Mark was working all the hours under the sun – they barely had time for a hug never mind anything else.

For you. He is working hard for you and the kids. She closed her eyes tight, wishing she could turn back the clock, had never gone for that drink with Phil when he'd phoned her, begging her to meet up as he needed someone to talk to, swearing her to secrecy, pretending he was scared of what Freya would do to him if she found out.

What if he wasn't pretending, though? What if he'd been telling the truth?

No, he'd been lying. She'd known that as soon as Freya had confided in her about his abuse – she had seen how nervous her sister was. And she'd had a glimpse of his true nature the other day when he had been aggressive towards her.

She jumped as the phone she'd been holding in her hand rang . She bit her lip nervously, hoping it wasn't Phil calling back. She didn't want to ever speak to him again but she knew she would have to and soon. She glanced at the name on the screen and her mouth went dry when she saw it was Freya. Had she guessed? Had Phil told her? She couldn't speak to her sister right now, not until she'd composed herself. She left the phone to ring, her eyes staring at the screen, her scrambled brain trying to think what to do. Then a message pinged in from Freya.

Hi Daisy, please phone me back when you can. I really need to talk to you.

Daisy trembled as she read the message. Had Freya found out about her and Phil?

CHAPTER THIRTY-THREE

Phil

Why the hell had he got Daisy's number in his phone under the name of Billy? As he quickly ended the call, he was literally shaking. There was only one explanation he could think of: Daisy had been telling the truth when she'd said they were having an affair. It hadn't been a trick; she'd only said that to cover her tracks because of his reaction.

How could he have been so stupid? Christ, he didn't even remotely fancy Daisy! He closed his eyes, guilt and anger surging through him. If Freya found out about this, their marriage would be over. He couldn't bear that. He loved Freya so much, he couldn't lose her. He wouldn't lose her. He had to do everything he could to keep this from her.

Then his eyes snapped open as another thought flashed across his mind. If Daisy was telling the truth about them having an affair, then she could also have been telling the truth about Phil saying that Freya was aggressive, violent. That he'd turned to Daisy, confided in her because he didn't know what to do about Freya's tantrums.

Another idea was seeding in his mind. Freya could have found out about his affair with Daisy and tampered with the brakes of his car out of revenge, deliberately provoking the argument so that

Phil would storm out and drive off. It could be Freya who was leaving the notes, pretending someone had broken in, wanting him to suffer for cheating on her. She could be feeding him a pack of lies, knowing he couldn't remember anything.

CHAPTER THIRTY-FOUR

Daisy

She could barely think straight all afternoon. Her life was a mess. She was pregnant, possibly by her brother-in-law, who it now seemed had remembered their affair. Only a couple of weeks ago she'd been hoping that Phil would change his mind, that he would leave Freya to be with her, as he'd promised he would. If he had done, they could have brought up the baby together, with Molly and Max. Except that Phil didn't want the twins. She thought back to the day they'd broken up, a week before the accident.

'I've nearly got everything in place; we'll be together soon,' Phil said as they lay in each other's arms. Phil had booked them into a hotel for the afternoon so Daisy had gone straight from work, arranging for Lisa to pick up Molly and Max from school for a playdate with her children, Holly and Jack. She and Phil had spent the afternoon making love, planning a future together.

'I can't wait for us to live together,' Daisy told him, wrapping her arms around his neck and kissing him. She loved him so much. She could hardly believe that they were going away together, making a new life.

'I've seen a two-bedroom cottage we can rent until the house is sold. It's in the Forest of Dean,' he told her.

'Is it near a school?' she asked. 'I don't want to have to travel too far with Molly and Max. And I'll have to look for another job.' She'd wanted to stay in the area but she knew that Phil was right: it would be impossible to remain here – the fallout from them running off together would be huge. It was best to put some distance between them and Freya and Mark.

'School?' Phil rolled away, edged himself up on his elbow, looking puzzled. 'What do you mean? I figured you'd leave the twins with Mark and they would come to stay in the holidays now and again.'

Now it was her turn to be puzzled. 'Of course they're coming with me, Phil. I thought that it was what you wanted too. You said that you always wanted a family. That Freya didn't want children…'

'Yes, I do want children. Our children. I don't want to bring up someone else's bloody kids, Daisy. I've done that once! I want my own child.'

She sat up, horrified. 'You can't seriously expect me to leave my children!'

'It's me or them,' he said and she knew that he meant it. Hurt and angry, she got out of bed, pulled on her clothes and drove home. She'd hoped Phil would phone her, tell her he was sorry and hadn't meant it. But she didn't hear from him again. That was it, they were over.

Now, she was ashamed that she had planned to run away with Phil and take the twins from Mark – who was so kind and supportive – to be with someone so manipulative and abusive as Phil.

'Are you all right, love? You're not still upset about being pregnant, are you?' Mark wrapped his arm around her waist and nuzzled into her neck.

The love in his action made her feel worse and the tears that she'd been holding back spilt down her cheeks. 'I'm sorry.'

'Hey, don't cry.' He wrapped her in his arms – strong, comforting arms that she should never have turned away from – and held her tight. 'We'll manage, I promise. Molly and Max are old enough to help a bit now, and your mum will be delighted to have another little one to fuss over. It'll be fine.'

How can it be fine when I don't even know if you're the father? Daisy thought as she sobbed on his shoulder. Her pregnancy with the twins had been so difficult, and she had been exhausted for the first eighteen months of their lives. She didn't want to be pregnant again, go through all that, lose control of her body, her life, her sleep. And she definitely didn't want to be pregnant by her sister's husband, a man who had ditched her so callously and didn't even remember their affair.

She had to pull herself together, get her head straight, think what to do. 'I'm okay, it's such a shock.' She wiped her eyes and smiled wanly up at Mark. 'I felt like we were finally getting our lives back together and now this.'

'I know, it's a shock for me too, but we'll be fine. Me and you, we'll always be fine.'

As she nestled her head on Mark's shoulder, Daisy felt overwhelmed with guilt. She'd never set out to have an affair with Phil. Yes, he was sexy and charming, but she loved Mark. She had never even thought of cheating on him. Then Phil had started confiding in her a little, telling her how Freya treated him, saying he didn't know where to turn… They'd started meeting for coffee, she'd tried to support him and one thing had led to another. Phil was a fantastic, adventurous lover, whereas she and Mark were first lovers, childhood sweethearts, had never dated anyone else never mind gone to bed with them. Phil had swept her off her feet and she regretted it so much. She had given up so much for him. And now she might be having his baby.

'I should go back to work now, love. Will you be okay? I could try and get cover if you need me here.'

He couldn't do that, he'd only just got promoted. Besides, she needed time on her own before she had to collect the twins, time to think.

'I'll be fine. You go to work and we'll talk more tonight.' She kissed him and he smiled down at her, eyes full of love, his hand gently caressing her cheek.

'Just remember that I'll always be here for you and together we can cope with anything.'

What had she done? If Mark ever found out, it would destroy him.

He won't find out, she thought determinedly. If Phil really had remembered it, she would simply deny it.

She closed her eyes, trying not to remember how much she had loved Phil. *It was just infatuation*, she told herself. She had to forget about him.

CHAPTER THIRTY-FIVE

Freya

Friday

Daisy had messaged her back last night saying she couldn't talk right now, the twins were being a handful, but she could meet her for lunch Friday as she had to go into town to get some shopping after work. Freya couldn't wait to see her, to talk to someone about what had being happening. Nadia was becoming a good friend, who she knew would listen to her, but she wanted to keep this out of work, and Daisy had been so supportive when Phil had been in hospital, she was the only one Freya felt she could confide in. The morning at work went quickly, and at one o'clock sharp she grabbed her bag.

'You off out for lunch?' Nadia asked, getting up too. 'Fancy keeping me company?'

'Oh, Nadia, normally I would love to but I'm meeting Daisy – she's shopping in town. Can we do lunch on Monday?'

'Sure we can, hun. I miss our chats now you only come in twice a week, but I know you've got that hunky husband of yours to look after.'

A husband who someone tried to kill and could be suffering from more trauma than we first realised, Freya thought. *A husband who has been like a stranger to me since the accident.* She didn't want to tell Nadia about that, though, scared things might get back to Stefan and he would think she needed to take more time off. Her work was keeping her sane at the moment, giving her a few hours' break from tiptoeing around Phil. She'd thought that she would have the upper hand when Phil came out of hospital but instead she felt like she was walking on eggshells; his moods were so up and down. *What do you expect after what he's gone through?* Phil had nearly died – watching her words and trying not to upset him wasn't that much of a big deal in the circumstances, was it?

Daisy was waiting for her when she walked into the café, sitting at a table with what looked like a herbal tea.

'What, no latte?' Freya asked in surprise. 'Are you still feeling sick?'

'Yes. It's more of an all-day queasiness than morning sickness. I'm hoping this peppermint tea will ease it,' Daisy replied.

'You do look a bit peaky,' Freya said, noticing her sister's pale face and dark-rimmed eyes. 'Do you want a muffin?'

Daisy shook her head. 'No, thanks, I'm good with this.'

Daisy really looked off-colour, Freya thought as she went up to the counter to get herself a cappuccino and a sandwich. She was worried about her sister. She'd looked tired and strained at the hospital too. This pregnancy was clearly taking its toll on her both mentally and physically.

'How are things now, Daisy?' she asked as she sat down at the table with her lunch. 'I feel awful I've been leaning on you so much the past couple of weeks and you have so much on your plate.' She leant over and squeezed her sister's hand. 'Are you still worried about the pregnancy?'

Daisy sniffed and nodded her head. 'It's just not what I need right now.' She forced a bright smile. 'Take no notice of me. I'll adjust, and we'll cope. It's a shock, that's all.' She picked up her cup. 'Now that's enough about me. What did you want to talk to me about?'

As Daisy sipped her peppermint tea, Freya told her about the police's visit. 'They said that the brakes of Phil's car were tampered with.'

Daisy's eyes widened. 'You're kidding! Are they absolutely sure?'

'Apparently the insurance assessors said there's no doubt at all.' She ran her finger around the rim of her cup. 'We both use that car. Someone wanted to injure, maybe kill, one of us.' She bit her bottom lip and glanced up at her sister. 'I'm scared, Daisy. Phil could have died. And the person responsible for tampering with the brakes is still out there.'

'No wonder you're scared! This is awful. Be careful, Frey.'

Freya kneaded the side of her neck. 'And weird things have been happening too.'

'What sort of things?'

She told Daisy about coming downstairs a couple of mornings to find the back door open. 'I was thinking it was Phil, that he'd been sleepwalking. He thought so too, but yesterday he went for a walk and I was working upstairs. I didn't go downstairs at all. But when Phil came back he yelled for me to come down – and the kitchen was flooded out. Someone had put the plug in the sink and left the tap running. And it wasn't me.'

Daisy frowned. 'So you think someone sneaked into your house and did it while you were upstairs? And that they've been breaking into your house in the middle of the night? Who would do that? And surely there would be signs of a break-in?'

'That's the thing, there's no sign of forced entry and nothing's been taken, so Phil thinks it's pointless telling the police. But now, after yesterday, I don't know if someone is trying to terrorise us, or if Phil has more severe brain trauma than we realised and he's doing things and forgetting...' A tremble ran through her.

She saw a flicker of something in Daisy's eyes but before she could put her finger on what it was, it had gone. Daisy leant forward. 'I think you're right and it has to be Phil. Maybe it is to do with his accident.' She paused, her expression serious. 'Or he's doing it on purpose to frighten you. Either way you need to be careful, Freya. He could be dangerous.'

CHAPTER THIRTY-SIX

Daisy's words played on Freya's mind for the rest of the day. Could Phil be doing all this to frighten her? Why? What would be the point? She felt more than a bit nervous about going home, wondering what might have happened in her absence and what mood she would find Phil in.

She opened the front door with trepidation. She could hear music playing in the kitchen and the smell of bolognaise wafting along the hall. Phil came out of the kitchen, wiping his hands on his apron, and gave her a kiss on the cheek. 'How's your day been?'

'Busy,' she said. 'It seems like you've been busy too. I take it we're having spaghetti bolognaise?' It had always been Phil's signature dish.

'Yes, with garlic bread. I haven't forgotten how to cook, thank goodness. It'll be ready in ten minutes. Does that give you time to freshen up?'

'It does.' She breathed out a silent sigh of relief that he was looking happier. 'You've cheered up.'

'I figured that losing two years of my memory isn't that big a deal, is it? I can still remember us and how much we love each other. That's what's important.' He grinned at her. 'Glass of wine? Merlot or Pinot?'

'Yes, please. Merlot. I'll be down in five,' she promised, heading for the stairs so she could freshen up, feeling a lot lighter herself.

She was silly to dwell on Daisy's words. Of course Phil wasn't playing tricks on her, and as for him being forgetful, it was just a blip, that's all. She had to expect him to have some confusion after such a terrible accident.

What about the brakes of Phil's car, though? That wasn't Phil being forgetful.

Forget about it for now, just enjoy the evening. She changed her top, brushed her hair and quickly patted a bit more powder on her face. She was determined that they were going to have a pleasant, relaxing evening and forget everything else.

'Perfect timing.' Phil glanced up as he put a basket of garlic bread down on the table and smiled. 'You look beautiful.'

'Thank you.' She glanced at the immaculately laid table – napkins, glasses of wine – her gaze resting on the vase of orange, cream and white roses standing in pride of place in the middle. She swallowed, remembering the last bunch of roses Phil had bought her, the night of the accident.

'See, I remember the important things,' he said, following her gaze. 'I do still buy you a mixed bunch of roses like that, don't I?'

'Yes.' She wouldn't think of that evening. This was going to be a fresh start for them. Phil had changed. 'They're gorgeous. Thank you.' She paused, not wanting to spoil the moment but a little anxious. 'Are you all right drinking wine, Phil? What about the painkillers?'

'I'm hardly taking any now, my ribs are a lot better,' he assured her, pulling out her chair. 'If madam would care to sit down, I'll serve up the starter.'

'I could get used to this,' she said lightly as she lowered herself into her seat.

'I want you to. I want to spoil you. These past couple of weeks must have been so hard for you. And I know I can get a bit edgy because I can't remember things but I'm not going to let it get to me and ruin things for us.' He poured her a glass of wine, then one for himself. He picked it up and held it out. 'To the future.'

'To the future,' she repeated, clinking glasses with him. Phil was right: the past was gone, and all that mattered was that they move on, build a good future together. And other than the moment with her phone and his mum's Facebook message, there had barely been a cross word between them. Phil's accident had been horrifying, but it seemed to have made him a better man. She'd done the right thing giving him another chance. Thinking about Aileen reminded her that she'd not received a reply to the message she'd sent her on Wednesday. Maybe Aileen had changed her mind about meeting up, after all.

It was a lovely evening. They chatted easily. Phil told her how he'd been going through his contacts, trying to get up to date with where he was with his work. 'I've had another article accepted by the *Climate Changer*, you know. I found the email in my inbox. I can't believe it!'

'Oh, Phil, that's marvellous,' she replied, raising her glass. 'Congratulations.'

'Thanks. I must say I'm really pleased.' He took a sip of his wine. 'Now, tell me about your day.'

It was so good to be sitting chatting like this – it was how they used to be when they were dating and in the early days of their marriage. Freya told Phil about the project that she was working on and he seemed really interested, asking lots of questions. 'And Daisy phoned me for a catch-up so I met her for lunch,' she added. Phil's expression tightened, his eyes darkened and he visibly tensed. It shook her for a minute. Surely he wasn't angry that she'd had lunch with her sister. 'She wanted to talk, Phil, and she was so supportive while you were in hospital,' she said quickly.

He took a sip of his wine and seemed to be considering his words. 'And how is she? Did she want to talk to you about anything in particular?'

'She looks tired, exhausted… I think she simply wanted someone to offload to. She's recently discovered that she's pregnant and is still a bit shocked about it.'

Phil's wine glass crashed to the floor.

CHAPTER THIRTY-SEVEN

Phil

The crashing of glass jolted Phil out of his daze. He jumped up out of his seat, his eyes resting on the red pool of wine spilling over the oak floorboards. He knew he should get a cloth, mop it up, but he couldn't move. Freya's words were spinning round and round in his mind. Daisy was pregnant. And she'd phoned Freya because she'd wanted to speak to her. Was that why Daisy had come to see him on Monday? She'd acted so strange, asking him if he had got his memory back, said they'd had an affair, warning him that she was keeping an eye on him. Was the baby his? Is that what she had come to tell him? Is that why she had got so angry when he couldn't remember anything from the past two years?

'It's okay, I've got it.' Freya was on her knees, soaking the wine with a soft, dry cloth.

Phil watched as she sprayed some furniture polish on the cloth and rubbed it into the wood.

'There.' She leant back on her ankles, triumphantly pointing to the floorboards, which looked – thank goodness – stain-free. 'Providing you soak up the wine straight away, it doesn't usually stain.'

'I'm sorry, I'm not sure how that happened – one minute I was holding the glass and the next…'

'It's okay. Don't worry.' Freya got to her feet and put a reassuring hand on his shoulder. 'No harm done. It's not the first time wine has been spilt on the floor.'

He wanted to ask whether the other times had been an accident or if a glass had been thrown down in an argument, like the vase. He wanted to ask her just how volatile their marriage had been, to question her and find out if he really was the instigator of the rows, or if it was Freya. But he didn't. He couldn't. He daren't voice the questions that were fighting for space in his head because he was scared to know the answers.

Freya put the polish and cloth back in the kitchen and returned to her seat with another wine glass, which she put on the table in front of Phil. 'Want a refill?'

Refill? He felt like drinking the whole bloody bottle. He was shocked to hear that Daisy was pregnant and horrified that the baby might be his. He could feel his head aching with the strain of it all.

'Are you all right, Phil? You're looking a bit pale. Is it the wine, do you think?' Freya asked gently.

'Maybe it is. Perhaps you were right and I shouldn't have drunk any.' He rubbed the back of his neck. 'I'm so sorry. I really wanted this evening to be special, to celebrate with you, but now I've ruined things.'

'Of course you haven't. It's been a lovely meal, but maybe you should have an early night? I bet you've been overdoing it today while I've been at work.'

'Yes, I will. I'll go on up now. You won't be long, will you?'

'No, I'll clear this away and load the dishwasher then I'll be with you.'

'I'm sorry to leave you with this mess.' Phil indicated the dirty dishes on the table. 'I've come over really tired and weak.'

'It's no problem. Honestly. Go to bed.'

Phil's head was pounding as he walked up the stairs. He'd been so worried that Daisy had asked to see Freya to spill the beans about their affair. He hadn't expected her to announce that she was pregnant. Had she come to see him the other day to let him know the baby was his, and that's why she was so angry he couldn't remember? He wondered if he had been the one to finish the affair and Daisy was furious about it. Perhaps that's why he'd booked the holiday at the last minute, bought Freya flowers and underwear. He'd been trying to make it up to her. Freya would leave him if she found out he'd had an affair and that Daisy was carrying his baby, he knew she would. He had to find out the truth, but he wasn't even sure who he could trust. He felt like everyone was playing with his head. Freya, Daisy, whoever was leaving the threatening notes. He opened the bedroom door and stepped inside. The bed looked so inviting – he wanted to lie down and sleep for days, weeks, and when he woke up for all this to have gone away.

Calm down, you don't even know for certain that you've had an affair with Daisy, he told himself. *She denied it afterwards, remember?*

A baby, though. He'd wanted a baby ever since he met Freya. A child, to replace the one he had lost all those years ago. The son he had loved like his own.

He shut down the memory. He wasn't going to think about that. He never thought about that; things happened and you had to move on with your life. And he'd moved on, with Freya. Daisy's baby was nothing to do with him.

He hoped Freya wouldn't be long. He felt a strong need to connect with her, reassure himself and Freya of their love for each other. He shouldn't have come up to bed yet; he should have helped Freya tidy away, then they could have gone to bed together. They hadn't made love since he'd come out of hospital, worried about his broken ribs; they'd cuddled and kissed, though. Maybe, if he was very careful, he could make love to her tonight.

He freshened up, cleaned his teeth and undressed, wondering whether to go back down and help Freya. To his relief he heard her footsteps on the stairs. He turned as she gently pushed open the door. 'I was about to come back down to help you. I'm sorry to leave you with all the tidying up to do.'

'It's fine. I put the dishes in the dishwasher. I'll deal with the rest in the morning.'

He climbed into bed as she disappeared into the en suite, joining him a few minutes later smelling of minty toothpaste and faint traces of perfume. He reached out for her and pulled her into his arms. 'It's been a long time,' he murmured in her ear.

'I thought you were tired.'

Was she trying to avoid sex, or was she genuinely concerned for his health?

'Not that tired…' He kissed her on the nose, the lips, then a trail down her neck.

'What about your ribs?'

'I'm sure you can be gentle with me…'

She was gentle. And distant, almost as if she was only going through the motions. He remembered their lovemaking as being wild and passionate – they hadn't been able to get enough of each other. Had two years of marriage taken the edge off it? Or was it something she – or he – had done that had extinguished the flame of desire he remembered so clearly?

The fact that all he knew of their marriage was what Freya chose to tell him ate away at him.

It was the early hours of the morning when he was woken by another vision. He blinked his eyes open, lay still for a while, trying to unscramble the jumbled images, making sure he had got it right. It was him and a woman with long, dark hair; they were rolling on the grass, laughing, a picnic laid out beside them. He lay on top of her and looked down at her. He couldn't see her face clearly but he knew who it was. The long, dark hair was a dead giveaway: it was Daisy. And it wasn't a dream, it was a memory. He was sure it was. It felt so real. They *had* been having an affair. His memories were returning. What would he remember next?

He quietly slid out of bed, not wanting to disturb Freya, pulled on his jeans and walked downstairs to have a cigarette to try and calm his nerves. If Daisy had been telling the truth about that, maybe she had been telling the truth about him confiding in her that Freya was abusing him. He walked into the kitchen, took a cigarette out of the packet then stopped in his tracks. Because, once again, the back door was wide open…

CHAPTER THIRTY-EIGHT

Freya

Saturday

Freya heard Phil get out of bed to go downstairs but pretended that she was still sleeping. She'd had a restless night, her mind plagued by unwanted memories, and when she and Phil had made love she'd found it difficult to relax. She had sensed that Phil was troubled too; he'd made love to her in a desperate sort of way, as if trying to erase the past, trying to show her how good they had been together, but it had lacked tenderness and feeling. They used to lie entwined after sex, as if they didn't want to let go of each other, sometimes talking, sometimes falling asleep in each other's arms. Last night though, as soon as it was over, they had both turned away, slept back to back.

It had taken Freya a long time to drift off to sleep – she kept thinking of Phil's reaction when she'd told him Daisy was pregnant and wondered if he was wishing it was Freya that was pregnant, if he'd remembered how much he had wanted a child but she hadn't. She wondered if that had been the reason behind his instigation of sex, not remembering that she was on the pill. The thing that had disturbed her most though was the way Phil had stared at the spilt wine, almost as if he had remembered the other time a glass of red wine had spilt on the floor. Only that time it had been thrown down in anger, by Phil. She had tried so hard to repress the memories of their arguments, of Phil's abuse, to give him another chance, but things kept triggering them back into her mind.

They'd been married six months. Phil was cooking a special dinner to celebrate. He did a lot of the cooking when he worked from home; weekdays it was usually basic stuff, often ready meals, and Sunday they often went out to lunch, but on Fridays or Saturdays Phil liked to cook something special. He really went to town that Saturday, cooking a Greek-themed menu of feta cheese with olives followed by a rich beef stifado, then homemade kataifi. It was a lovely evening. Phil was on top form, smiling, joking, affectionate.

'What are we celebrating?' Freya asked as Phil opened the Cabernet Sauvignon and poured out two glasses. They were both chatting in the kitchen as he put the finishing touches to the meal and she got the plates out of the cupboard, ready for him to dish out.

'Six months of being happily married.' Phil put the bottle down and held his arms out to her. She slid into them, raising her head to meet his lips. She loved it when he was like this, happy, teasing, loving. If only he was always this way. *He is most of the time*, she reminded herself. It was only the odd occasion.

'You are happy, aren't you?' he asked, raising his head slightly, his deep blue eyes gazing at her.

'Of course,' she assured him, and he held her tight, told her how much he loved her. Then they sat down to eat their meal, talking, laughing as they did so. It was a perfect evening until after the dessert, she rose, saying, 'Shall I do us a coffee?'

'In a minute, let's finish the wine first.' Phil took a long sip, his eyes meeting hers over the rim of his glass, then put the wine down. 'I've been thinking, Freya. We're in a great position financially now. I've got regular features with the *Telegraph* and a couple of magazines, as well as my university work.'

'And I've just been given a pay rise,' she replied, smiling. She had been so pleased about that; she loved her job at IPA Studio.

'So, I think it's the ideal time for us to have a family.' Phil reached over the table to hold her hand. 'What do you think?'

Freya felt a little nervous as she thought about her reply. They had both talked about having children sometime in the future but she hadn't expected Phil to mention it yet. Especially given their marriage felt a bit… volatile… at times. She wasn't sure it was a good idea to bring a child into the equation right now but she couldn't say that to Phil – he'd be hurt. And maybe angry. Perhaps she could fob it off by saying that she wasn't ready yet.

'We have discussed it. We both said that we wanted children.' There was a slight edge to Phil's voice now as he obviously sensed her reluctance.

'Yes, I know, and I do want children, of course I do, at some point. We haven't been married long, and it would be nice to spend more time together, to do the things we want, to have a few holidays abroad before we have a family, don't you think?'

'Having a family won't stop us doing anything. Your mum would love to babysit, so we'd still have plenty of nights out.' He squeezed her hand tighter. 'Just imagine a little Freya or Phil. Our very own baby.' His tone was soft, wheedling now, the usual tone when he wanted his own way. She knew what happened next, when he didn't get it, and she desperately wanted to prevent that. It had been such a lovely day, a perfect evening; she didn't want to spoil it.

'It would be lovely, and yes, I want a family too, Phil. Not yet though, Maybe next year…'

Phil gazed at her adoringly, his tone coaxing. 'Why wait? We can afford it. I can earn enough to support us both, you wouldn't even have to go back to work.'

There it was. She knew that Phil wanted a family, but part of her felt that Phil also wanted a child to prevent her from working at IPA. Since their wedding she had realised that he hated her going to work, hated her going anywhere without him. Ever since they'd got married, it was as if he wanted them to be joined at the hip. He'd repeatedly asked her to stop working but she had refused, saying they needed the money and she loved her job. Sometimes she felt that Phil hated her having a life that he wasn't involved in. He never had a night out with his friends – actually, he didn't seem to have friends except Tom, who was more of a work colleague – and was always miffed if Freya went out with her friends. So much so that she often didn't bother any more, because the sulks and arguments before and after the event simply weren't worth the hassle. 'It's only because I love you and want to be with you,' Phil would tell her. 'Don't you want to be with me too?' He would look so hurt that she'd always fight back the retort, 'Not all the bloody time!'

'I like working,' she pointed out. 'I'm not ready to have a baby yet, Phil. Can we please talk about it in another year or so?'

'But darling, why wait another year when we can start trying for one now? Neither of us is getting any younger, and they say it's harder to have children the older you get, and it would be nice to have more than one child. I don't want to risk us not having our kids, do you?' He leant over to kiss her, that engaging twinkle in his eye, a teasing smile on his face, the full charm offensive. Well, she wasn't going to be charmed into taking such a big decision when she wasn't sure it was a good idea.

'I'm only thirty-three, Phil, not exactly over the hill yet,' she reminded him, a smile on her lips to take the edge off her words. 'I do want kids but not right now. Having a child is a life-changing commitment. Please, let's put it on the back-burner for another year or so.'

His eyes darkened, a furrow creasing between his eyebrows. 'What about what I want? Doesn't that count? You know how much having a child means to me. How devasted I was to find out that Danny wasn't mine. And now you want to deprive me of the chance of having a child with you.' There was an edge to his voice now and the air was thick with tension.

Yes, she did know how hurt he was about his ex-wife cheating and having a child with someone else, and she did want a child with Phil. Not yet, though – she was too wary of his temper. She felt that they needed more time to get used to each other, for their relationship to settle, and his attitude now only served to prove to her that she was right to be cautious. 'I know, Phil, and we will have a child. But not yet. This has to be a joint decision, taken when we are both ready. I'll be the one carrying the baby, the one who has to give up work, whose life will change dramatically, and I'm not ready for all that. Let's wait a little longer, perhaps until we've been married a year.'

It was as if a mask had been pulled off. His face contorted with anger, he rose to his feet, leant over and thumped his fist on the table. 'It's all about you, isn't it?' He slammed his fist again. 'You never care what I want. I thought when we got married that we would be a couple, a partnership, sharing our lives completely. But no, you always want your bloody independence, and sod everything else.'

The injustice of his remarks had stung and she instantly retaliated. 'And you always want your own way! Well, there are two of us in this marriage and I have a right to my say too.'

His face turned red, eyes bulging, and her throat tightened. Suddenly, he grabbed his glass and threw it on the floor.

Freya jumped up as it smashed and trickled red wine all over the floorboards. 'Now look what you've done!' she shouted.

Phil stormed around the table until he was standing right in front of her, pointing his finger at her, so close she could see his enlarged pupils and the vein throbbing in his forehead, smell the wine on his breath. She stepped back, her heart pounding, suddenly afraid what he would do. 'You always do this, you selfish cow! You always push and push. I think you like to make me bloody angry. You get a fucking kick out of it.' He jabbed his finger into her chest. 'Well, you'd better watch it because one day you'll push me too far.' Then he grabbed his car keys and stormed out of the house, leaving her shaking and stunned.

What the hell had happened there?

Her legs gave way and she sank down into her chair, wrapping her arms around herself to try and still the trembles that were coursing through her body. She had been terrified. Phil had looked so furious and for a minute she had really thought he was going to hit her. She took a deep breath, then another, until she felt calmer. She had overreacted. Phil wouldn't hit her. He got angry, yes, but he wasn't a violent man. Although that scene had been pretty close. She looked down at the broken glass on the floor and the dark red stain over the floorboards. She really ought to clear that up.

Why should she? He was the one who threw the wine glass; let *him* clean it up.

Determined not to sit up waiting for him, or to clean up after his tantrum, she went up to bed. She was far too upset and angry to sleep, though, and spent the night tossing and turning restlessly, continually glancing at the clock as the hours ticked by. Where had he gone?

Anger was replaced by anxiety and finally, at half past five, seriously worried that Phil might have been in an accident, she gave up trying to sleep and went downstairs. She walked into the kitchen, where the remains of last night's romantic dinner, the smashed wine glass, the red stain on the floor all awaited her. Overwhelmed with it all, she sat down in a chair and, head in her hands, sobbed.

That was how Phil found her half an hour later when he finally returned home. She looked up as the door opened, tears streaming down her face, and there he was, pale, tired and contrite. He rushed over to her, wrapped his arms around her, smothered her with kisses, told her that he was sorry, really sorry, asked her to forgive him. And she was so pleased to see him, so happy that the dreadful argument was over, that she readily forgave him, went back up to bed with him, made love to him then slept in his arms until he woke her up at noon with a cup of coffee and toast. When she'd showered and gone downstairs, she found the table bare, the dishwasher on, the broken glass swept up and only a slight stain on the floorboards. Neither of them mentioned it again.

Now, seeing Phil's reaction to the smashed wine glass, she wondered if he had remembered the row and would bring up the subject of them having a child again. She hoped not because, though she really did want a child – and within the next couple of years if possible – she wouldn't risk bringing a baby into their marriage. Not until she felt completely confident Phil had changed.

CHAPTER THIRTY-NINE

Phil

What the hell? Phil ran over to the open door and peered out into the darkness. Was there someone out there? He stepped outside, still barefoot, and looked around the garden. It was too dark to see clearly. He grabbed a torch and went back out, shining its beam everywhere. Nothing. How long had the door been open? Had the intruder heard him coming down the stairs and quickly made their escape? Would they have got over the fence that fast? Or had the door been open for hours? The questions were bombarding his mind, making him feel dizzy. He held on to the table to support himself and took a few deep breaths, slowly so as not to hurt his broken ribs. He hated this, feeling so weak and vulnerable. If he'd run into the intruder, he wasn't even sure he would have had the strength to fight them. Well, whoever they were, there was no sign of them now. Hell, he needed a smoke. Taking the lighter out of his jeans pocket, he lit up the cigarette he was still holding, inhaling then exhaling deeply. A couple of deep puffs and he felt calmer.

He'd better go inside, check that nothing was taken. And to see if there was another note. He didn't want Freya to come down and find it. He went back inside, firmly locked the door behind him and checked the kitchen and lounge. Nothing seemed to be missing, not that he was surprised – the intruder didn't seem to have burglary in mind. Then he made his way to his study and over to his desk. There it was. The same typed bold black capital letters:

YOU'LL PAY FOR WHAT YOU DID.

Phil sat down on the desk chair, reading and rereading the note, wondering what he had done to make someone so desperate to punish him, and how they were getting into the house. His first thought was Daisy, angry maybe that he hadn't remembered their affair. He dismissed the thought – he and Freya had visited Daisy and Mark a couple of times before they got married and he remembered that they lived about twenty minutes away, too far for her to slip out in the middle of the night without Mark noticing. Freya had said that Mark worked nights sometimes but then surely if he was on the night shift, Daisy wouldn't leave the twins at home alone. It had to be someone else.

He put the note in the dictionary with the other two and leant back in his chair, his head throbbing. Every day he was overwhelmed by questions and fragments of memories he didn't understand.

He thought back to last night when Freya had told him about Daisy being pregnant, which had shocked him so much he'd dropped the wine glass. He'd felt a spark of memory: that they'd had an argument and wine had been spilt before, but he didn't want to ask Freya about it, didn't know if he could believe her reply. He wished he could remember for himself.

He walked back into the dining area of the kitchen and sat down at the table, staring at the slight stain on the wooden floor. There was no doubt that wine had been spilt here before and he felt sure that it hadn't been an accident. He put his head in his hands, trying to peel back the fog, to get a hint of the memory.

His head started to buzz and a fleeting image came into his mind. He couldn't see it clearly – it was like he was wearing too-strong glasses that made everything blurry – but he could make out that he and Freya were both standing up and shouting at each other, either side of the kitchen table. Then there was a smash and a wine glass was on the floor, red wine flowing over the floorboards like a stream of blood.

It was a memory, he was sure it was. It felt so real. Who had thrown the glass, him or Freya? And what had they argued over?

Then there was the crazy dream that had woken him up. About him and Daisy. He was sure this was a memory, it had felt so real. But he guessed it could just be a dream, brought on by his fears over what Daisy had said. He massaged the back of his neck, trying to ease the tension away.

He glanced at his watch: 4.35. He was tired but he didn't think he could sleep now – there was too much going on in his mind. He wanted to go for a walk and clear his head but as he'd come down clad in only his jeans, that would mean going back up to their room for a T-shirt and probably waking Freya. No, he'd stay here and try to make sense of things. Maybe it would help if he wrote things down. So much was happening it was hard to keep track of everything. He went back into his office and sat down in his chair, reaching for the spiral notebook and black biro lying on the desk, then flicked through to find a clean page. He wrote across the top of it:

Things I remember – everything up to the past two years:
My childhood.
Marrying Marianne.

He wished he could forget his first marriage – it had been the biggest mistake of his life. As for his childhood, spent constantly in Graham's shadow, never living up to his parents' expectations… that was definitely best forgotten. He moved on to better, more recent memories.

Meeting Freya.
Going out together.
Getting married.
Our honeymoon.

He chewed the end of his pen. There were other things he remembered, surely? What about his job? He added:

Teaching at the university.
Writing articles.

Although he couldn't remember finally having that article published by the *Climate Changer.*

It was a start anyway. He could add to it if he remembered anything else. He turned the paper over and wrote:

Things I don't know:
What our marriage was like.
Why we don't have children.
Who caused the big argument the night I left.
Who tampered with the brakes of my car.
Who is sneaking into the house during the night.
Who flooded the kitchen.
Who is leaving me threatening notes.

He tapped on the desk with the pen as he tried to think of more things. Then he remembered the holiday Freya said he had booked.

If I did book a holiday to Dubai, and if so, what I did with the booking details.

He paused, scared to put the next things in writing, but he had to – it was so big he had to try and sort them.

If I was having an affair with Daisy.
If Daisy's baby is mine.
If Freya is abusive to me.
Whether I can trust Freya.
Whether Freya tampered with the brakes, is pretending someone is breaking in and is writing the notes.
Whether Freya is trying to mess with my head.
If I am in danger.

He read through all the items again; it made him realise how much he had forgotten, how vulnerable he was. Two years didn't seem much of his life to lose, but those two years held so many secrets and he had no idea how he was going to unravel them all when he didn't know who he could trust.

Weary now, he ripped the page out of the notebook and slipped it between the front page and cover of the dictionary, with the notes. *It should be safe there.*

He yawned, his eyes heavy. He didn't want to go upstairs and wake Freya, face the inevitable questions, so he went into the lounge, wrapped himself in the throw that was draped over the sofa and drifted into an exhausted sleep.

*

That was close! I'd only just got out of the door when I saw him walk into the kitchen. I had to leg it into the garden quick and squat down by the bins when he came out to have a look around. He looked pretty shook up – good. Let him know how it feels to be frightened.

I left him another note on his desk. I want him to know that I've been here, that I can get in anytime I want. I'm so glad I made a copy of the spare key – it's easier than climbing in through the kitchen window. I've returned their key… I bet they didn't even realise it was missing.

I wonder if he tells her about the notes I leave. I don't think he does. I don't think he will go to the police either but it doesn't matter if he does. No one will guess it's me. I bet no one even knows about me. I'm his Big Secret.

I need to up the game a bit, though. Something a bit scarier than notes.

CHAPTER FORTY

Freya

Phil was fast asleep on the sofa, wrapped in the throw, when Freya got up. She guessed that he hadn't wanted to come back to bed in case he disturbed her. She stood watching him for a while, trying to imagine how he must be feeling. *It must be so frustrating – and confusing – to lose two years of your life.* She thought of the things she would have forgotten if she'd lost the last two years: the holidays she'd had with Phil, the different projects she'd worked on, the new furniture they'd bought for the house, doing the garden.

The arguments with Phil. The fights. The bruises. The scars inside that would never heal.

She wished she could forget those. Phil was lucky that he didn't remember. She would love to wipe the slate clean, to come to their marriage with no memory of what had happened before like Phil could do; it would make things so much easier. The memories were there, though, somewhere in Phil's mind. That was why he had reacted the way he had to the news that Daisy was pregnant. It had taken him back to the argument they had had over having a child, only he couldn't remember the argument right now, he could only remember the feeling. She wondered if he would ever remember it. The doctor said it was likely Phil's memory would come back but no one knew when – it could be days, weeks, months, years.

She went into the kitchen – thankfully Phil had closed the door after him this time – poured herself a glass of orange juice and took it outside to sit in the garden. It was a lovely sunny day, the sort of day to go out for a drive, or a stroll along the river. Perhaps she should suggest they go to the Mill Pond again; they'd enjoyed it last weekend.

The garden looked so pretty now, with the pots full of bright flowers – pansies, lobelias, petunias, nasturtiums, sweet peas. She sat down at the table, sipping her orange juice as she listened to the birds singing in the trees, gazing up at the almost cloudless cobalt-blue sky, enjoying the peace and tranquillity of it all.

'How long have you been up?'

She turned at the sound of Phil's voice. He was barefoot, jeans slung low on his waist, belt half-buckled; he'd obviously pulled them on quickly in the early hours of the morning, not wanting to disturb her. She let her gaze linger over his body for a few seconds: at forty-one he was still fit and worked out regularly. Still handsome too, with those ink-blue piercing eyes you could drown in, his hair all tousled. In spite of herself, she loved him. But she was scared of him too.

'About half an hour. I didn't want to disturb you,' she replied. 'You looked so peaceful on the sofa.'

He pulled out a chair and sat down beside her. 'I had a bit of a restless night so I came down for a drink.'

He looked so tired that she reached out and touched his hand. 'How are you feeling now? I was thinking that maybe we could go for a walk, or a drive somewhere. Are you up for it?'

'I'd like that,' he said, nodding. 'Can we pop into a DIY shop, do you think? Get a bolt for the back door? I don't want to risk coming down in the night and forgetting to lock it again. We could get burgled.'

'Yes, that's a good idea.' It worried her that Phil was still sleep-walking and leaving the back door open even though they now put the key on a hook. Would a bolt across the top deter him from going outside or would he open that too? Still, it had to be worth a try. She smiled at him. 'How about we grab a bit of breakfast then set off? We could have lunch out at the Mill Pond again.'

'That sounds good. I'll go and have a shower, I won't be long.'

It was a pleasant day. They ambled around the large DIY store, buying a sturdy bolt for the back door, and some more flowering plants, which they placed in the boot of Freya's Fiesta, making sure they parked in a cool spot while they stopped for a ploughman's lunch at the Mill Pond before a slow stroll by the river.

When they returned home, the first thing Phil did was put the bolt in place at the top of the door.

'There, that should do it,' he said, standing back triumphantly when he'd put in the last screw. 'That'll stop my nocturnal wanderings.' He seemed so certain. 'Now, let's figure out where we're going to put the new tubs.'

They spent a couple of hours planting the new flowers in the garden then had a quiet evening watching the TV. Before he went to bed, Phil locked the back door and slid the bolt firmly across the top. As she watched him, Freya had the feeling that he was trying to keep someone out rather than himself in.

CHAPTER FORTY-ONE

Phil

Monday

The house was quiet without Freya. A long, lonely day loomed ahead and Phil didn't quite know what to do with himself. He'd found a couple of news apps on his phone and had occupied himself finding out what had been going on in the world for a while, getting up to speed with world politics, but staring at the small screen soon made his head ache. The amnesia was making him feel fragile and anxious, wondering what else would come out of the woodwork, what else he had done. It was as if he was an imposter, living someone else's life. He knew that he should be grateful it was only the last two years he had forgotten – he could have forgotten everything, not have recognised Freya or remembered Tom or his work at the university. But how could he be grateful when actually he was so bloody angry that someone had tried to kill him, someone had caused this to happen to him, and he had no idea who it was? All he could think about was unlocking his memory so he could recall the last two years, remember his life with Freya, whether he'd had an affair with Daisy, and work out why someone might want him dead.

He hated this not being in control. There were so many questions in his mind and he had no idea who to ask for the answers.

He felt at the mercy of everyone around him, that the previous two years were an empty book in which anyone could rewrite his history. He so desperately wanted to remember; the truth couldn't be worse than not knowing.

The doctor at the hospital had told him that retrograde amnesia after brain trauma like his was quite common and often the sufferer recovered their memory fully. Phil wondered if the memories just came back to them in one block, or if something jolted their return bit by bit. Was there something he could do to trigger them back, perhaps? There must be a lot of information about it on the internet. He'd go and do a search on his computer – he'd had enough of reading the small screen on his phone – and see what he could find out. He made himself a black coffee, locked the back door, pulling the bolt across to secure it, and took the coffee into the study with him.

He was amazed at the information he came across and read through a few case studies of people who had suffered retrograde amnesia after a traumatic event, like him. Some of them had regained some memory of their missing years by meeting someone from their past, visiting a place they used to be familiar with, or after hearing a verbal clue such as the name of someone they had known. He'd thought coming home might help him, and yes, a couple of memories had come back. Was the answer to visit familiar places – the university perhaps – and meet up with people he knew? Like Tom. He had known Tom for years and worked closely with him at the university. Perhaps seeing Tom might jog his memory. He pulled out his phone, scrolled for Tom's name and sent him a text asking if he was free to catch up and bring Phil up to speed on what was happening at the university.

Then he returned to his internet search, which was far more informative than he'd expected. There were several therapies he could try, and even a guide on what to eat to help memory recall – apparently alcohol and sugar were both big no-nos.

He read on, fascinated by the different cases studies, many of the subjects forgetting the last couple of years prior to an accident or traumatic event, as he had. And many eventually regaining those memories. It made him feel more hopeful about the future. Some people never recovered their memories, though, but he didn't think he would be one of them. He had already had flashbacks to some memories. He was sure it would all come back in time, and the sooner the better.

A text pinged in. It was Tom.

Good to hear from you, mate. Yes, a catch-up would be good. How does tomorrow about 11.30 suit? I've got a couple of tutorials in the morning and one in the afternoon so can see you in between.

That was perfect. Phil hadn't fancied another day home alone, and goodness knew how long Freya's meeting would last. He messaged back:

Yeah, that works. See you at the Miller's Arms?

Tom replied with a thumbs up.

Feeling a lot more upbeat now, Phil went into the kitchen to make himself a sandwich. He was spreading the bread when he heard the landline ringing. It was the first time he'd heard it ring since he'd been home. He ignored it and carried on making his cheese and pickle sandwich – Freya had said most of the landline calls were spam anyway. The phone stopped ringing then started again. Maybe it was important – it could be the hospital, rearranging his check-up appointment. He placed the sandwich on a plate and went into the lounge to answer the phone.

'Hello.'

'Phil! Thank goodness! I was worried you'd collapsed or something.'

The woman on the other end of the phone talked loud and fast. Phil moved the phone away from his ear as he tried to recall who it was. The voice sounded familiar but he couldn't remember who.

'It's Yvonne, Freya's mum. Freya said you're suffering from amnesia,' the woman told him. 'I'm sure you remember me, though. We are very close.'

Are we? 'Er, I'm afraid I don't, really. Sorry. Freya is at work. Could you call back later this evening?'

'I don't want to speak to Freya, I want to talk to you.'

Anxiety stroked his stomach. Had she phoned to tell him off about his treatment of Freya?

'I wanted to see how you were. Freya wouldn't let me visit you in hospital; she said you weren't strong enough.'

Phil remembered Daisy saying their mum was desperate to come and see him. Were they really that close? Freya didn't speak about her mum much. 'Er… yes. I'm fine, thank you. My ribs are still a bit sore, and as you know I'm struggling with my memories of the last two years, but otherwise I'm okay.'

'I can't believe that Freya has gone to work and left you to cope alone. I told her that she shouldn't. She should be looking after you. You've had a terrible accident.'

That was exactly what he thought too – it was nice for someone else to show him some sympathy. Maybe he and Freya's mum did get on pretty well after all.

'I've told Freya she'd better take care of you. She's lucky you weren't killed. Freya is too obsessed with her work, I've told her that. Too obstinate and headstrong. She always has been.'

Her words resonated in Phil's mind. What was Yvonne saying? Did she suspect that Freya didn't treat him right? That Freya might have been responsible for the crash?

'Well, I'd better go now. I just wanted to check on you. Take care, Phil.'

'I will. Thank you.'

Phil sat down, his sandwich forgotten as he thought over the conversation with Freya's mother. First Freya's sister had come to check on him and now her mother had phoned. They had both seemed very concerned about him, even though Daisy had backtracked later and said she believed Freya that Phil was the abuser. Yvonne said she and Phil were close but Freya had stopped her from coming over to see him. Why? Was she afraid of what her mum might say?

The niggling thought that Freya was lying, making out that Phil had abused her when really it was Freya abusing him, was growing bigger in his mind.

CHAPTER FORTY-TWO

Freya

Tuesday

'How long will you be at your meeting?' Phil asked, looking over the newspaper he was reading as she walked into the lounge.

'It should only take me a couple of hours but then there's travelling there and back. You'll be okay here, won't you?' Aileen had replied on Sunday evening, apologising for the delay in replying, explaining that Charles had taken a turn for the worse and suggesting meeting at a café in the town centre for lunch on Tuesday, so Freya had booked the day off.

Obviously she couldn't tell Phil yet that she was meeting his mother so had avoided telling an outright lie by simply saying she had a meeting. She hated deceiving him. *He'll understand why I did it and be pleased when I manage to reunite him with his family*, she told herself. Although Phil had been adamant he didn't want to see his parents again, she was convinced that if she could tell him how much his mother regretted the rift, and how ill his dad was, she would be able to persuade him to give them another chance. She had to admit that she was curious about Phil's childhood. It would be good to chat with his mother although she was a bit nervous about meeting her – it was such an awkward situation.

She'd spent ages getting ready, wanting to make the right impression. She indicated the navy linen trousers and white short-sleeved top she'd finally decided to wear, thinking it was smart but not too formal – after all, Phil thought she was going to a business meeting. 'Do you think this outfit looks okay?'

He nodded his approval. 'Smart casual, just right I'd say.' He folded up the newspaper and placed it on the table. 'I'm off out myself soon. I'm meeting Tom at the Miller's Arms in a bit – we arranged it yesterday. I want him to update me on what we've been doing the last couple of years, and the course details for September so I can start thinking about my lesson plans. It'll be good to focus my mind on something apart from the accident.'

The Miller's Arms was only a ten-minute walk away. And a short stroll would do Phil good, as would a chat with Tom, thought Freya, although she wished he'd arranged the meeting for tomorrow so that she could have some peace to work with him out of the house. She was finding it increasingly difficult to work from home. Phil was constantly interrupting her and she was beginning to feel claustrophobic being in the house with him most days, but he insisted that he felt too vulnerable for her to return to working in the office all week. She hoped he wasn't manipulating her to persuade her to work from home full-time, especially given that was something he'd always wanted.

'I'd better dash. My train leaves soon. Take it easy, don't exert yourself,' she said, kissing him on the forehead.

She parked her car in the station car park. It was easier to take the train into Birmingham rather than to drive. Parking was always a nightmare, and it would mean that she would arrive more relaxed. Normally, Phil would have dropped her off at the station and picked her up again, but he'd been advised not to drive yet. He didn't seem to mind that, though. He hadn't asked for a courtesy car from the insurance company, happy to wait for the pay-out to buy another car. She was sure the accident had shaken him up more than he let on, too. It certainly had her. If she were Phil, she'd be in no rush to get behind the wheel again either. At least not until the person who had sabotaged his brakes was under lock and key.

As she sat on the train, Freya reread Aileen's messages and tried to imagine what Phil's mother would be like. The profile picture showed a mature woman with short dark hair, almost the same colour as Phil's, but she knew that profile pictures were often not a true likeness. Phil was forty-one so his mother must be in her sixties at least.

Freya was familiar with the restaurant they were meeting at, having passed it a few times when shopping with friends, but had never actually gone inside. Now, she took a deep breath to calm herself then pushed the doors open and walked inside, glancing around the room for a woman looking in any way similar to Aileen's profile picture. The restaurant wasn't very busy yet – there were a few couples here and there, two groups of women, two men, but no woman sitting alone. *Aileen must still be on her way.* Freya decided to grab a table, order a coffee and wait. She sat down at a table in the corner, thinking that would give them more privacy to talk, and a waiter immediately approached her, notepad and pen in hand.

'I'm waiting for someone so just a latte for now, please,' she said.

When it arrived, she sipped her coffee, trying to shake off the apprehension that had seized her now she was finally about to meet Aileen. She wondered not for the first time if she should have come – if Phil found out that she had gone behind his back to meet his mother, he would be furious. *I can't deny a mother the chance to make up with her son,* she reminded herself. *And I will tell Phil, I just need to choose the right moment.*

She glanced over as the door opened and a good-looking woman glided in, immediately recognisable from her profile photo as Aileen. Even from this distance Freya could see that her features, hair and the confident way Aileen held herself were the same as Phil. The woman glanced around, caught Freya's eye, waved and made her way over.

As Aileen came closer, Freya could see that her eyes were the same inky blue as Phil's and held the same twinkle in them. Her hair was slightly darker – probably helped by a hair dye now – but there was no mistaking the resemblance. She was smartly dressed in what Freya was sure was a designer blouse, beige fitted cropped trousers and multi-coloured soft leather sandals. A matching bag hung from her shoulder and the waft of an expensive perfume floated around her as she reached the table. Phil's family obviously had money. Not quite sure what to do, Freya stood up awkwardly.

'Aileen?'

'Freya. Hello, my dear.' Aileen hugged her warmly. 'Thank you so much for agreeing to meet me.'

'It's a pleasure,' Freya said with a smile. *What a lovely woman*, was her first reaction as Aileen pulled out the chair opposite Freya, hung her bag on the side and sat down.

Freya sat down again. 'I ordered a coffee while I was waiting. Would you like one?' she asked as she saw the waiter walking over towards them.

Aileen ordered a coffee too, black – like Phil.

'I really am grateful that you came. I've been dying to meet my new daughter-in-law,' Aileen said. 'You must have been surprised to get a message from me.'

'I was,' Freya admitted. 'Phil isn't on Facebook. He tends to keep off social media. I guess that's why you contacted me.'

'Yes. My brother Richard – Philip's uncle – saw the newspaper article about the terrible accident and showed it to me. I knew then that I had to get in touch… Philip could have died.' She paused for a moment to compose herself. 'To be honest, I've been wanting to get in touch with Philip for some time but Graham, our other son, said it was up to Philip to contact us and to apologise. I kept hoping that would happen. None of us had contact details for Philip, you see, and we had no idea where he was living until we read the newspaper article.' She reached in her bag for a tissue and dabbed her eyes.

Freya took a sip of her coffee and waited patiently for Aileen to continue, not knowing what to say until she had heard the story. Phil had told her that his parents didn't care about him but his mother was clearly distressed about the fallout.

The waiter returned with Aileen's black coffee and left them with menus to browse.

'I did think about contacting Philip via the newspaper or the university that the article said he worked for, but it's such a personal issue, I thought it best to contact you, that if I explained the situation, you could talk to him. I would never have forgiven myself if Philip had died in that accident and I'd made no attempt to get in touch with him, to heal the family rift. Especially now.' Her dark blue eyes rested on Freya's face, serious now and uncannily like Phil's. 'Does Philip talk about us much?'

Freya didn't want to be cruel but she sensed that Aileen wanted the truth so she shook her head. 'No, he never mentions you. All I know is that you all had a fallout years ago, so he walked out and hasn't seen any of you since.'

Aileen was silent for a moment, staring down into her cup as if hoping to find the words she wanted to say there. When she did finally speak, her voice was so soft that Freya could barely hear her. 'He didn't just walk out. I told him to get out and never come back.' She paused, raised her troubled eyes to Freya. 'I've regretted it so many times but that afternoon I was so angry and upset, so worried for Charles. Because I thought Philip had killed him.'

CHAPTER FORTY-THREE

Aileen thought that Phil had killed his father? Freya stared at her, horrified. No wonder Phil didn't want to talk about it!

'I'm sorry, I can see that this is a shock to you.'

'He said… he said that you both always favoured Graham over him and one day he'd had enough so he left.'

Aileen's eyes clouded over. 'I know that Philip always felt that, but it wasn't true. Philip and Graham, they wound each other up as brothers do. I certainly didn't favour Graham when they were growing up. I adored both my boys, and so did Charles. But Philip, he always had such anger inside him – the slightest thing would inflame him and he found it so difficult to control his temper. Graham was… easier to be around.'

Freya was shocked by her words. Phil had a temper right back from when he was young? He had always told her that she was the one who'd made him that way, that she provoked him. Another lie. 'What happened?' Her eyes were glued to Phil's mother's face. She couldn't move. She was waiting for her next revelation.

'Graham and Phil came home for a week to celebrate Charles's birthday with us. They squabbled, as usual, but then one night Philip came home drunk. It was very late. He and Graham had words. Charles and I were in bed but heard a commotion and got up to see what was happening. We came downstairs to see Graham flat on his back on the hallway floor and Philip on top of him, hammering him with his fists. I was so horrified I was rooted to the spot, I thought he was going to kill him, there was blood all over Graham's face.' She closed her eyes briefly as if to shut away the memory. Then she took a breath and continued, 'Charles yelled at him to stop, then ran over and pulled Philip off.' She swallowed and Freya saw tears glistening in her eyes. 'Philip… he turned around and punched Charles, knocked his father to the floor. I thought he'd killed him. I was in such a panic. I ran over to Charles, and Graham crawled over to check on Charles too.' She paused again and Freya could see that this was difficult for her to talk about. 'Philip, he just stood there, his fists clenched, like he couldn't decide who to attack next…'

Yes, she'd seen him like that, the veins pulsing in his forehead as he struggled to control the fury that was engulfing him. It was terrifying.

'I looked up at him and in that moment I hated him. I yelled at him to get out and never come back. He went upstairs, packed his bag and walked out into the night just as an ambulance arrived for Charles. I haven't seen my son, my firstborn, since then.' She dabbed her eyes with the tissue again. 'Later that night Charles had a stroke.'

Freya stared at her, horrified – she hadn't expected to hear this, that Phil had set about his brother and then his father. She didn't blame Aileen for telling him to get out; she would have done the same when faced with such a horrendous scene. She couldn't believe that Phil hadn't gone back and apologised when he'd sobered up. That he'd stayed away, refused to contact them, to invite them to his wedding, to even talk about them, as if it was their fault that they were estranged rather than his. She hadn't expected to hear such a shocking story but deep down she knew that Aileen was telling the truth. The painful look in the woman's eyes, the way she was twisting the tissue around her finger, the wobble in her voice were all proof that this was really distressing for her.

'I was angry for quite a while, I admit that,' Aileen continued. 'I should have tried to contact Philip earlier, not left it so long. But I expected – wanted – him to come to us, to apologise. He didn't. We never heard from him after that night. When I finally tried to reach out to him it was too late, he'd changed his phone number, his address, vanished without a trace. I thought that he would get in touch when he was ready. But that was over twenty years ago.' Aileen's eyes brimmed with tears. 'And I can't wait any longer. Not now Charles has only weeks to live and it's his dying wish to see Philip again.'

'I'm so sorry,' Freya said softly.

'Charles has come to terms with it. He's very brave and has made his peace. But he wants to make his peace with Philip too. Even though Philip hurt Graham and Charles, he was very young. He'd had a drink and the situation got out of hand. And to marry a lovely girl like you, I know he must have turned over a new leaf.' She took a sip of her coffee and Freya could see that she was struggling to compose herself. 'It's a huge ask. But would you talk to him? Let him know about Charles? Tell him we forgive him and want to see him?' She opened her purse and took out a white card with fancy black lettering. 'This is our new address and my phone number.'

Freya took the card. 'I'll try,' she promised.

CHAPTER FORTY-FOUR

Phil

'You're looking well, considering.' Tom surveyed Phil over the rim of his lager glass. 'You're lucky not to be dead. And you say it was deliberate? Someone messed with your brakes?'

'Yes. The insurance company are positive. The police are investigating.' Phil couldn't stop thinking about it. He could have died. Someone wanted him dead, had tried to murder him. It was a chilling thought. The accident still haunted him; the memory of practically standing on the brakes and not being able to stop his car hurtling down the hill towards the lorry, once retrieved, would not now leave him. He didn't know how he would ever pick up the courage to drive a car again. He would have to at some point, he needed to for work, and also because he wasn't going to let the bastard who tampered with his brakes win, but thankfully he had time before he had to face that step. First, he wanted his ribs to heal, to feel fit again. And to get his memories back.

'Any idea who it could be? I guess your memory loss makes that difficult if whoever it is who has such a big grudge against you is someone you met recently?'

'I know,' Phil said again. He could do with a stiff drink rather than the orange juice he'd ordered but he needed to keep his head clear – it felt fuzzy enough as it was half the time, as if he was barely present. 'I was wondering if you knew anyone I'd upset. Someone at the university maybe? One of the students? Freya reminded me of a student' – he paused, searching for her name – 'Katrina, who apparently had a thing for me a couple of years ago. She hasn't done anything since, has she?'

Tom frowned. 'No, but there have been a couple of other incidents. Actually, I'd been meaning to talk to you about it but then you had the accident. You got a little friendly with a student called Georgie a few months back and then the poor girl took an overdose. Her parents were threatening to sue. I had a hell of a job hushing it up.'

'What?' Phil could hardly believe it. 'Are you saying that I had an affair with one of my students?'

'Not a full-on affair, no, but she claimed that you got close, too close, and she was besotted with you. She followed you home one day, tried to get you to go to bed with her, and when you rejected her, she went home and took an overdose.'

'Bloody hell! Does Freya know about this?'

'I've no idea. You were desperately trying to keep it from her.' Tom's disapproval was evident. 'I've got to be honest, Phil, you've been becoming a bit of a liability. You're too touchy-feely with the female students. You've had two warnings so far. One more strike and you'll be out. I hope the silver lining of this situation is that you use the opportunity to turn over a new leaf.'

Phil took a long swig of his orange juice. He hadn't expected this. 'You said I rejected her, though. So, I didn't do anything wrong, Tom. Surely that's unfair?'

'Your behaviour hasn't been professional, Phil. That girl could have died…'

'Because I rejected her unwanted advances? How's that my bloody fault? She's obviously unhinged.' He took another gulp of his drink, wishing he could add a double whisky to it. 'And I can't even remember it so can't defend myself,' he added bitterly.

'I stuck up for you the best I could but there's only so much I can do. You really need to toe the line from now on.'

Phil felt narked. The things he could say about Tom – and he bet there were more over the last couple of years that he couldn't remember. Tom was known for playing the field, admittedly not with students, but if his wife got wind of it… bang would go his marriage. Besides, it wasn't Phil's fault if the girls fancied him; he hadn't gone to bed with them like some people would have. And, anyway, they were adults for God's sake. You weren't talking schoolkids here! 'So, would you say her parents might be upset enough to try and kill me?' he asked. 'Because now someone is breaking into my house and leaving me threatening notes.'

'What?' Tom placed his elbows on the table and leant forward, his expression intent. 'Tell me.'

Phil explained about finding the back door open, the notes. He took one of the notes out of his pocket and showed it to Tom.

Tom read it, his eyes widening. 'Blimey, Phil, this is serious stuff. Have you told the police? What does Freya think?'

'I haven't told the police, or Freya. Not yet.'

'Why the hell not?'

Phil hesitated. Should he confide in Tom? They'd been friends for years, ever since Phil started working at the university, and had always had each other's backs, but Tom hadn't been exactly friendly today, had he? Phil squashed down the anger at Tom's abruptness about the student – he was just trying to warn Phil what was going on. Tom was the only friend he had, and he needed someone; it was driving him crazy. So he took a deep breath and told Tom all about Daisy's visit, and how she had said they'd been having an affair, but then said that it wasn't true and she was just testing him to see if he had lost his memory. He didn't mention that Daisy had told him he'd been confiding in her that Freya was abusing him, or that Daisy thought he'd abused Freya. No need to offload everything. 'And then Freya told me that Daisy's pregnant,' he added.

Tom had just taken a mouthful of lager but at Phil's last remark he almost spluttered it out. He grabbed a napkin and wiped his mouth. 'Blimey, Phil, that's a bit of a mess,' he said when he could finally speak.

'The thing is I don't know whether Daisy is telling the truth or just trying to trick me to see what I can remember, as she said. But if we were having an affair, then surely the baby could be mine?' He hated this not knowing, this powerlessness.

'I don't understand why she would say something like that to trick you, though. And why would she think that you'd pretend to lose your memory?' Tom looked as puzzled as he sounded. 'It doesn't make sense.'

'I know.' He regretted saying anything to Tom now. He didn't want to tell him about the argument the night of the accident, that Freya had said he'd been abusive. But he had to say something to convince Tom. He was looking really suspicious now.

'Apparently Freya and I had an argument the night of the accident. She thought I was having an affair.' He wasn't even sure if that was a lie, he only had Freya's word for it that they were arguing because he'd booked a last-minute holiday. A holiday he could find no details about.

'And you don't know if you were?'

'I wouldn't cheat on Freya. I love her. And certainly not with her perishing sister. I don't even fancy Daisy, never have.'

Tom gulped back a mouthful of lager then leant back in the chair. 'This opens a right can of worms. If you were having an affair with Freya's sister and her husband found out, that would also give him a motive for wanting revenge.'

Phil had already considered that. He'd met Mark a couple of times before the wedding, and from what he remembered he was a quiet bloke, hardly went to the pub, was focused on his family. He remembered Freya saying that Daisy and Mark had been child-hood sweethearts, though. He'd take it badly if he discovered that his wife was having an affair, especially with her sister's husband. Badly enough to try and kill Phil?

'I wouldn't have an affair with Daisy. I just know I wouldn't,' he said adamantly even though the image he'd had the other day of him kissing Daisy flashed back into his mind.

Tom must have picked up on his uncertainty because he gave him a long, hard look. 'The thing is you don't know, do you, Phil? You can't remember the past two years. All you know is that someone is out to get you. You need to speak to Freya's sister and find out for certain if you did have an affair. And you need to tell the police about those notes, and your nocturnal visitor.'

'I can't.' He struggled to stop his voice from shaking. 'I'm scared what else is going to come out, Tom. Have you any idea what it's like not to know what you've done over the past two years?'

'You have to!' Tom leant forward. 'If you can't do it for you, then do it for Freya. She could be the one who gets hurt next time. What if whoever it is decides to set fire to your house? You can't keep this to yourself, Phil. It's too risky.'

He was right, Phil knew he was, but what if he had been having an affair with Daisy? What then?

He voiced his concern to Tom, who advised, 'First find out if her husband knows. If he doesn't, then she won't want it made public, especially now she's pregnant. So you both agree to say nothing and then you go to the police and tell them what's been happening, leaving out the bit about you having an affair.'

'If Freya finds out, she'll leave me.' It was the thing he dreaded most. He'd fallen in love with Freya at first sight, known she was the one for him, and couldn't believe his luck when she'd agreed to go out with him, then that she'd agreed to marry him. If she left him, it would destroy him. Surely he hadn't risked their happiness for a sordid affair with her sister?

Then he remembered Daisy's words: 'You told me she was abusive, showed me some cuts and bruises.'

Maybe he and Freya weren't happy after all. Maybe that was why he'd had an affair with Daisy – if he had, that was. Tom was right. He had to find out.

'Daisy said that I turned to her for help because Freya had a temper and was abusive sometimes,' he confessed.

Tom raised an eyebrow. 'She seems nice, Freya, pleasant, easy-going, but…'

'But what? Come on, Tom, have you any idea how horrible it is not to remember things? Not to know who to believe?'

'Well, you did turn up for work with a big bruise on your cheek once. You said you'd walked into the door.'

CHAPTER FORTY-FIVE

Daisy

'Mum, where's my smiley jumper? I want to wear my smiley top.' Molly bounced in wearing pink shorts and no top. Already, at only six years old, Molly had clear ideas of what she wanted to wear. She was so sure of herself, brimming with confidence. Not like Max.

Daisy's heart sank. The yellow top with the big smiley face on the front was still in the wash. She hadn't got around to putting the washing machine on the last couple of days, she'd felt so sick. And worried. It was all she could do to get herself out of bed, get the twins off to school and herself to work. And Mark was no help – although he was being kind and supportive, he was either working or sleeping, often not getting home before the twins went to bed. Honestly, he practically lived at the supermarket since he'd been made regional manager.

'It won't be for long, babe, we're just short-staffed right now. So many people on holiday,' he'd told her before he'd left at six that morning.

'Lucky them.' The words had slipped out of her mouth before she could stop them and she instantly regretted them. It wasn't Mark's fault that they hadn't been on holiday since the twins had been born. She shouldn't have had a dig at him. The twins had come along unexpectedly, and the labour and birth had been difficult, then Max had been so ill most of his first year, Daisy had had to take such a lot of time off work and it had seriously affected their income. Not that Mark had complained, he'd just taken on more work himself and now been promoted as a reward, meaning he was away from home even more. Leaving the twins, the housework and everything else for Daisy to fit in alongside her part-time job as a dental receptionist.

'Mummy!' Molly tugged at her sleeve. 'I want my smiley top.'

'Well, you can't, I haven't had time to wash it,' Daisy snapped then instantly regretted it as Molly's face fell. She really could do without a tantrum right now. Yellow was her daughter's favourite colour, and the smiley top her nan had given her for her birthday was her all-time favourite at the moment. 'I'll get it ready for tomorrow. Why don't you go and wear your unicorn one? It will match your pink shorts,' she suggested gently.

Max walked in wearing yesterday's stripy T-shirt with an egg stain down the front and navy shorts. The twins were so different – Max didn't care what he wore; food and playing with his tablet were his priorities. 'I'm hungry,' he said.

'I'm just doing breakfast. Sit down – you too, Molly, you can get your T-shirt in a minute.' Knowing Molly, she'd only get chocolate cereal all over her top and have to get changed again.

Daisy took two plastic bowls out of the cupboard and a box of chocolate cereal, pouring some into the bowls and adding milk then passing them over to the twins, who were now sitting at the table. Molly still had the sulky expression on her face, and Max was already playing on his tablet, from which an annoying jingle was repeating over and over.

Daisy's head was thumping and she felt nauseous. She hoped it would ease soon; she couldn't take another morning off work.

She made herself a peppermint tea and sat down at the kitchen table to sip it slowly. Finally the nausea in her stomach was bearable and she set off to take the twins to school, then herself on to work.

It had been a hectic morning and she was just having a much-needed refreshment break when a text came in. Idly she glanced at the screen and almost dropped the phone when she saw the name Phil. She had been trying to decide what to do ever since he'd phoned her the other day and hadn't replied to her message. Her hand shaking, she opened the text:

Need to see you. Urgent. Can you meet me in an hour at the Miller's Arms?

Damn. He must have remembered something. Well, she wasn't going to meet him. She couldn't face seeing him. Not after how he'd acted the other day. She texted back:

Sorry, I'm busy. I'm working all morning. And I've got nothing to say to you.

A few minutes later a text pinged back.

Meet me after work then. Or shall I wait until Mark comes home and talk to you both?

She read his message twice, trying to figure out his motive. He had to be bluffing because surely if Phil had remembered their affair, he wouldn't want Mark to find out about it, or Freya? She wanted to tell him to get lost but didn't dare take the risk of him coming to the house when Mark was home. She couldn't afford for Mark to have any doubts that this baby was his. She would have to meet Phil. *He probably just wants to make sure I keep schtum and don't tell Freya about our affair*, she thought. Well, he needn't worry about that. She wanted to forget it as much as he did.

You really are a slimeball, aren't you? Well, I'm not meeting you at the pub, someone might see us. I'll meet you at the park nearby at 1.30. And you'll have to make it quick because I need to pick the kids up from school at 3.

She put her phone down, rested her head back in the chair and closed her eyes. Why the hell had she gone to see Phil and mentioned the affair to him? Why hadn't she just kept her mouth shut? *Because it made you angry that he had dumped you so callously then forgotten all about you after what you had risked for him. Because you believe Freya and realised Phil was feeding you lies for months. Because you suddenly realised what a total scumbag he is.*

She took a deep breath and calmed herself down. She was jumping to conclusions. Phil might not have remembered the affair. He might have been thinking about what she had said and wanted to meet her for an explanation, an assurance that it wasn't true. She hoped she could be convincing about that. She shouldn't have told Freya about the baby either, not yet. Why couldn't she keep her mouth shut instead of blurting things out? If Freya had told Phil, he might want to meet Daisy to ask her if the baby was his. She placed her hand over her stomach, where a new life was already forming. If only Mark hadn't guessed that she was pregnant, she could have had an abortion and nobody would have been any the wiser, but now… It had to be Mark's baby, it had to be. *Even though you rarely have sex with him but were at it with Phil a few times a week?*

She had been so stupid and reckless to risk her home, her family, her marriage for a meaningless fling. Because that was evidently all it was for Phil.

She buried her head in her hands. If only she could turn back the clock.

CHAPTER FORTY-SIX

Phil

'Was that her?' Tom asked, putting another glass of orange juice on the table in front of Phil before sitting down, pint of lager in his hand.

Phil nodded. 'I'm meeting her at the park at one thirty.'

'Make sure you get the truth, Phil. You need to deal with this. It isn't going to go away.'

'Don't worry. I will,' Phil promised. He glanced anxiously at Tom. 'You won't tell anyone, will you?'

Tom zipped across his mouth with his finger. 'My lips are sealed. We always keep each other's secrets. Mind you, you probably can't remember my recent ones, thank God.' He laughed. 'Now, let me fill you in on where we are with the course.'

The time went so quickly that Phil had a shock when he saw that it was quarter past one. 'I've got to go, I'm meeting Daisy in a quarter of an hour,' he said to Tom. He downed the rest of his orange juice and stood up.

'Good luck… and Phil?'

'Yeah?'

'Sort out your bloody life, mate, because it's a right mess.'

Phil shot him a steely look. 'Don't worry. I intend to.'

Daisy was sitting on a bench in the park, her eyes closed. He'd been expecting her to be watching, waiting for him, but he had almost reached her when she finally opened her eyes and spotted him.

'You look tired,' he said, sitting down beside her.

She edged away. 'What do you want, Phil?'

'The truth.' He was facing her now, his eyes fixed on her face, determined to get to the answers he wanted. 'Is that baby you're carrying mine?'

She gasped and her hand flew to her mouth, her eyes wide, but he couldn't make out if she was scared or shocked by his question.

Then she pulled herself together and threw him a contemptuous look. 'What?' She scoffed incredulously. 'Of course it isn't! Why would you even think that?'

'Because you told me we were having an affair and I think you might have been telling the truth.'

She stood up, anger all over her face. 'I told you I was just testing you. I love Mark and would never cheat on him. Especially not with you. I'm going now. I don't want to have this conversation again.'

He sprang to his feet and grabbed her arm. 'Then why did I have your number saved in my phone under the name of Billy? Did we have code names for each other?'

'How the hell should I know?' She got out her phone, swiped the screen and showed him his name and number. 'See? No code name here.'

He was flummoxed for a moment. None of this made sense.

'I told you, you kept phoning me, telling me Freya was abusing you. That's probably why you gave me a false name. You didn't want Freya to know that you were phoning her sister and telling lies about her.'

Daisy was staring at him defiantly. Was she telling the truth?

'I had a flashback the other night, of me and you together...'

'A dream, you mean, brought on by your own stupid imagination!' she retorted.

If she was lying, she was a good at it. He kept his eyes on hers. 'Look me in the face and tell me that we weren't having an affair.'

She raised her eyes to meet his, held his gaze and said emphatically, 'We were not having an affair. And this baby is most definitely not yours.'

He believed her. Relief surged through him and he nodded. 'Good, because I'm quite certain I would never cheat on Freya, and if I did, it wouldn't be with *you*.'

'Believe me, the feeling is mutual.' He could hear the loathing in her voice.

'Then why did you say it?'

'Oh, for God's sake, how many times? I told you to trick you. To see if you really were the nice guy you pretended to be, or if you were aggressive as Freya said.' She looked pointedly down at his arm still gripping hers. 'Well, I can see that Freya was telling the truth.' He released his grip and stared at her. 'I saw the cut on Freya's arm. You'd better not hurt her again, Phil. If you do, I'll report you myself.'

Phil watched her as she walked away; was she lying to cover up the fact that they had had an affair, not wanting Mark to find out now she was pregnant? She'd sounded so convincing, though.

Then he remembered what Tom had said about the student and being on a second warning at the university. 'Sort your life out, mate,' he'd advised.

He was right. Phil couldn't risk any of this getting back to Freya. He didn't want to lose her.

CHAPTER FORTY-SEVEN

Freya

'Phil had such a rage in him.' Aileen's words repeated in Freya's mind as she sat on the train on the way home. The meeting with Phil's mother hadn't turned out at all as she'd expected it to. Aileen had seemed nice, genuinely upset about the rift between Phil and the rest of his family, desperately wanting to see Phil again, ready to forgive him for nearly killing his father and causing him to have a stroke. Not that Phil knew about the stroke. Aileen said that she had tried to phone Phil a couple of days later to tell him that but couldn't get through. Phil had blocked her, blocked all of them. They never heard from him again. The stroke had affected Charles's mobility so after a few years they had moved into a bungalow, near to where Graham and his new wife lived. Aileen had left a forwarding address with the people who bought the house from them, in case Phil turned up. But he never did.

They'd ordered lunch – both choosing an omelette and salad – and chatted for a couple of hours. Aileen had been easy to talk to, so happy to meet Freya and eager for information about Phil. She had wanted to know how Freya and Phil had met, about their wedding, their life, and was clearly upset about the occasions she'd missed. Freya showed her some photos on her phone, even texting her a couple of Phil. It had been a pleasant couple of hours and the conversation had flowed easily. Aileen had insisted on paying the bill, begging Freya one more time as she left to try to persuade Phil to meet up with her and Charles. Freya was determined to try her best, but she wasn't sure how to go about it.

Phil had told her he'd walked out because he was sick of his family choosing Graham over him. Freya believed Aileen's story, though. She had seen that rage of Phil's and knew that he could get violent. The first time Phil had actually hit her, it had shaken her to the core. They had only been married ten months, one week and two days.

*

It was February and had been cold and drizzly for weeks. Freya was off work with a bad cold and cough and had had a restless night. It seemed like she'd only just dozed off when she heard Phil jump out of bed.

'What the hell, Freya! Why didn't you wake me?'

Her eyes snapped open and she stared at the clock. Quarter to eight. Phil had to be at the university for eight thirty and it was a half-hour drive in the morning traffic.

'Didn't the alarm go off?' she mumbled, still groggy.

'I was so bloody tired I must have slept through it. You were coughing and sniffing half the perishing night.'

He was right, she had been. She felt bad for keeping him awake. She should have slept in the spare room. 'Sorry. I'll go and make you a coffee.' She stumbled out of bed as Phil disappeared into the en suite for a shower. Freya went to the main bathroom to use the loo and wash her hands. She felt dreadful, and a glance in the mirror over the sink showed that her face was all red and puffy. *It's only a cold and it will be gone in a couple of days*, she told herself. Right now, though, she felt really miserable.

She headed downstairs, filled the kettle and flicked it on then grabbed the jar of instant coffee out of the cupboard – there was no time to put the coffee machine on.

She was taking two mugs out of the cupboard and the kettle had just boiled when Phil walked in. 'Almost done,' Freya said cheerily, her stomach sinking when she noticed that Phil had his moody face on. *Uh-oh, you'd better tread carefully*, she warned herself, fighting down the resentment. She was ill; he could have been more sympathetic. She desperately needed a hot drink – her head was thudding from lack of sleep as much as the cold. Phil probably felt the same way, she reminded herself as she started to spoon coffee into one of the mugs, her hand so unsteady she spilt some on the worktop. God, she was so exhausted she couldn't even focus.

'Leave it. I'll do it!' Phil snapped, pulling the mug away.

'I'm sorry. I'm just so tired!'

'You're tired! What about me? I've got a half-hour drive before I get to work. Then I've got to do an eight-hour day.' He poured hot water from the kettle into his mug, ignoring Freya's, and added milk. 'It's okay for you, you can go back to bed.'

She glared at him, annoyed because he hadn't made her a coffee and was being so unsympathetic about her being ill. 'You could have made me one!' She reached for the kettle and accidently knocked Phil's arm as he picked up his mug of coffee. 'Gosh, sorry,' she apologised, staring in dismay at the coffee stain on his shirt.

'Bloody hell, Freya. Look at the mess you've made of my shirt and I haven't got another good one ironed!'

'Sorry! Here, let me dab it out.' She grabbed a towel, ran it under the cold water tap and started to dab the coffee stain on Phil's shirt, making a massive wet patch.

Phil lashed out, his hand hitting the side of her cheek. 'Bloody well leave it, you're just making it worse!'

Her cheek was stinging. She put her hand to it, shocked that Phil had actually struck her. 'You hit me!' she accused him, tears springing to her eyes.

He glared at her. 'No, I didn't. You got in the way. I was just trying to stop you making more of a mess of my shirt. I'm going to have to bloody change now, and I'm already late!'

He stormed upstairs, coming down still buttoning up one of his old shirts, then rushed straight out of the house without apologising or kissing her goodbye.

Tears rolling down Freya's cheeks, she sank onto a chair at the table, going over and over the events. Maybe she should have left his shirt alone when he told her to; maybe he was only trying to stop her making more of a mess of it and hadn't meant to hit her. But he should have said sorry. He should have wrapped her in his arms and told her how sorry he was, not stormed out without even a goodbye kiss.

She sat there for ages, so upset and bewildered she couldn't move. Didn't even touch her coffee. Finally, exhausted, she decided to go back to bed. She caught her reflection in the wardrobe mirror and saw a big red mark on her cheek. It hadn't been a 'get off' push. It had been a hard slap and had left its mark.

He didn't mean it. He's tired, she thought as she crawled into bed. *We're both tired. I should have left his shirt alone.*

Later that night Phil came home with an apology bouquet of fifteen red roses and told her he was sorry. That he was tired and overworked, he hadn't meant to hurt her, just push her hand away. That he was ashamed and promised that it wouldn't happen again. Then he begged her not to leave him, said he couldn't live without her. He made her a hot lemon drink and made a fuss over her all evening. 'I promise that it'll never happen again,' he said, kissing her before he went into the spare room to sleep so that she wouldn't disturb him with her cold.

But it did happen again, and it got worse.

*

And now she knew that he had always had this rage, that he had hit out before, his brother and his father and goodness knew who else. All this time she'd blamed herself, believed Phil when he'd told her that it was her fault, that she provoked him, nagged him, confronted him, challenged him, annoyed him, she made him do it. That he was never like this with anyone else.

What else had he lied about? And who else had he hurt so badly that they wanted him dead? The night of the accident she'd been about to leave Phil; now she wondered if she should have done that, if she was in danger being with him. She shivered. Had she made a mistake giving Phil another chance?

CHAPTER FORTY-EIGHT

Wednesday

Sleep eluded her. Phil's mother's words kept going through her mind and the knowledge that Phil had been so violent when he was younger stunned her. She edged away from Phil as he lay snoring softly beside her, wanting to keep a bit of distance between them. She felt like she was sleeping with a stranger, that she had never really known the man she had married.

She had thought all evening about how to tell Phil she had met his mother. She wanted to tell him as soon as she returned home but he'd seemed preoccupied so she'd decided to put it off until the next day. Things were always better said in the morning, and she needed to choose her moment carefully. With Phil's father so ill, she had to tell him soon but was nervous about how he'd take it. Phil used to hate being undermined, and that's what she'd done. He'd told her not to have any contact with his family, had blocked his mother from contacting her, and Freya had gone behind his back, unblocked her, replied to her. Met her.

I'm an adult, we're a partnership, I have a right to make my own decisions, she told herself. She hoped Phil would see it that way. He used to hate it if she challenged him about anything or offered a different opinion on a subject. Had he really changed now?

Another memory she'd tried hard to suppress jolted into her mind, this time of when she'd attended the open evening at the university with Phil last year. She'd only met Tom – a tall, gangly, fair-haired man with a scruffy beard – once briefly before. Within a few minutes of chatting to him about the course she could see how much he loved his job, and the students. He and Phil were talking about trying to garner more interest in the university and the courses, and she suggested a few promotion strategies, which Tom seemed really interested in. They were locked in conversation for quite a while until eventually Phil cut in, a fixed smile across his face, suggesting that Freya mingle a little and stop monopolising Tom. Freya was horrified – had she got too carried away? She knew she was prone to when she was on her favourite subject, so she smiled apologetically at Tom, excused herself and went to have a look at some of the exhibitions. Later that night, when they got home, Phil was furious. 'You really like to show me up, don't you?' he said through gritted teeth.

'What?' Freya stared at him, puzzled.

'All that cosying up to Tom, giving him ideas to promote the course. You're so up yourself because you work at IPA Studio, you think you know it all.'

'Of course I don't. I was just trying to help…' She backed away a little, alarmed at how furious Phil looked.

'Help? Demean me, you mean! Tom and I were discussing strategies, no one asked you to butt in.'

'So what was I supposed to do? Stand there with my mouth closed?' She could feel anger rising in herself too. This was unfair! Tom had been listening to her and had seemed interested in her opinion.

'Yes! You came along to support me, not to take over and show everyone what a clever little thing you are. That programme you were dissing, that was my idea.'

His eyes were bulging now, the vein throbbing in the middle of his forehead, but she was still too angry to take heed. His idea? So that was why he was annoyed: she had dared to disagree with his idea. Well, she hadn't known he'd dreamt it up, had she? He never discussed his work with her.

'I'm sorry but I didn't know that, did I?' she replied. 'Anyway, what does it matter if I disagree with you? It's the twenty-first century, women have their own opinions now. No one takes any notice if a couple have different opinions.'

Phil lunged at her, grabbed her by the tops of her arms and pushed her up against the wall, standing right in front of her. 'I do. I take notice when my own wife rubbishes me!' he screamed, his face inches from hers. 'Don't you ever do that again! Do you fucking understand?' His hands still gripping her arms, he shook her as he spoke.

She nodded, tears springing to her eyes, scared to speak because he looked so furious. When he finally let her go she crumpled into a heap on the floor, barely registering that he had walked out – as he always did after a row. She was shaking so much she couldn't move. Never in her entire life had she felt so frightened. What the hell had that been all about? Finally, she sat up, hugging her knees, fighting back the tears, trying to make sense of what had happened. She had never seen Phil so angry before.

Her arms hurt where he had held them tight; she pulled up the sleeves of her thin top and saw that bruises were already forming. God, he'd actually marked her.

I have to get away from him, she told herself. *Phil could have really hurt me then. I'm not safe here.* She went upstairs and started packing her bag. When she came back down she saw Phil standing by the back door. 'Where are you going?' he asked, spotting the suitcase she was holding.

'Away from you. You really hurt me.' She stood in front of him, inwardly shaking but determined not to show it.

Phil looked horrified. 'I would never hurt you. You know I wouldn't.'

'What do you think you just did?' she screeched, yanking up her right sleeve to show him the bruise. 'There's a matching one on the other arm too.'

He stared at them aghast, running his fingers through his hair. 'I'm sorry, I didn't mean to do that. But it's you, you always provoke me. I told you how upset I was, how you'd shown me up, but you didn't care. You had to keep justifying it. Anyone else would have apologised but not you; everything is a battle with you.'

'It's you who makes things a battle. I'm not allowed to have an opinion.'

'See, you're at it again. You never want to listen to how I feel, how you hurt me. You always have to argue.' He took a deep breath. 'I'm sorry I grabbed your arms and bruised them, really I am. But please will you accept how much you push me? How much you provoke? How would you like it if I came to IPA Studio and rubbished one of the projects you were working on?'

She'd hate it, she admitted to herself. But she hadn't done that to him, had she? Tom had asked her opinion and she'd answered. She hadn't known it had been Phil's idea. Her head felt a bit woozy. Had she had too much wine? Was Phil right and she'd shown him up?

Suddenly his arms were around her and he was hugging her tight. 'I'm sorry I hurt you, I didn't mean to, but you hurt me too. Please don't leave me. I can't live without you. I wouldn't have anything to live for.'

It was what he always said, that unspoken threat that if she left him he wouldn't want to live any more. He'd never actually said he would take his own life, but the meaning was clear.

'Please, Freya. I love you so much. Can't we both say sorry and forget this?' He was hugging her, caressing her and she nestled her head into his shoulder, feeling confused. Had she caused this?

'I'm sorry too,' she whispered.

He held her tight and they embraced for a long time, as if they were both scared to let go. Finally, they went to bed, wrapped in each other's arms, silent tears spilling down her cheeks until she finally fell asleep. In the morning they made love and neither of them ever mentioned it again, but Freya thought of it a lot. And from then on when she was out with Phil, she was careful not to disagree with him in public.

Now, she had met his mother, against his wishes, and she was pretty sure that he was going to be mad about that. *He might be a little angry, but he won't get violent*, she told herself. *The old Phil has gone. Hasn't he?*

She glanced at the clock. Almost three in the morning. She'd go down and heat up some milk – maybe that would help her sleep.

She was just about to put the light on in the kitchen when she heard a sound, as if someone was turning a key in the back door. She put her hand over her mouth to stifle a scream, her eyes fixed on the door handle as it rattled. Someone was trying to open it! She stepped back, pressing herself against the wall. *They can't get in*, she told herself. *That bolt across the top will stop them.* After a few moments the rattling stopped. Freya crept over to the kitchen window and quietly opened the venetian blinds a little so that she could peep out. A shadow went past the window then disappeared.

CHAPTER FORTY-NINE

'Phil! Someone tried to break into our house!' Freya shouted, flicking the light on as she hurried into the bedroom.

'What?' Phil opened his eyes groggily, throwing his arm across his face to shield them from the light.

'I just saw them, in the back garden.' She grabbed her phone from the bedside table. 'I went down for a drink, and as I walked into the kitchen I heard a key rattling in the lock of the back door, as if someone was trying to open it. Then it stopped and I went over to the window and saw a shadow move past.'

'What the hell! Was it a man or a woman?' Phil jumped out of bed and pulled on his jeans.

'I've no idea, it was too dark to make out. I'm going to phone the police.'

Phil was already out of the bedroom, heading for the stairs.

'Be careful!' Freya called, dialling the police as she followed him.

He fled down the stairs and into the kitchen, unbolting the back door, hitting the outside switch and running out into the garden in his bare feet. There was no one in the garden. Whoever it was had gone.

When he went back into the kitchen Freya was standing by the sink, talking to the police. Phil listened as she replied that nothing had been taken and no, the intruder hadn't got in because there was a bolt across the back door for extra security.

She looked disappointed when she ended the call. 'They've made a note of it all but the officer said there isn't much to go on because nothing was taken and there was no actual break-in,' she told him. 'I'm scared, Phil. How has anyone got a key to our door?'

'Are you sure they had a key? It could have been an opportunist thief, trying the handle to see if the door was locked.'

Freya nodded emphatically. 'I definitely heard a key in the lock. I think someone has been sneaking into the house, Phil. It must be this person, they've got a key somehow!' Her eyes widened as if she'd just had a horrible thought. 'It could be them who caused your accident?' He could hear the panic in her voice.

Phil's mind was racing. Was this person responsible for leaving those notes on his desk? If so, why? What grudge did they have against him? 'Look, maybe someone found a key in the street and has been trying all the doors in the neighbourhood hoping it would work in one of them. And remember we don't know for sure that anyone has come in previously. We only know that the back door was left open and I'm sure that was me sleepwalking.' He was lying but he didn't want Freya to know about the notes, not until he found out who was breaking into their house and threatening him.

'What about the flood in the kitchen, though?' she pointed out. 'I didn't turn the taps on and you were out.'

'I know, but I did have a glass of water before I went out. Maybe I left the tap dripping and didn't notice that the plug was in the sink.'

'You didn't mention this before.' She sounded dubious.

'Look, try to stop worrying and let's go back to bed. Whoever it was has gone now. Thank goodness we put that bolt on the door.'

'I won't be able to sleep now. I'll be scared they'll come back,' Freya said.

Phil put his arms around her to comfort her. 'I'll stay down here for a bit to make sure. You have to work in a couple of hours, you need your rest.'

'Okay, but if they do come back don't tackle them. Call the police right away. Promise?'

'I promise.'

Phil waited for Freya to go back upstairs and into the bedroom then headed straight for his study. Taking the dictionary from the shelf, he opened it and spread the notes out on his desk.

'Phil…' The door opened and Freya walked in. 'I've just remembered…' She paused as Phil quickly tried to cover the notes with the dictionary. One of them fell to the floor and she reached down to pick it up. 'Sorry… what?' Her eyes widened in alarm as she read out the note. '"**YOU'LL PAY FOR WHAT YOU DID**." Phil, where did this come from?' She snatched up the other notes and read them too. 'Who sent these and why didn't you tell me about them?'

Phil thought fast. 'I didn't want to worry you. Someone put them through the letterbox. I wondered maybe if I'd upset one of the students at the university, not given them the grades they wanted. That's one of the reasons I met Tom, to ask him, but he said there was no problem as far as he knew. So then I wondered if they were meant for you.'

'For me?' Freya looked stunned. 'I've no idea why anyone would leave me threatening letters. You should have told me, Phil. It's more evidence that someone has a grudge against one of us. This person could be dangerous. I'm going to phone the police again, right away!'

CHAPTER FIFTY

Freya

The police came later that morning and were really concerned when they saw the letters. Phil insisted that he'd found them folded up on the mat by the front door, not in an envelope, as if they had been pushed through the letterbox, but Freya sensed he was lying. She was pretty sure that whoever had the key had walked in and left the letters, and that they were meant for Phil. And as she was the one who had found the back door open and not seen any notes, they must have left them in his study, maybe on his desk. That was probably why he had got a bolt for the back door because he knew that it wasn't him accidentally leaving the door open, that someone had been coming in and he wanted to keep them out. Was it the same person who tried the door last night?

'You should have told us about these sooner, sir. This is a serious situation. Someone tampered with the brakes of your car, and you are now receiving threatening letters.' The police officer looked very grave. 'If the sender is the same person who tried to enter your property tonight – and if they have been entering before – you could both be in real danger.'

'They have a key too.' Freya could feel herself trembling. 'They can come in anytime.'

'I suggest you consider getting the locks changed but in the meantime make sure you bolt both doors when you are in the house, especially at night-time.' The second police officer looked up from the notes she'd just made. 'As the letters were put through the door they could have been meant for either of you. Are you sure that you can't think of anyone who might have a grudge against you?'

Freya shook her head. She could hardly believe this was actually happening. 'We will definitely have the locks changed. I'm literally terrified by all this. I didn't even know anything about the notes until today – Phil didn't tell me as he didn't want me to worry.'

'And you, sir?'

Phil agitatedly rubbed the top of his arm. 'I'm sorry, officer. I wish I could remember but, as you know, the last two years are a complete blank to me. It's freaking me out, to be honest.'

When the police officers had gone, taking the notes with them, Phil turned to Freya, looking contrite. 'I'm sorry for not telling you about the notes. Do you forgive me? I was only trying to protect you. I wasn't sure if they were for you – I don't know if you've upset a client at work, perhaps.' He reached out and held her hand in his. 'I would do anything to protect you, Freya. You're everything to me.'

'You should have told me, Phil. This affects both of us. I don't want there to be secrets between us.' As the words were out of her mouth, she realised how ironic they were, when she was keeping such a big secret from him. She had to tell him. He probably hadn't told her the truth about the row with his family because he was ashamed, she told herself. But it was years ago, he had been young, and had been drinking – perhaps his brother had started it and Phil had lost his temper. Surely when he knew that his parents had forgiven him and were desperate to see him, he would be pleased and want to meet them? She took a deep breath. 'Phil, I have to tell you something and I don't want you to get mad…'

His eyes met hers. 'Go ahead.' His tone was quiet, measured. He was bracing himself for whatever it was she was about to tell him.

'I met up with your mother yesterday.'

It was as if his face had turned to stone. She swallowed nervously at the steely glint in his eyes, the set of his jaw.

'So you lied about having a meeting to go to?'

'Not exactly, I just didn't tell you who the meeting was with,' she pointed out.

'Why would you do that when I specifically told you not to have any further contact with my mother?' His voice was ice-cold.

She fought to keep her voice steady. 'She's your mother, Phil, and she's just found out that you almost died. I imagined how I would feel if I were her. I couldn't just ignore her. So I unblocked her and replied to her message that she wasn't to worry, you were on the mend, and explained that I was sorry but you didn't want any contact with her.'

Phil stood motionless, his face like thunder, waiting for her to continue.

Freya swallowed. 'Then she messaged back and begged me to meet her, said she had a message for you. So I did.'

'You lied. You said you were going to a business meeting.'

'To protect you. Like you lied about the notes to protect me.'

His eyes narrowed. 'That isn't the same.'

She continued quickly, before she lost her nerve. 'She seems such a nice woman, and she's so upset about not having any contact with you. And Phil…' She lowered her tone, knowing that no matter how angry he was with his parents, he would be upset to hear that his father was dying. 'Look, I don't know how to tell you this. But your dad has cancer. And it's terminal. He's desperate to see you one more time before he dies.' She reached out to hold his hand but he jerked it away from her.

'I suppose she told you a pack of lies, said it was all my fault.'

'She told me what happened but said she was sure you had lashed out in anger, not meaning to hurt your dad, and that she regretted telling you to go. She desperately wants to see you again, Phil.'

'She's twisting things, as usual, to protect her precious Graham. It was Graham who attacked me, then my father waded in. I was simply trying to get them both off me. I didn't attack my father, they both attacked me. Did she tell you that?'

Freya was surprised at his attitude. She'd expected him to be upset that his father was dying. 'Phil, your father is dying. And your parents are desperate to see you. They both want to make it up with you.'

Phil clenched his fists. 'They can never make it up to me. They made their choice: they chose Graham, like they always did. I went back the next day, to apologise and ask how Dad was, but Graham told me they never wanted to see me again.' Anger blazed in his eyes. 'My parents have been dead to me a long time, as I have been to them. So no, I will not meet up with them. Please never mention this to me again.'

Freya watched wordlessly as he turned and walked away. He looked so cold, so distant, and she remembered times he had been like that with her too, but she had thought he had changed. Now she realised he hadn't. His father was dying and he didn't care. It had been nearly three weeks since the accident and Phil had shown several signs of his old anger, and now this. *As soon as Phil has had his check-up at the hospital and been given the all-clear, I'm leaving him*, she decided. *Before he completely loses his temper.*

CHAPTER FIFTY-ONE

Phil

White-hot rage surged through him. How dare Freya defy him when he had specifically asked her not to have any contact with his mother? Did she always do this? Is that what had caused their argument the night of the accident? Freya said he'd booked a holiday without checking with her first and was annoyed because she said she couldn't get away from work. But he only had her word for it. He hadn't been able to find any trace of the holiday. She could be lying, twisting things like Marianne used to do. He might not be able to remember his marriage to Freya but he could remember his first marriage to Marianne. She was always nagging, prodding him, nothing was ever good enough for her, and then he'd discovered that she'd been having an affair and the son he had loved so much wasn't really his. Marianne had manipulated him, lied to him. Then she had upped and left without as much as a goodbye, probably moved in with her new man. He'd been well rid of her.

He walked into the kitchen, poured himself a glass of water and went outside, sitting down on the bench in the garden. He felt like a stranger living someone else's life. His wife, house and job were all the same but everything else was different. He might have been having an affair with his wife's sister, who was now pregnant, and someone had tried to kill him, was still after him. And he had no idea why.

He put the glass down on the table and buried his head in his hands. He wanted to wake up from this nightmare, longed to feel like he had some control of his life again.

How do you know it's you they're after?

There it was again, the question that kept niggling him. He raised his head and considered it properly. As the notes had been left on his desk, he had presumed they were meant for him, even though he had pretended otherwise to Freya, but the intruder might have thought it was Freya's desk. And the police had already said that whoever had tampered with the brakes of the car could have been intending to hurt either of them. It could have been Freya who'd got into the car and drove off that night.

He got to his feet and paced around as the thoughts took root, trying to make sense of it all.

Freya said that he had abused her, several times. But Daisy had said he'd told her that Freya was abusing him. And she seemed to have believed that until Freya had convinced her otherwise. Freya could have been lying. Phil might have turned to Daisy because he hadn't known what to do, hadn't wanted to hit back but couldn't stop Freya lashing out. Even Freya's mother had telephoned him, concerned for his wellbeing.

Maybe he did have an affair with Daisy but only because Freya had driven him to it, then Freya had found out about it and was so furious she had tampered with the brakes of his car out of revenge. The idea was taking flight now, making more sense as he explored it. He didn't even know if there was an intruder – he hadn't seen one. He'd found the back door open one morning, and there was the day he had gone for a walk, leaving Freya working upstairs, and come back to find the kitchen flooded. He hadn't heard someone put a key in the lock, or seen someone out in the garden.

Freya could be manipulating him, pretending someone was out to get him. She could have left the notes. Maybe this was all payback because she had found out about the affair. And now she was contacting his parents, probably telling them how abusive he was. Telling everyone. And he had no memory of the last two years, so how could he deny it? Freya could tell him anything and he wouldn't know if it was a lie or not.

He paced around the garden, thoughts whirring in his mind. He had to be careful, very careful. He shouldn't just believe what Freya told him. He had no idea what their marriage had been like. Freya could be a danger to him. He had to keep his wits about him. He clenched his fists so tight he could feel his nails digging into the palms of his hands. If Freya had been lying to him, was tricking him, she would regret it. He'd make sure of that.

CHAPTER FIFTY-TWO

Daisy

Thursday

Daisy felt so nauseous, so exhausted, that it was all she could do to drag herself out of bed and get the twins ready for school. She couldn't eat, couldn't sleep. She wished to God she had never said anything to Phil. Why the hell hadn't she left things alone? *Because he might have been faking his memory loss, or it might have come back – you needed to be sure.*

Well, she knew for certain that he wasn't faking it – the look of disgust on his face when he'd realised she'd been telling the truth about their affair replayed in her mind, making her sick to the core. She'd cheated on her husband for him, betrayed her sister, and all the time the bastard had been playing her. She wished he had died in that crash. She sat at the kitchen table, her head in her hands, trying to summon up the strength to get through the day.

'Go back to bed, Daisy, you look exhausted. I'll take the twins to school and phone up the surgery, let them know that you're too sick to come in.' There was such a tender look in Mark's eyes that she wanted to weep, to get down on her knees and beg for his forgiveness, but she stopped herself because she knew that Mark could never find out how she had betrayed him. The truth would destroy him. She wished she could be sure that Phil wouldn't tell him. She shook the worry from her mind. Of course he wouldn't; Phil wouldn't risk losing Freya.

But what if Freya left him? If Phil was violent towards her again, she was sure that her sister would walk out; she'd be mad not to. Freya had told her she'd have left Phil already, if it hadn't been for his accident. If Freya did leave him, Phil would have nothing to lose then and could easily tell Mark out of spite.

God, it would have been a lot simpler if Phil had died in that crash, then she wouldn't have to worry about anyone finding out.

'Cheer up, love.' Mark wound his arms around her, hugging her to him. 'Are you fretting about the baby? There's no need to. We can manage, I promise you.'

Daisy nestled into him. 'We're struggling as it is,' she mumbled.

'We'll be fine.' Mark lifted up her chin with his finger so that she was looking at him. 'I love you, Daisy. I would do anything for you. Do you love me?'

She nodded, tears springing to her eyes. She did, so very much. She wished she had realised that before, instead of cheating on him.

'Then nothing else matters. Do you hear me?' His hazel eyes were holding hers, as if there was a hidden message inside them. 'Nothing matters as long as we love each other and are together, do you understand?'

Was he saying…? No, he couldn't be. He couldn't know about her and Phil. Yet there was something about the way he was looking at her that made her wonder.

'I know we lost our way a bit – we were both working so hard, and the twins… it's been a difficult few years for us but it's over now. The twins are at school, I've got a promotion and life's easier. This baby can be a new start for us, it can bring us back together, if we allow it to.'

He seemed so earnest, so happy about the baby she almost choked on her tears. 'Mark…'

He put his finger on her lips. 'Shhh. It doesn't matter. I've told you, all that matters is that me and you are together.' He pulled her head into his chest, caressing her hair. 'I love you so much, Daisy. Always have, always will. Now you go back to bed and I'll take the twins to school and phone work for you.' His hands moved down to her shoulders, softly massaging them. 'I want you to take today to rest, to come to terms with the baby, to accept that the past is done and that I love you.'

He did know! She jerked her head up, staring into his face.

'Will you do that?' he asked softly, and all she could do was nod, tears spilling down her face.

She let Mark lead her back to bed and pull the cover over her, then he shouted out to the twins to get ready. Half an hour later he came up with a cup of tea and the twins, dressed and ready for school. He put the cup down on the bedside table then kissed her on the forehead and told her to rest. Both children kissed her goodbye and happily went off with their father.

Daisy sat up, sipped her tea and told herself that she didn't deserve Mark, but she was going to put this right and be a good wife to him. Like Mark had said, she had to come to terms with the past and live for their future. And that's what she intended to do.

CHAPTER FIFTY-THREE

Freya

Phil had barely spoken to her all evening or this morning. It was obvious that he was still annoyed with her because she had met his mother. He had that set look on his face that she had learnt to dread, so Freya shut herself in her study to work, hoping he would come to terms with it, not wanting to say or do anything to make the situation worse. She wondered if she should have done as he had said and ignored his mother's message. They were his parents after all, not hers – how would she have felt if she had told him that she didn't want anything to do with her parents and he had ignored her? But then she kept reminding herself that Phil's father was dying. What if she hadn't told him and then he found out later? He might have blamed her then, been angry that she didn't give him the chance to say goodbye.

And if she hadn't met Phil's mum, she wouldn't know the truth of what had happened, and that Phil had always had a temper. She would have still thought that it was all her fault. She was angry about that. And angry that Phil had kept from her that someone had been sneaking into the house and leaving notes. What else had happened that she didn't know about? Had he remembered more than he was letting on? Was he playing her, trying to keep her sympathy for him and all the time concealing something terrible that he'd done? So terrible that the person he had hurt wanted him dead? She had to have this out with him, stand her ground, she decided, instead of hiding away upstairs as if it was her in the wrong.

Daisy's words flashed across her mind. 'Be careful, Freya. You can't be sure that Phil has changed. At the first sign of him being abusive, get yourself out of there.'

She would be careful. And yes, if Phil raised a hand to her again, she would leave and never come back, never mind waiting for him to get the all-clear from the hospital.

She went downstairs; no sign of Phil in the lounge, kitchen or garden, so she went to his study. He was sitting at his desk, staring at a sheet of paper. He must have heard her come in but he made no acknowledgement of that. She bit her lip as he determinedly ignored her, concentrating on reading the papers in his hand. She had to bite the bullet. *Keep calm*, she told herself. She coughed. Phil's eyes remained glued to the paper.

'Phil. Can we talk?'

His eyes slid up to her face and the coldness in them made her stomach turn to ice. 'I don't think we have anything to talk about, do you?'

She couldn't speak for a moment, unsure of what to say. *Don't let him do this to you*, she told herself. 'Yes, actually, I do. I'm sorry I went behind your back to meet your mother but it was with the best of intentions. Please can we not fall out over this? There's so much other stuff we need to figure out.'

'Really? Like what?' It was as if he was a stranger. So cold and distant. He was looking at her as if he hated her. Memories of other times he had looked at her like this flashed into her head and she fought back the panic that was welling inside her at the fear that he hadn't changed after all.

'Like who tampered with the brakes of your car? Who has been breaking into our house and leaving you threatening notes?

Someone has a grudge against you, Phil, and we need to find out who and why.'

He got up slowly and the expression on his face sent a snake of fear down her spine. 'Well, let's see. Who has the most to gain if something happens to me?'

Freya stared at him, dumbstruck. What was he getting at?

'Let me tell you, shall I?' He held up the sheets of paper. 'You have. I've found my insurance papers and it seems that you will get a lot of money if I die. Thousands. You'll be very rich.'

She could hardly believe what she was hearing. He was actually suggesting that she had tried to kill him so she could get his insurance money. He couldn't really believe that. 'For goodness' sake, Phil, why would I want to kill you? I love you.'

'So you say, but you weren't very loving at the hospital, were you?'

'I told you, we had just had a big argument. You stormed out. I was packing a bag when the police called to say you were in an accident.' She licked her lips. 'You scared me, Phil. You smashed the vase of flowers up the wall and I thought you were going to hit me. Again. And you're scaring me now,' she added, wrapping her arms around her shoulders to try to stop the trembling. And it was true, he was scaring her. Make that terrifying her. Her instincts were all telling her to turn and run, to get out while she still had the chance.

She was just about to do that when suddenly Phil slumped into the chair, his head in his hands. 'I'm sorry, Freya. I'm so sorry. I just can't think straight at the moment. It's so hard not being able to remember.'

She gazed at him, wondering what to do. He raised his head and looked imploringly at her. 'Please don't leave me, Freya. You're all I've got. I can't live without you.'

Maybe it was the brain trauma making him act like this. Was she being unfair? 'It's okay.' She went to him and put her arms around his shoulders, holding him close as he sobbed, sympathy replacing her fear.

Finally, he calmed down and wiped his eyes. 'God, I'm so sorry. What a bloody wimp you must think I am, bawling like that. My head is all over the place. I can't remember anything. You said I booked a holiday but I can't find any details of the bookings. I don't know why anyone has got a grudge against me. And when I found this insurance proposal I remembered what Daisy had said and thought it was you.'

'What?' Freya said, astonished. 'What do you mean? What did Daisy say?'

'She came to see me when you went to work last week, asked me if I could remember anything and I said I couldn't.' He held Freya's hand, gazing earnestly into her eyes. 'Then she told me to be careful and I sort of got the impression that she was warning me about something. So when I found this insurance policy I thought maybe she was saying I should be careful of you. I'm so sorry, Freya. I don't know how I could think such a dreadful thing. Please forgive me.'

His words were like a blow to her stomach. Phil hadn't mentioned that Daisy had been around, and Daisy hadn't mentioned it either. Surely Daisy wouldn't suggest that Freya would harm Phil. Why would she? It didn't make sense.

'Why didn't you tell me about this?'

'Daisy begged me not to. She didn't want you to know she'd been to see me. She made it sound as if I was in some sort of danger.'

She stood up. 'I'm going to phone Daisy and find out what's going on.'

Phil grabbed her hand. 'No, please don't. I must have got it mixed up. I do get confused since the accident, you know I do. I don't want to cause trouble between you and your sister.'

Freya hesitated. It didn't sound like Daisy to say stuff like that to Phil. But then it was strange that she had come to visit him when she knew Freya was at work. She thought back to how she'd confided in Daisy that Phil had been abusive to her. Had her sister been so worried that she'd visited Phil to warn him to be careful how he treated Freya, but Phil had misunderstood? Maybe Daisy had thought it best not to tell Freya about her visit, thinking that she would be annoyed.

'Don't look so worried.' Phil squeezed her hand. 'I'm sure I got it wrong. I think Daisy just came to check on me, knowing you were at work, and was warning me not to overdo things. I got a bit muddled.' He put his hand to his forehead. 'It's all so foggy in here sometimes. I feel like I'm wading through cotton wool trying to find a memory I can cling to.'

Freya hesitated, trying to decide if Phil was playing her so she wouldn't leave him or if the accident was really to blame for his mood swings.

'Can we please forget all about it. I was just being silly.'

'Forgotten already,' Freya told him, knowing it was best to play along and keep the peace. But she couldn't help feeling uneasy. She didn't like how Phil had accused her of trying to kill him for the insurance money. Someone had to have put that thought in his head. Surely it wasn't Daisy, though?

CHAPTER FIFTY-FOUR

Friday

'Please don't go into work today. I don't feel well,' Phil begged as Freya got up to shower the next morning.

He did look a bit pale and they had both had yet another restless night. Phil's actions yesterday, accusing her of causing his accident so she could get his insurance money, had chilled her to the core, and even though he had apologised, Freya felt nervous around him. She wanted to get out of the house, and was desperate to see Daisy and find out exactly what she'd said to Phil, and confide in her sister her fears about how Phil was acting.

'I've got such a lot of work to do in the office, Phil, I could really do with going in.' She hesitated. 'Is it your ribs? Are they hurting you?'

Phil struggled to sit up in bed, his face twisting in pain. 'They are a bit sore but mainly it's my head. It's thumping so much and I feel dizzy. I don't want to be left on my own in case I pass out.' He sighed and smiled wanly. 'If you really need to go to work, I guess I can manage. I'll make sure I sit down as much as I can and that I keep my phone on me in case I feel faint.'

She couldn't go into work if he felt that bad; she'd have to work from home. Meeting Daisy would have to wait. 'It's okay,

I'll phone in and explain. Stefan won't mind me working from home,' she said.

'Thank you, I really appreciate it.' He lay back down again. 'I feel so tired. Do you mind if I rest up a bit?'

'Of course not. I'll phone work now and then get a bit done while you're having a rest. And I'll check in on you in an hour to see how you are.'

Stefan was understanding, as she'd expected. 'No problem, Freya, work at home for as long as you need, and if you need to take some of your holiday, then do. Nadia can take over from you,' Stefan told her. 'Phil's health has to come first.'

She was lucky to have such an understanding boss, and that her work could be done remotely, Freya thought as she ended the call. She had to admit that she was worried about Phil this morning. He had seemed genuinely desperate not to be left alone. *He's had a major accident and lost part of his memory*, she reminded herself. *That must make him feel vulnerable.* Plus someone was out to get one of them, she reminded herself as she went down to make a cup of coffee.

The letterbox flapped as the postman shoved a letter through. She picked it up, glancing at the envelope. A credit card statement for Phil. She frowned when she saw the company name; this wasn't from his usual credit card company. He must have applied for a new card. Maybe he'd used this to book the holiday and that was why he hadn't found any record of it, because he'd forgotten that he had this new card. She never opened Phil's mail but this could solve the mystery of the missing holiday details, so she carefully slit open the envelope and scanned the list of purchases. There it was, right at the top. A booking with Sunshine Holidays. Thank goodness for that! Phil would be so relieved now he could sort out the insurance claim. Her gaze fell on the previous items: a meal at a very expensive restaurant, a trip to the cinema… neither occasion had been with her and must have been during the day when she was working, as Phil rarely went out in the evening. She guessed Phil and Tom might have gone to the cinema to see a film related to the university course they were both tutoring but why hadn't he mentioned it to Freya? And she didn't think Phil would pay for him and Tom to dine at an expensive restaurant. Besides, if it was something to do with the university, they would charge it to expenses.

Her hands shook as she clutched the statement, her mind going back to Phil asking her if he had ever cheated on her. Looking at this, it seemed like he definitely had. Her husband had been taking someone to posh restaurants for lunch, and cinema trips while she was at work. The question was, who was it?

Then another thought hit her. Had Daisy found out about this? Perhaps she had come round when Freya was at work to warn Phil that if he continued with the affair, she would tell Freya.

She felt sick. God, how could she have been so stupid as to not see it? And who was the woman he'd been having an affair with? Was he going to meet her the night of the accident when he had stormed out? Yet no one had come to visit him at the hospital or contacted Phil to see how he was. He would have told Freya if someone had, surely, wondering who the woman was.

Unless he hadn't really lost his memory, and he had just pretended so that Freya wouldn't leave him. Perhaps he was still seeing this woman. She could feel the anger rising at how she had been tricked.

Stop jumping to conclusions, she told herself, but the unease nagged away at her and she decided to see if she could find more evidence. She stood at the bottom of the stairs for a moment to check that there was no sound from Phil then went to his study.

She knew he would have kept his credit card and bank statements. Phil was very organised about things like that and always had paper copies so he had receipts for things he could claim as expenses. She glanced around then her eyes rested on his silver filing cabinet. They would probably be in there. It was unlocked so she pulled it open; unsurprisingly, everything was filed in alphabetical order. She flicked through: council tax, electric, his usual credit card statement. Of course the new card statements wouldn't be in here otherwise surely Phil would have found them when he searched his office. He must have put them away somewhere, before his accident, so that she wouldn't find them. Not that she ever went in his office. She scanned the room, wondering where Phil would hide something like that. Then her gaze rested on the bookshelf over his desk. Still clutching the credit card statement, she pulled out the big dictionary where he'd hidden the letters. A piece of paper fell out.

She picked it up and opened it. It was a list, in Phil's handwriting. Her eyes rested on the heading.

Things I remember—

'What the fucking hell do you think you're doing, Freya?'

She swirled around. Phil was standing by the doorway, his face contorted with fury. Freya faced him, her own anger making her brave. How dare he take that tone with her after what she had discovered?

'Give me that!' he roared, charging over to her and making a grab for the piece of paper in her hand. She swerved, dodged past him and shot out of the room into the hall, running into the kitchen towards the back door. She was getting out of here fast and never coming back. She reached the back door then remembered it was bolted at the top. Shit. She could hear Phil's footsteps in the hall. She reached up for the bolt, her hands shaking as she yanked it across and pulled open the back door.

'Where the fucking hell do you think you're going?' Phil seized her arm and dragged her back inside. A piece of paper fell out of her hand onto the tiled floor.

Freya winced as pain shot up her arm. 'Stop it, you're hurting me!' she yelled. God, he looked so angry, she was terrified what he would do. Desperate to escape his clutches, she kicked out, her foot hitting him in the shin.

'Ouch! You little bitch!' He released her arm and she dashed for the door again, but before she could escape through it, he grabbed her, threw her against the wall, his hands around her neck. 'You're not going anywhere! You're not leaving me!' he snarled.

His face was contorted with fury, his eyes bulging and his hands were tightening around her throat. Fear snaked up her spine and coursed through every nerve in her body. She couldn't move; he had her pinned tight against the wall. Bile rose into her throat as she realised she was trapped. She should have got out earlier, when she realised that Phil had always had a temper. She should never have given their marriage another chance. She had to fight him off somehow then get out of here and never come back.

Phil's face was so twisted in red rage it was almost unrecognisable. It was as if he had become someone else. Someone who in that moment hated her. Someone who might kill her.

CHAPTER FIFTY-FIVE

'Get your hands off her, you bloody bully. You're not beating her up too!'

Suddenly someone launched themselves at Phil, jumped on his back and started thumping it until he released his hands from Freya's throat.

Freya gasped in a lungful of air, her shocked eyes fixed on the attacker's face. It was a teenage lad. Who was he? She had never seen him before.

'What the fuck!' Phil wriggled about, elbowing, trying to get the teenager off his back, but the boy was like something possessed, screaming and pummelling away at Phil with his fists. Finally Phil managed to throw him onto the floor and stood over him, breathing heavily. 'Who the fuck are you and what are you doing in my house?' he gasped.

'You don't recognise me, do you, *Dad*? You've forgotten all about the three-year-old son you walked out on after beating up my mum.' The teenager scrambled to his feet and stood in front of Phil, glaring at him with such hatred, fists clenched by his side. 'Well, I've come to make you pay.' Every word dripped with venom.

Dad? Freya caught her breath, her eyes shooting to Phil's astonished face as he gaped at the lad. He was half-bent over now, his arm across his chest. She guessed the fighting had hurt his not-quite-healed ribs. It served him right.

'Danny?'

'This is your son?' Freya asked, running her hands around her sore and throbbing neck. Part of her wanted to run out of the back door to safety but another part of her wanted answers. And she felt a lot safer with this teenager here to defend her, especially as it looked like Phil's ribs were hurting too much to fight both of them off. 'You said that your wife had cheated on you. That you were devasted when you discovered that the son you adored wasn't really yours.' She turned back to the teenager: the dark hair, thick-set eyebrows and nose were definitely Phil's. 'Look at him, Phil. He's so obviously your son!'

'I… told… you… Marianne… had… an… affair…' Every word was punctuated by a long breath.

'No, she didn't! It was you who had the affair. I know you're my dad, we had a DNA test and it proved it.'

'What? When?' Phil looked stunned.

'A few weeks ago. It was Uncle Graham's suggestion.'

'Graham!' Phil nearly exploded at the mention of his hated brother. 'What the hell has he got to do with this?'

'My mum met him. She's a store detective and he's a barrister dealing with a case she's connected to. They got talking, and when she realised who Uncle Graham was, she told him about you, how you hit her, and wouldn't believe that you were my father. He said we should do a DNA test and make you pay maintenance. He said that you shouldn't get away with what you did. Mum wouldn't hear of it, but I thought he was right,' Danny shouted at him. 'So I found out where you lived and watched the house, waited for a chance to get something to test. I saw you drop a cigarette butt in the garden and put it in the bag Uncle Graham gave me and we sent it off. We had to send a couple of my hairs too. You're my dad, all right, but I wish you weren't. I hate you! I hate what you did to my mum. You're a bully.'

'You hit your ex-wife too!' Freya exclaimed, stunned.

Danny squared up to Phil and pushed back his floppy fringe; his eyes flashed with anger. 'Yes. He beat my mum up so much we had to run away, go into hiding. He hasn't seen us for ten years. He's scum!'

Freya listened to it all in shock, knowing that Danny was telling the truth. The hurt, the fury were oozing out of him. He had tracked Phil down, left him notes, wanted to scare him – all as revenge for what Phil had done to his mum, Marianne.

'So those are the lies your mum has told you, are they?' Phil retorted, his breathing regular now, although he was still clutching his ribs. 'Well, here's the truth. She provoked me, pushing my buttons, cheating on me. Yes, we had an argument, but—'

'Don't you call my mum a liar. You're the liar and a bully!' Danny yelled at him. 'Anyway, Mum never spoke about it to me. I think she hoped I'd forgotten because I was so little. And I had. I'd pushed it to the back of my mind until a couple of months ago when I heard my aunt and mum talking about you. I'd been asking about you, I wanted to know who my dad was, and Mum had been fobbing me off, saying she didn't know where you were, that you had just walked out and she'd never seen you again.' The angry words were spilling out with hardly a breath in between. 'I heard them talking about how Mum had met Uncle Graham and he said that you'd beat him up and your dad. Like you did my mum. You knocked her out – my aunt came round and found her, and found me crying under the table, so she took us both away. Mum got a restraining order against you so that you couldn't hurt us ever again. I was too young to stick up for my mum then but I'm not now. I'm going to make you pay for what you did to her.'

'You! It was you who tampered with the brakes of my car! Why you little…' Phil took a step forward and the lad flexed his shoulders.

'What are you going to do? Beat me up too? I'd like to see you try, old man.'

Freya had heard enough. She stood between them, holding up her phone, ready to start taking a video if Phil did hit Danny. 'Stop it. If you touch him, Phil, I'll film you and call the police.' She turned to Danny. 'Did you tamper with the brakes of his car?'

'Of course not. I don't know how to do anything like that. But I saw the accident. I've been watching him for ages, trying to think of a way to get him back for what he did to my mum.' He turned to Phil. 'I wish you'd died in that accident. That's what you deserve. I wish you weren't my dad. I hate you.'

CHAPTER FIFTY-SIX

Phil

They were ganging up on him, all of them, trying to make out he was violent. He wasn't. He was sticking up for himself. They all pushed him, prodded him, provoked until he erupted. They lit the gunpowder then complained about the explosion. It wasn't fucking fair. He clenched his fists.

'I can explain everything,' he said, turning to face Freya. 'I'm sorry about your neck. I didn't mean to hurt you. You made me angry, snooping through my things.' He picked up the piece of paper Freya had dropped on the floor; thank goodness she hadn't had a chance to read it – he'd mentioned his affair and that he wasn't sure he could trust Freya. He was about to shove it in his pocket when he noticed that it wasn't his list, it was a credit card statement – but it wasn't his usual credit card. He stared at it, dumbfounded.

'It's your secret credit card. The one you use to treat someone for lunch and take them out to the cinema while I'm working,' Freya was glaring at him, accusingly. 'You used it to pay for the holiday too. Maybe you caused the row so you could take your girlfriend on holiday instead of me.'

Damn! He had to talk fast to get out of this one. 'Don't be ridiculous, Freya. I haven't got a girlfriend. I must have gone with someone from work, as research, for part of the course.'

'Liar! You do have a girlfriend. She's got long, dark hair. I've seen her come here when she's at work.' The teenager nodded at Freya. 'I've seen you both out together. I told you, I've been following you.'

Long, dark hair. This bloody kid had seen him and Daisy together. He needed to close this down before Freya put two and two together.

It was too late. He saw shock and realisation dawn on Freya's face then she took out her phone, slid her finger across the screen and held it up. There was a picture of Daisy and Mark on the screen. Freya pointed to Daisy. 'Is this the lady?'

Danny nodded. 'That's her.'

'My God! You've really had me fooled, haven't you?' Freya asked furiously. 'You've not only got a son you lied to me about, you've been having an affair with my bloody sister!'

'Of course I haven't! You can't believe a word he says, he's just trying to cover his back. I bet he *was* the one who tampered with my brakes. He tried to kill me!' He stepped towards Danny, eyes blazing. This kid was really getting on his nerves. 'I've had enough of this. I'm going to call the cops, get you charged with breaking and entering and leaving threatening notes. We can let them decide if you're guilty of attempted murder.' He jabbed his finger in the lad's chest. 'You don't get to break into my house, threaten me and tell lies about me.'

'Is there a problem, sir?'

Phil spun around to find two police officers standing by the open back door. 'The neighbours reported a disturbance and in view of recent events we thought we had better check it out, especially when we heard shouting out the back here,' one of them said.

'I was about to call you. This kid—' Phil said but Danny had bolted. Freya went out into the hall just in time to see the teenager dash out of the front door. She had to admit she was glad he'd got away, although there were a lot of questions she'd liked to have asked him. She turned back into the kitchen as Phil was saying. 'He's run off but I know who he is. He's the one responsible for messing with my brakes and who's been breaking in and leaving me threatening notes.'

'Are you okay, madam?' the policeman asked, looking in concern at Freya, who was rubbing her sore neck.

She shook her head. 'My husband has just attacked me. And it's not the first time.' She showed them the red marks on her neck. 'I'd like him charged with assault and to take out a restraining order against him. If it wasn't for Danny, I think he might have killed me.'

CHAPTER FIFTY-SEVEN

Freya

Freya let herself into the house and sank down wearily on the sofa. The police had insisted that she go to hospital for a check-up because her neck was so badly bruised, then she had to give a statement about Phil's assault, and how Danny had pulled him off her. The police had soon found the teenager and questioned him. Graham had come to the station to represent him legally. The police told Freya that Danny had confessed to seeing Phil's car accident; he'd been outside, hoping to catch a glimpse of his dad when Phil had stormed out of the house and driven off. Danny had also admitted to sneaking into the house, through an open window at first then getting a key cut, and leaving the notes. He explained that he'd come to finally confront Phil when he heard screaming and had rushed in to rescue Freya.

Graham spoke up for him, giving an assurance that he was certain Danny wasn't responsible for tampering with the brakes, so the police asked if Freya wanted him charged. Freya didn't condone what Danny had done, breaking into their house and leaving threatening notes, but she could understand his anger when she found out that Phil had attacked his mother. And he had almost certainly saved Freya's life, so she asked the police not to press charges and they gave Danny a caution instead.

She rested her head back wearily. She'd been astonished to hear of Graham's part in all this, and that he had known where Phil was but hadn't told their mother. Graham had actually stopped to talk to her at the police station, and she'd found him to be very pleasant, although it was obvious that there was no love lost between the two brothers. He'd promised to let his mother know of the recent events, which was a relief as Freya didn't want to be the one to break the news to Aileen.

Phil was due in court on Monday morning and was being kept in custody until then. He had begged Freya to withdraw the charges, protesting that she knew it was an accident and he hadn't meant to hurt her, that Danny was lying, that he had never slept with Daisy. Freya had refused to listen to him. She'd listened to his lies and excuses enough, given him chance after chance. He had almost killed her. She wasn't going to let him get away with that.

All this time Phil had been telling Freya that she was the cause of their problems, she was the only one who ever made him mad, and she had believed him, not knowing that this was a long-standing pattern of behaviour. That he had attacked his brother, father, ex-wife and goodness knew who else. It was hearing Danny, the teenage son she had no idea Phil had, furiously relating how Phil had beaten up Danny's mother so badly she had fled for her life, taking Danny with her, that had made Freya bring the charges against Phil.

She had finally come to her senses and realised that Phil was a dangerous abuser. There was so much of Phil's life she didn't know about, Freya realised, and maybe would never have found out if it hadn't been for the accident. She couldn't believe that he had been having an affair with her sister, right under her nose. How could she have not spotted that? He denied it, of course, and maybe he couldn't actually *remember* his affair with Daisy, but he had looked so guilty it was obvious he had found out about it. She remembered how he had been so shocked when she had told him about Daisy being pregnant that he'd dropped his glass of wine. He must have known then that he'd had an affair with her and wondered if the baby was his. That was probably why Daisy had come to see him while Freya was at work, to see if he remembered. Well, not remembering didn't make him less guilty.

She sighed wearily. What a fool she had been; she should have walked out the first time Phil had lost his temper with her, and never come back. Still, what was done was done, and she had to figure out what to do from here. Right now, though, she needed to sleep.

She was about to go upstairs to lie down when the doorbell rang. Freya stopped and turned to the door. Was it the police again? She hoped not; she couldn't face any more questions today.

She tentatively opened the door and was surprised to see Danny standing on the doorstep beside a woman with short, dark hair. A car was parked at the bottom of the drive.

'Hello, Freya. I'm Marianne, Danny's mother,' the woman said with a soft smile. 'I hope you don't mind us coming. Danny wanted to apologise to you and try to explain himself, and I thought I should come with him.'

'I'm sorry for breaking into your house. I didn't want to hurt you – it was him I was after,' Danny blurted out.

He looked so young, vulnerable and hurt that her heart went out to him. 'I'm fine, thanks to you. It was very brave of you to stick up for me like that.'

He pushed his floppy fringe back. 'I wasn't going to stand by and let him beat up another woman. I wish I could have stuck up for my mum.'

'You were only a toddler, Danny. There is nothing you could have done,' Marianne assured him, putting her arm around his shoulder.

Freya surveyed them both thoughtfully and decided that she wanted to hear their story before they left.

'I had no idea Phil had a son,' she said softly. 'He told me about Danny, but said that you'd cheated, that it'd broken his heart because you'd told him Danny wasn't his. He'd made out he was the victim. I'm really sorry for what you have both gone through. Why don't you come in and have a coffee? We should talk.'

Danny looked over at his mum and she nodded. 'Thank you, I'd like that.'

Freya led them into the kitchen, where she made coffee for her and Marianne and poured a glass of Coke for Danny. Then they sat down at the table and talked for a long time. Marianne explained that Phil was eight years older than her, and she'd been taken in by his charm, swept off her feet, just like Freya had been. She had blamed herself for the arguments like Freya had done, until the one day Phil had attacked her so badly she feared for her life. She had fled with Danny, got far away, and started a new life.

'Danny started asking questions about his father, wanting to find him, and I wasn't sure what to do so I talked to my sister, Stacey, about it. That's the conversation Danny overheard. I also told Stacey about meeting Phil's brother, Graham. He was the barrister on a shoplifting case I was a witness in. The surname obviously rang a bell but I thought it was just a coincidence, then when I was checking my phone, Graham was behind me and saw the photo of Danny on the screen and said how much he looked like his brother, and it clicked. When I told Graham what had happened, how I had run from Phil, he gave me his card in case I ever wanted to chase Phil for maintenance. I told him that I didn't and that Phil had denied Danny was his. But Danny overheard me tell my sister this and took the card from my purse and contacted Graham, wanting to know how to find his father.'

'I was so mad about how he bullied my mum, what he did to her, that I was determined to find him and make him pay.' Danny took up the tale, pausing to push his fringe out of his eyes again. 'Uncle Graham wouldn't help me – he said we should go through the proper channels – but it didn't take me long to track him down. Mum said he was a journalist so I googled his name. A couple of articles came up that he'd written, then I found out that he wrote for the local paper and his bio said he taught part-time at Birmingham University, so I hung about outside and followed him home on my bike one day.'

'You should have talked to me and told me what was going on,' Marianne told him. 'What you did was wrong and dangerous.'

'You would have told me not to do it, and I wanted to prove that you weren't lying about him being my father and show what a bully he was.' He turned to Freya. 'I'm sorry for breaking into your house. I didn't want to hurt or frighten you. It was him I was after,' he apologised.

'I understand, and as you possibly saved my life, all is forgiven.' Freya picked up her phone and showed Danny the photo of Daisy and Mark again. 'And this is definitely the woman you saw Phil with?' She didn't say 'your dad'. She wasn't sure Danny would want that.

He nodded then pointed to Mark. 'And I saw that man standing by Phil's car the night of the accident.'

'What? Are you sure? You saw this man by Phil's car?' Freya was astonished at this revelation.

'Positive.'

'Did you see him do anything to the car?' she asked, wondering why Danny hadn't mentioned this to the police.

Danny shook his head. 'No, I was cycling past and just saw him standing there.'

'Are you telling the truth, Danny? This is serious.' Marianne's eyes were glued to her son's face as she questioned him.

He nodded. 'I swear.'

Was he telling the truth? Freya sighed. She didn't really care who had tampered with the brakes. Phil hadn't been killed; maybe it would teach him a lesson.

When Danny and Marianne finally went, Freya sat thinking for a long time. The events of that morning had shaken her. She had been living with a stranger, someone who had lied to her throughout all their marriage; her sister, who she thought she'd been getting closer to, had betrayed her; she couldn't even trust her brother-in-law. Her world had come crashing down. She had nothing and no one. From the moment those brakes had been tampered with, her life had changed forever, and she had no idea what to do now.

Then she remembered the piece of paper that had kicked off the events of that morning. She must have dropped it in the garage when Phil had chased her. He had been desperate for her to not read it. She went into Phil's study to retrieve it, finding it lying scrunched up on the floor by the desk. She picked up the piece of paper and went back into the lounge, not wanting to spend any more time in this room than she had to.

She sat down on the sofa, braced herself for whatever she might find, and smoothed out the paper. Phil's neat handwriting, in black biro, filled the page.

Things I remember – everything up to the past two years:
My childhood.
Marrying Marianne.
Meeting Freya.
Going out together.
Getting married.
Our honeymoon.
Teaching at the university.
Writing articles.

She turned the paper over.

Things I don't know:
What our marriage was like.

Why we don't have children.
Who caused the big argument the night I left.
Who tampered with the brakes of my car.
Who is sneaking into the house during the night.
Who flooded the kitchen.
Who is leaving me threatening notes.

So Phil really had lost his memory then. It hadn't been a trick to persuade her to give their marriage another go. He had evidently been writing things down so he could try and make sense of them. She continued reading.

If I did book a holiday to Dubai, and if so, what I did with the booking details.
If I was having an affair with Daisy.
If Daisy's baby is mine.
If Freya is abusive to me.
Whether I can trust Freya.
Whether Freya tampered with the brakes, is pretending someone is breaking in and is writing the notes.
Whether Freya is trying to mess with my head.
If I am in danger.

Her hands shook as she finished reading. No wonder Phil hadn't wanted her to see this. It proved that he had known about Daisy for some time and, more scarily, that he didn't trust Freya and had been wondering if she was behind everything that had happened. She had been in danger ever since Phil had come out of hospital.

She jumped, startled, as her phone rang. She didn't recognise the number on the screen but thinking it might be the police she answered it, her heart thumping in her chest when she heard Phil's voice. 'The police let me use the landline to call,' he told her, his words spilling out. 'I've started remembering things, Freya, my memory is coming back. I'm so sorry for everything. You're the only one who can help me get through this. Please give me another chance. I'll change. I swear I will.'

This time she wasn't falling for it. She knew he would never change. 'We're over, Phil. I never want to see you again,' she said, ending the call. Then she blocked his mobile number in case he tried to call her on that when he was free. She never wanted to hear from Phil again.

Making that decision gave her a new strength. She wasn't going to let Phil destroy her life. This wasn't the end; this was the beginning of her being in charge of her own life, of living it her way. She was going to get a solicitor, file for divorce, put the house up for sale and move on. She was going to build a bright new future for herself, and would never let anyone manipulate, control or abuse her again.

CHAPTER FIFTY-EIGHT

Saturday

'Freya.' Daisy stared at her in surprise. Freya was obviously the last person she expected to see early on a Saturday morning. 'Is everything all right?'

'Not really. Can I come in?'

'Of course.' Daisy stepped aside to let Freya enter, an anxious expression on her face.

And so you should be worried, Freya thought, anger burning brightly inside her.

'Come into the kitchen and we can talk uninterrupted,' she said but Freya carried on into the lounge, pushing the door open and walking straight in. 'Actually, I'd rather Mark heard what I have to say too.'

'Freya.' Daisy stood in the doorway, her eyes beseeching. *She's guessed that I know*, Freya thought, shooting her a cold look back.

'Auntie Freya!' The twins both scrambled to their feet and bounded over to her. Freya hugged them and wondered if she should do this, shatter their happy family life.

It's not me who's ruined this family, it's Daisy and Phil, she reminded herself.

Mark's eyes flitted to Freya's face then to the twins. 'You two go upstairs and play please, we have some grown-up talking to do.'

'Aw…' Molly started to protest but Mark took their hands and led them out of the room.

Daisy looked imploringly at Freya. 'Freya, can we just talk—'

'Phil got arrested yesterday,' Freya informed her. She pulled back her hair to show her bruised neck. 'He attacked me and probably would have killed me if his son hadn't arrived and pulled him off me.'

'Oh God! Are you okay?' Daisy asked, her eyes glued to Freya's bruised neck. Then they widened as she released what else Freya had said. 'His son!' she repeated incredulously. 'I didn't know Phil had a son!'

'I knew there was a child from his first marriage but Phil told me he'd found out Marianne, his ex, had an affair and that Danny wasn't his. It was another lie. The truth is that he attacked Marianne too and she had to go into hiding. Phil has a track record of being violent. So you see,' she retorted, glaring at Daisy, 'all those things he told you about me hitting him were lies.'

'What?' Mark had come back into the room now. He shot a glance at Daisy. 'Phil told you that about Freya?'

The colour drained from Daisy's face and she held on to the back of the sofa for support.

'Oh, yes, they shared a lot of pillow talk, didn't you? And expensive restaurant meals too. Was the holiday for you too? Did Phil cause an argument with me just so he could go off in a huff, and go away with you?'

Daisy looked like she was going to faint. She sat down in the chair, her arms shaking. 'I don't know what you mean…'

'I do.' Mark was standing behind her now. 'I knew you two were having an affair. It's been going on for months.'

Freya swivelled around to face him. 'So you did know about it?'

He nodded. 'I'm not a fool. I've noticed the difference in Daisy, the sexy underwear, the afternoons out "with friends". I picked up her phone one night and saw a message from Phil. Only it seemed more like a message from a lover.'

'I'm so sorry.' Tears spilt out of Daisy's eyes. She looked distraught. She turned her head to Freya. 'I'm so sorry I hurt both of you. I wish I could undo it all. I got taken in by Phil – he targeted me, flattered me.'

'Oh, don't worry, I know how Phil works, but that doesn't excuse you. What I want to know is…' Freya met Mark's gaze full on. 'Was it you who tampered with the brakes on Phil's car? Did you cause the accident?'

'Of course it wasn't!' Daisy said indignantly. 'What kind of person do you think he is?'

'A husband who had got cheated on. People do a lot of things for revenge,' Freya said, watching Mark carefully. He had gone pale and hadn't yet denied it.

'Danny – Phil's son – said he saw you by Phil's car earlier that evening,' she told him.

Mark swallowed then licked his lips but still didn't reply.

'Mark?' Daisy stared at him in horror. 'Please tell me that you didn't.'

Mark sank down into the chair and put his head into his hands. 'I wasn't trying to kill him, just put him out of action for a bit,' he mumbled.

'Well, you certainly did that,' replied Freya.

Daisy looked appalled. 'I don't believe you! You wouldn't do something like that. You wouldn't. You're not like that!' she shouted.

Mark raised his head, a defiant look on his face. 'No, I wouldn't have thought it was something I would do either. But then I wouldn't have thought you'd cheat on me. And when your wife is having an affair with another man, when you think she's going to run away with him and take your kids with her, then you do desperate things.'

'You were going to run away with Phil?' Freya repeated in disbelief. 'How could you do that to me? And to Mark?' Then a thought occurred to her. 'That's why you came to the hospital!

Why you kept me company all the time Phil was in a coma. It wasn't to comfort and support me. It was because you were worried about him. Because you and him were…' She couldn't say the word 'lovers'; it made it sound romantic instead of seedy. 'You disgust me.'

'I *was* supporting you. Phil and I ended things weeks before. I realised I wanted to be with Mark, that I'd made a mistake.'

'Really? And when you realised Phil had amnesia, you wanted to make sure he'd forgotten about your affair? Or did you hope he remembered it? That you could pick up where you had left off?' Contempt dripped from her voice. She pointed to Daisy's stomach. 'Is the baby Phil's? Is that why you were so upset when you discovered you were pregnant?'

'No, it isn't!' Daisy protested. She turned pleading eyes to Mark. 'I am sure that this baby is yours.'

'Look, I'd already figured there's a chance it isn't. But I'll love it just the same,' Mark told her. He turned to Freya. 'You're not going to tell the police, are you?' he asked, his face strained, his voice breaking. 'I didn't intend to kill him, honestly. I just meant him to get a bit hurt so that they couldn't run off together. I can't lose Daisy. I don't want my family to break up. Please don't tell the police.'

Freya couldn't help but feel sorry for him. He looked a pitiful sight. Yes, what he did was wrong – he could have killed Phil, but he hadn't. And she could see that he had been tortured, desperate. She felt sorry for him that he loved her sister so much he was willing to forgive her and take on the baby she was having, even if it wasn't his. She wondered if Phil would fight for contact, though. He had always wanted to have a child with Freya, conveniently forgetting the son he already had. She doubted it; he was too selfish. It wasn't her problem anyway.

'No, I'm not telling the police,' she said. She turned to Daisy. 'But I'll never forgive you for what you did. I'm going away and never want to see you again.'

As she turned to walk out, Mark shouted to her: 'Freya. Thank you, I know I don't deserve it.'

She looked back at him. 'I think you've been through enough, Mark, and I don't want to punish you – or the children – any further. But I pity you for loving someone like her.'

She walked out. From now on her sister was dead to her.

'I'm sorry, Freya. I really am,' Daisy shouted after her.

Freya carried on walking.

*

Mum passes me the newspaper and I see his photo on the front page. There's a big article about how he's been charged with assault on his wife. The paper is ripping him to shreds, dragging up stuff from his past, how he's sexually assaulted a couple of his students, and then there's a big piece about how he beat my mum up years ago and she had to run away and get a restraining order against him. I know it must have been Freya who told them about him – she was getting justice for herself and us. The article says that he's on remand until the case can be heard, has been suspended from the university, and she's got a restraining order against him and is filing for divorce. He's well and truly screwed, and I'm glad. It's payback.

'Well, I guess he's finally got what he deserves,' Mum says.

That's what I think too. That's why I didn't tell the police about the man I saw tampering with the brakes of the car. I didn't think Freya would tell them either – she's nice, too nice for him. I knew the man was his girlfriend's husband. He was a bit of a dope, though, didn't really know what he was doing, so I finished it off for him when he left.

A LETTER FROM KAREN

I want to say a huge thank you for choosing to read *The Stranger in My Bed*. If you did enjoy it and want to keep up to date with all my latest releases, just sign up at the following link. Your email address will never be shared and you can unsubscribe at any time.

www.bookouture.com/karen-king

This story is a change of direction for me. If you have read any of my previous books, you will know that I usually write romance novels, but this story has been brewing in my head for over ten years now. Rather than a relationship that finally goes right, this is a story about a relationship that goes dramatically wrong. There are many people who have been in, or are still in, abusive relationships. It's a common trait of abusers to gaslight their victims, to deny all knowledge of the abuse, to say that their partner has imagined it, that they caused the injury themselves, to even pretend to other people that they are the victim. It's this behaviour that gave me the idea to write this story. I know that many people stay with abusive partners, or go back to them, because of their memories of the good times, because they want their partner to be the person they know they can be, the one they fell in love with. I wondered what would happen if the abuser really did forget what had happened – would their partner forgive them and try to give the marriage another chance? If the abuser couldn't remember the abuse within the marriage, could they change? That is the concept this story explores.

If you're reading this book and are in an abusive relationship, I want to say to you that the abuse isn't your fault and that no amount of your love, understanding or squashing of yourself will make your partner change. Please look after yourself, walk out, stay safe.

I hope you loved *The Stranger in My Bed*, and if you did, I would be very grateful if you could write a review. I'd love to hear what you think, and it makes such a difference helping new readers to discover one of my books for the first time.

I love hearing from my readers – you can get in touch on my Facebook page, through Twitter, Goodreads or my website.

Thanks,
Karen

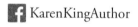 KarenKingAuthor

 @karen_king

🌐 www.karenking.net

ACKNOWLEDGEMENTS

I always find this part of the book difficult; there are so many people involved in writing and publishing a book that it's easy to forget someone. I will try my best not to, but please forgive me if I do.

The first person I want to thank is my wonderful editor, Isobel Akenhead, for believing in this story and encouraging me to write it, for her invaluable advice, expertise and guidance. You have been a shining star lighting up my way. For all the Bookouture editorial team, you are truly marvellous. And special thanks to the dynamic promotion and marketing team of Kim Nash, Noelle Holten and Sarah Hardy, who go above and beyond in their support of all us authors. We love you ladies. The authors in the Bookouture Lounge, who are always ready with a kind word, a virtual hug and a word of advice. In particular Rona Halsall, whose books I really admire, and who has been my sounding board while writing this book. Thank you.

As always, huge thanks to Dave, the love of my life, who keeps me sane, fed and watered while I am in my writing world, and to my wonderful family and friends, who all support me so much. I love you all.

To the incredible bloggers who read and review my books, host me on their blogs, cheer me on, retweet and share my posts. The authors and online writing community who are always there to answer questions and encourage. Thank you, every one of you.

Finally, massive thanks to you, my readers, for buying, reading and reviewing my books. Your support means so much. I especially appreciate you for believing in me enough to buy this book, a new genre for me. Thank you from the bottom of my heart.

Printed in Great Britain
by Amazon

51558537R00159